THE TROUBLE WITH LOVE

THE FORBIDDEN LOVE SERIES

KAT T. MASEN

The Trouble With Love

Kat T. Masen

ISBN: 9798736615964

Editing by Nicki at Swish Design & Editing
Proofing by Amy at Briggs Consulting LLC
Cover design by Outlined with Love Designs
Cover Image Copyright 2021
First Edition 2021
All Rights Reserved

"Sometimes it's not the butterflies that tell you you're in love, but the pain." - Unknown

PROLOGUE

WILL

The silver tip of the pen hovers above the piece of paper in front of me.

My lips press together in a slight grimace as all eyes inside the boardroom fall upon my every move.

All I have to do is sign my name—a simple task I've done many times.

Yet, the repercussion of such an easy action will onset tremendous suffering. I felt it the moment I stepped into the room only an hour ago, to last night when I laid wide awake unable to shut down my thoughts. Everywhere I turn and every breath I take isn't without a constant ache that has long buried itself inside me.

This pain, unbearable and consuming, is what *we* have become.

"Is there a problem, Mr. Romano?"

My gaze lifts. Jeff, the head of our legal team, quizzes me with a frustrated stare. His team worked nonstop to make this deal happen. Our company was against all odds, yet we persisted and won the final bid. Purchasing this other company will expand our name in the tech industry and officially make us a billion-dollar empire.

This is everything I have worked hard for in my career—the long hours, non-existent social life, constant travel, and stress associated with starting up a new company. All of it has come to fruition.

Then she walked back into my life.

Amelia Edwards.

She's no longer the annoying kid who would torment me with her childish games, and I'm no longer the teenage boy who would entertain her to avoid the wrath of my mother and aunt.

Our families have ties, strong ties, something neither of our mothers let us forget over the years. Unlike many other families, we're bonded by the timing of the past and not connected through sharing the same blood or gene pool.

Perhaps, in the chaos of what we have become, it's our way of justifying our actions.

But the biggest surprise, the one I never expected to take my breath away that afternoon several months ago is how Amelia turned into this beautiful woman. The very reason why my emotions fucked with my head, causing me to hesitate in front of our executive team.

Her body isn't supposed to be so irresistible to the point that I crave her every goddamn moment. I've been with many women, but no one has ever owned me like she does when we're alone. Maybe I shouldn't have succumbed to my desires and taken her selfishly to satisfy my craving of her innocence.

But in return, she did something which rendered me speechless. Something an older and more experienced man should've known better.

She made me fall in *love* with her.

"I'll repeat Jeff's question since perhaps you didn't hear it," Lex voices coldly, unforgiving with his tone. *"Is there a problem?"*

Across the room, the most powerful man I know watches me with an uninviting stare. His fingertips drum against the woodgrain table. The shade of his usually vibrant green eyes has turned almost black.

Anyone else caught in his unrelenting stare would've recoiled and signed the contract. But as the sick feeling in the pit of my stomach begins to alleviate, it's instantly replaced with resentment.

He leaves me no choice.

My company's future is in his hands. We need his investment to complete this purchase, and all I have to do is sign this contract and move to London.

Away from Manhattan and away from his oldest daughter.

Beside me, my phone vibrates with a text appearing on the screen. Slowly, my eyes shift across to the notification. I keep my expression flat as the words tear through me like bullets ricocheting from a loaded gun.

Amelia: *I will always choose him.*

These five words end everything between us; I'm left with no choice. Even if I give this all up for her, she'll never be happy unless her father approves.

And I know for a fact he doesn't want a man like me to be in a relationship with his daughter. We've been friends well before this, and for many years, he's been a mentor and a father figure who treats me like his own son.

He knows I never cared for women unless it was for my own selfish physical needs. We often joked about my inability to settle down with anyone since all I care about is work. We had spent many nights just sitting at bars, drinking while talking about life. He knows me better than my father, better than any man I've called a friend over the years.

But then it all shifted.

A complete turn of events in which, if he knew the extent of our relationship, he'd never approve.

I'm not stupid. He taught me everything I know, and when the master himself has taught you all his tricks, you know well enough that his proposal for me to move is because he knows the secret we've been keeping.

The forbidden affair between his nineteen-year-old daughter and me.

My throat begins to tighten at the same time my knuckles turn white around the pen still resting in my hand. Pressing hard against the paper, the pen glides across as the blank spot above the line is filled with my signature.

Without a thought, the pen falls against the table as my head slowly lifts to the ruthless stare of the man who pulls all the strings.

The same man who Amelia chose over me.

Her father.

Lex Edwards.

The new stakeholder in my soon-to-be billion-dollar company.

ONE

AMELIA

I stare at the three envelopes sitting in front of me.

For the last two years, it was all I could think about —college.

What exactly do I want to do with my life, and more importantly, what sacrifices am I willing to make for a future that may *not* be right for me?

I gave up parties and social gatherings, opting to study and earn college credits. I'm blessed with a boyfriend who's equally as focused as me. We've spent numerous hours cramming for exams and it all boils down to this very moment. I sought comfort in knowing I'm not alone. Most of my peers have received their acceptance letters in the last few weeks, each one getting into their first or second choice of colleges.

My cousin, Andy, is still waiting to hear back from two colleges. He and I have followed the same method—our personal choice, our mother's choice, and our father's choice.

However, Andy has been fortunate to have both his parents support his decision, never mentioning a preference as to where they thought he should apply. Unlike myself, Andy is creative, so I wasn't surprised when he told me one of the colleges he applied to was NYU, and being the amazing human being he is, he got accepted. So, all his applications were of his own doing—three different colleges for three various reasons.

I'm not that lucky.

My mom lets out a sigh, sitting beside me as I hold the letter opener in my hand, staring blankly at the envelopes.

"They're thick," Mom comments, touching my hand softly. "Go ahead."

I take a deep breath, counting down in my head while giving myself a pep talk.

Don't define yourself just because you get rejected.

Remember, each school has its pros and cons.

Jamming the opener into the corner, I slice the envelope open. Pulling out the letter, my eyes move toward *Dear Amelia, Congratulations! I am pleased to offer you admission to the University of Southern California.*

My shoulders slump as I slide the acceptance letter toward my father, who sits across from me. Within moments, his eyes beam with triumph. I'm not surprised by his reaction since he chose the college, which means I can stay as close as possible to home. He doesn't say a word, especially after we butted heads earlier over a party I want to attend tonight. I rarely ask for much these days, but granted myself a pardon from studying since the pressure is causing many emotions of late. I am beyond burned out, yet in his eyes, I'm just a kid wanting to go to parties to have sex, drink alcohol, and smoke weed.

"What's going on?" My sister, Ava, enters the room while munching on an apple.

Wearing her denim shorts and white midriff top, I'm

shocked Dad hasn't reprimanded her for showing skin since the rule is either the short top or short shorts—not both.

Ava wraps her hands around my father, hugging him tightly. She has always been his favorite, unlike me—the black sheep. When it comes to Ava, she gets anything she wants, and I swear, when she enters the room, he looks somewhat relieved to see her rather than having to focus on me.

"Amelia has received her college responses," Mom softly says before scowling. "Ava, what's with that top? Don't you think it's a bit too tight?"

"All the more reason to go shopping," Ava responds with a grin, taking a seat beside my father and grabbing the letter. "Oh, USC, you can live at home."

I ignore her, knowing all too well she understands my hesitation in remaining close to home. Dragging the letter opener through the next envelope, I pull it out quickly to read, *Dear Amelia, Congratulations! I am pleased to offer you admission to the University of California, Berkeley.*

With a pleasing smile, I slide it over to Mom. Her chocolate-brown eyes dart back and forth until the corners of her mouth turn upward. Momentarily, she glances toward my father, who offers no emotion upon reading the acceptance letter.

It's an option, and San Francisco is only a five-hour drive from home. It would be a long enough distance for me to live on campus yet still be able to visit home occasionally on the weekends.

The final envelope sits in front of me, the most crucial one of all. The college I chose, the college I have dreamed of attending for as long as I can remember, Mom's alma mater —Yale.

The navy logo sits in the corner, the envelope not as

thick as the others. I prepare myself for the worst, the possibility of my dreams being shattered all in this one moment.

I have so desperately wanted to study law, and aside from Harvard, which I opted not to apply to, this is the one place where I want to start my future just like my mom did many years ago.

The sharp blade glides once again across the seal as I take a deep breath, my stomach tied in knots. I close my eyes briefly before pulling the letter out and opening it wide.

"What is it?" Ava asks in anticipation.

Dear Amelia, Welcome to Yale!

I release a loud breath, falling back onto the chair, overjoyed at the words which seal my fate. The straight A's, and everything I did to make my college application as best as it could be, has paid off—this letter proof of exactly that.

My eyes do a doubletake before Mom's hand rests on mine. "Congratulations, honey. You've worked so hard for this."

Clearing her throat, she follows with, "Lex, would you like to say something?"

Slowly, my eyes lift to meet my father's. Unlike Mom, who's on the verge of tears, his reaction is the complete opposite. The hard stare and the way his hands clench against the tabletop is anything but welcoming.

Growing up with a father who also happens to run a billion-dollar empire wasn't always easy. Sure, we had a beautiful home and nice cars—money was never an issue. But Lex Edwards is a known tycoon. His intimidating stare alone frightens anyone who dares to challenge him. All but Mom, she somehow has him under some sort of weird spell.

And being the oldest has its disadvantages. I am the guinea pig of his rules. The only saving grace has been

Mom. She understands me and has often played the medi-
ator between us. The last few years have been the hardest.
We've had somewhat of a distant relationship, though I
never truly understood why.

However, this time, I doubt he'll listen to her.

Yale is across the other side of the country, and even
though it has been my dream, my father's slow and steady
gait warns me that the battle has only begun.

I hold his stare, crossing my arms, knowing we're about
to get heated.

"I don't expect a congratulations from you, Dad. But
you, of all people, understand the importance of working
hard toward your goals, unlike some other children of yours
who'll remain nameless." I purposely ignore Ava's roll of her
eyes. "I have studied hard to get straight A's. I don't spend
my weekends shopping or attending parties. In fact, I've
declined almost every social invitation aside from tonight's,
which you so easily refused my attendance. I've done
nothing but invest my time into making sure I got the results
needed to get into an Ivy League school."

His eyes soften, and perhaps, my words finally get
through to him.

But, of course, my victory is only momentary. He toys
with his cufflink, still wearing the suit he wore to work
today. Although he has removed his jacket, his white business shirt and navy tie remain. Steadily, his gaze fixates on
mine. The emerald-green orbs I've grown so accustomed to
are slowly shifting to a darker shade.

"Congratulations, Amelia. You have worked hard to
achieve the result you desired," he says in a significantly
neutral tone, "But I'm sorry, you'll not be moving across the
country."

Pushing his chair out, he stands up, his tall stature

demanding attention. "You've got other excellent choices. I suggest you pick one of them."

And just like that, he exits the room, an audible breath expelling as the reality of his words begins to sink in.

Everything I've worked so hard for seems impossible to attain because of the one man who controls my life.

Lex Edwards.

My father.

TWO

AMELIA

"Millie, can you imagine all the hot college guys?" Ava jumps onto my bed, causing the mattress to shuffle and disturb my momentary silence. Her golden-brown hair falls messily against the lavender bedspread, and the scent of her cherry-flavored gum lingers in the air between us.

"California guys, since it's obvious where I'm going," I answer bitterly.

Beside me, Ava lays on her back, hands resting on her exposed stomach as we both stare at the ceiling. "He'll come around."

I rub my eyes, letting out a frustrated breath. "Maybe with you. He treats me differently."

"Well, it's not exactly like you make an effort with him either."

"Two-way street," I quickly inform her. "You're his favorite."

I recall a childhood full of great memories, and given our closeness in age, the two of us were inseparable. I'd been dubbed the so-called daredevil in my earlier years, never a moment of fear as I jumped off things, out of things, rode my bike at a fast speed without a care in the world. Ava and Andy were unfortunate that I bullied them with my over-bearing ways, and on more than one occasion, I dared them to do things that landed us all in trouble.

My body is covered in scars from my knees being scraped numerous times to the several ER visits from concussions and broken bones. It's fair to say I've given my parents multiple coronaries.

Though somewhere along the way, I guess I changed, unaware I had done so. I became more cautious of my actions, and perhaps, I matured as I grew older, knowing certain situations carried heavy consequences.

I swapped adventure for studying, outdoor activities for reading. The daredevil in me no longer existed, but the memories still lingered. Ava and Andy made up a huge part of my life, two people I'll miss dearly once I go to college.

My younger sister, Addison, arrived years later, then the youngest, Alexandra, much later than all of us. According to my parents, a surprise baby. I don't need any more details.

Unlike some of my friends who have fathers from divorced marriages or those who run wealthy companies, my father has been present. He often attends our sporting events and every school milestone, Mom ensuring he never misses out. With certain things, her word holds more weight. I know my father works hard, and Mom often calls him a workaholic, which has led to several arguments, but he never made us feel unworthy by absence. He travels, but when he is home, the attention is on my sisters and me. Being one of four girls, I do feel sorry for him since he suffers through more gymnastics and ballet than most other fathers I know.

Yet, it must have been in middle school when our relationship began to shift, and my interests changed. I started to like *boys*. My friendship circle grew in junior high, which included more of the opposite sex, prompting my parents to give me "the talk." It was uncomfortable, awkward, and I'd never seen my father so quiet. Mom carried the whole conversation, and, of course, in front of him, I kept my questions at bay.

"Let's talk about the party tonight." Ava changes the topic.

"The one Dad won't let me go to?"

"Austin will be there..."

"I know." I sigh, knowing this is the biggest party of the year, the one I've been anticipating as the reward should my hard efforts pay off.

"It's not fair that juniors aren't allowed," Ava whines.

"Madison wanted it to be a pre-graduation event," I remind her, my frustration deepening as the minutes pass. "Besides, it's the only weekend her parents are away."

Ava sits up, her long hair swooshing at her sudden movements. "You mean, there's no chaperone?"

"Not exactly. Her older sister and brother are there."

"Do Dad and Mom know?"

"They know there's adult supervision. That's it."

I feel terrible for lying, but it doesn't matter anyway since I'm not allowed to go. I never felt the need to lie to either of them, nor have I disrespected their rules despite disagreeing. On the other hand, Ava often pushes the limits, sneaking out whenever she gets a chance. I wouldn't be surprised if she turns up at the party after our parents fall asleep.

"I think you should go anyway. Just sneak out once Dad's asleep."

"It's not even worth it," I tell her, less than enthused.

And just at that moment, my phone lights up beside me with a text from Austin, my boyfriend.

Austin: *Can't wait to see you tonight. I miss you. I can't believe senior year is almost over.*

A smile spreads across my face. Typing fast, I send a reply.

Me: *I miss you too.*

I hop off the bed, darting to my closet, which consists of more comfortable attire, the complete opposite to Ava's wardrobe.

"I need to borrow a dress," I yell out to her.

Ava runs into my closet, barefoot with excitement. "I have just the one."

She disappears, to return moments later with a red off-the-shoulder dress which sits mid-thigh. When it comes to shopping, Ava and Mom are experts. If Ava owns this dress, Mom approved it.

"Perfect." I grin, holding it up. "Shoes?"

Ava huffs, leaving the room again to return with a pair of gold heels. Handing them to me, I scowl at the height.

"I'll fall over in these," I point out, my eyes gravitating toward my closet floor. "I mean, how wrong would it be to wear my Chucks?"

"Very wrong," Ava exaggerates, eyes wide. "We need to raid Mom's closet."

"Uh, in case you forgot, how can we raid her closet without her knowing?"

The sound of a throat clearing causes us to shift our heads

abruptly. Mom is wearing a pair of sweats, still looking beauti-ful, though I heard her complain earlier that she'd spent an hour cleaning my sister, Alexandra's, room. Her hair is tied in a messy bun, but I'm always in awe of her beauty no matter what she wears. As far as mothers go, Mom looks years younger than her actual age, often mistaken for my older sister.

"Hey, Mom," Ava drags, her lips parting with worried eyes. "We were just talking about clothes and how your wardrobe is every girl's dream."

"Uh-huh." Mom nods, standing still while watching us with her arms crossed beneath her chest. "Ava, could I have a word with your sister, please?"

Ava bolts out of the room, quick to escape the lecture I'm about to receive for attempting to sneak into Mom's closet. So typical of her, and the worst part—this was all her idea.

"Can we talk, please?"

I follow Mom to my bed, sitting beside her as the guilt sets in over my brief lapse of judgment. I could blame Ava. After all, she's a bad influence and not the angel everyone makes her out to be.

"Amelia, I know you're upset, and you have every right to be. I'm not here to defend your father's actions." She takes a deep breath, choosing her words carefully. "Your father loves you. And believe it or not, he's very proud of you."

"It doesn't feel like it. I can never please him."

"That's not true," she informs me with a loving gaze. "He just struggles with his emotions. You'll always be his baby. And in the blink of an eye, you've grown up into this beautiful woman ready to embark on a very important jour-ney. I'm not excusing his behavior. I'm merely trying to point out he's trying to come to terms with all these changes."

I think about what she says. I don't feel that at all. Dad treats me so differently from Ava.

"Mom? I really want to go to that party tonight. I wouldn't normally ask once I've been given a no, but I want to clear my head. I didn't think this whole process could be so stressful, but I was wrong," I say honestly, continuing, "I know Dad said no, but..."

Mom places her hand on mine with a smile. "You can go, Amelia. As for your father, give him time to process all this."

Leaning in, I hug her tightly, grateful for her support and friendship. Many of my friends have mothers they can't call their best friend. I count myself lucky for having both, plus she's much more level-headed than Ava.

"Now, exactly what shoes are you on the hunt for?"

I laugh softly. "Ava's idea, not mine. It's okay, Mom. I'm sure I can find something."

"The offer is there. Just don't tell your sisters." She chuckles but slowly calms down at my expression. "What's wrong, honey?"

"Can I ask you a question? Only between you and me?"

"You can ask me anything. You know we've always been open with each other."

"It's about your..." I clear my throat, unsure how to raise the topic without my thoughts coming out in a jumbled mess. "Your, um... first time."

"Oh..."

"Unless, of course, it was with Dad in which maybe we shouldn't discuss this."

Mom's shoulders relax. "No, it wasn't your dad, but if

there's anything he wishes he could change, that would most likely be one of them."

"Did you love him? The guy?"

Mom hesitates, then smiles fondly. "I do now, as a friend, but at the time, we were kids just fooling around and curious."

"Wait, a friend? Have I met this person?"

"Yes, though some things are better left a mystery."

I remain quiet, opting not to pry into who this mystery man is.

"How old were you?"

"Seventeen."

"I see..." My mind has so many questions, but I try to focus on the most pressing. "Do you regret it? I mean, do you wish you waited for a perfect moment with someone you did love?"

Growing quiet, she touches her wedding ring before deepening her breath. "I think the timing is everything. It wasn't pleasant. In fact, it was awful. But I guess, when I look back now, it meant that the next time I gave myself to a man, I did so with better judgment."

"It makes sense..." I trail off.

"Amelia, I'm not going to tell you what's right or wrong. Only you can decide that, but that moment is something you'll never get back. If you have the opportunity to share it with someone special, then it will stick with you forever."

"It's okay, Mom," I reassure her. "I know that most of the girls my age have already had sex, some with more than one boyfriend, but just because I'm eighteen doesn't mean I have to follow them."

Mom smiles while patting my leg. "I don't know what I did to deserve such a beautiful and smart daughter like you."

"I don't know what I did to deserve a beautiful and smart mom like you," I repeat the sentiment.

"You better get ready for tonight. The offer is there in case you need shoes."

"I'll keep it in mind," I say while grinning. Mom stands up, about to leave the room when I call her name again. "About tonight, Madison's parents won't be home. It's just her older brother and sister. I completely understand if you don't want me to go."

Mom hesitates, but her eyes never leave mine. Staring back at me is a woman who loves me unconditionally, a woman I've always admired and hoped to be when I grew up. With her guidance, there's nothing I can't do. I just need to muster up the courage to go head-to-head with my father because Yale is the only thing I want.

"I trust you, Amelia. Just be home by midnight, okay?"

"Thank you, Mom. I love you."

"I love you too, kid."

THREE

AMELIA

Madison Sloan knows how to throw a party.

Her house is located in Bel Air, and according to the stories she tells everyone, the property was given as a wedding gift to her parents almost twenty years ago. Veronica Sloan, a well-known actress, married her father, who happens to be one of LA's top realtors. Veronica's grandfather, a prominent director in Hollywood, was said to have cast his daughter in several blockbusters until his death a few years ago.

Madison is never shy in sharing her family's secrets, including her dad's affair with their maid, which apparently her mother turns a blind eye to.

Nevertheless, their house is a mansion with sweeping views of the canyons. Its style, a mixture of modern and contemporary, makes for an interesting design choice. Wherever you look, there's glass everything—large glass windows, glass walls, display cabinets, side tables—I'd never seen so much glass in a house. Everyone from our senior class is here, including others from neighboring schools. This doesn't look like it will end well, especially given the jocks are knocking each other around as usual, oblivious to their fragile surroundings.

"What a place." My cousin, Andy, drops his head to whisper beside me. "It's like a museum... of glass."

I nod along, hiding my laughter. I'm doing my best to be careful and not slip in the heels I ended up borrowing from Mom, clutching to Andy's arm for much-needed support.

Andy and I have been inseparable since the day we were born. My father and his mother are siblings. Although I'm a few months older than him, his entrance into this world was met with mixed emotions, according to my mom. Of course, Andrew Elijah Evans, named after our grandfather and his father, had been a long-awaited blessing for my Aunt Adriana. It was just unfortunate that Andy's father passed away from terminal cancer a week later. Having been a baby, I have no recollection of any of this or how it almost tore our family apart. I'm just glad that Aunt Adriana remarried because Andy has an amazing stepfather, one who, according to Ava, used to be engaged to Mom.

When Ava first mentioned it, it seemed absolutely ludicrous. It sounded like a plot from a poorly written soap opera. Yet, Ava was adamant it had been the truth, throwing in some additional information that began to add up. I thought about raising the topic with Mom since Ava is dead certain she's right, but the more I tried, the more I chickened out. Sometimes, it's best that secrets remain exactly that, no need to taint the perfect love story my parents appear to have.

"Amelia, Andy! You came!" Madison throws herself onto us, squeezing us both simultaneously while we glance at each other uncomfortably. Her platinum blonde hair is tied back into a ponytail, enhancing her perfect bone structure and flawless skin. The short dress she wears, designer most likely, is white and barely covers her chest. "How amazing is this party?"

"Amazing," we both say in unison.

Madison links her arm into mine, leaving Andy to walk behind us. "You know, Austin is here."

"I figured, since he said he'd come."

Madison leans in, her perfume stronger than usual. "No one is allowed upstairs but say the word, and it's all yours."

I'm about to switch the topic with a nervous smile when thankfully, Madison gets pulled outside. Bouncing in her pink heels, she joins a group of boys and begins to dance in the middle of a circle, basking in all the attention.

"Let's go get something to eat," I suggest to Andy.

We head outside, hovering near a table spread out with catered food. I have to hand it to Madison, she went all out, not that anyone else cares. Most of the teenagers here are self-absorbed, eager to get laid by some jock or cheerleader.

The music blares from a DJ booth stationed near the large swimming pool. A few people jump in the pool on a dare—the goofy boys—who I often enjoy spending time with when I need a good laugh.

Andy nods his head, spotting a few of his friends by the drinks.

"Will you be okay?" he asks, though his eyes are fixated on Skylar Fischer, a girl he's crushed on since middle school.

"I do know how to socialize," I remind him with a pat on his shoulder. "Will you just go and have fun? And when are you going to ask Skylar out? It's senior year. You've got nothing left to lose."

"Um... my ego? Besides, she's out of my league."

"Just because she's a cheerleader doesn't mean she is out

of your league. You're a good-looking guy, your mom is a top fashion designer, and your dad is one of America's well-known journalists. You come from a good family. Why wouldn't she like you?"

"You're just saying all this because you're my cousin. But I'll agree with you, it's my senior year and time to get my shit together."

He takes a deep breath, his blue eyes widening with slight fear until the usually confident boy I love so dearly walks away toward his crush. When it comes to girls, they often throw themselves at Andy. It's hard for me to look at him in any other way, but I guess, if I'm honest, his dark blond hair and bright blue eyes along with his tall and toned physique, make him extremely handsome. Yet unlike all the arrogant jocks in our year, Andy isn't the type of guy to sleep around and use girls for the sake of being macho. I'm just glad he broke up with Giselle Monaghan after she acted like a maniac. If luck is on his side, she won't be here tonight to ruin his life again.

I watch from across the pool until arms wrap around my waist as the familiar masculine scent invades the air around me, radiating warmth throughout my chest.

"My girl," his voice whispers in my ear.

Unable to hide my smile, I turn around and wrap my arms around Austin's neck. In his eyes, the warm honey hues mixed with caramel reflect a hazel color I've only ever seen when he gazes upon me. Austin is dressed in a hoodie, blue jeans, and sneakers—looking deliciously handsome as always.

"You're here."

"I said I would be." His smile is so wide, baring his perfectly straight white teeth. "Besides, I'm kind of fond of you."

I smack his chest softly, his face pained, though only momentarily.

We've dated all through senior year. In terms of relationships in high school, this is considered long-term. Being the gentlemen he is, Austin offered to meet my father, and much to my surprise, it wasn't as bad as I thought it might be. It started off shaky, my father, of course, interrogating poor Austin. But when Austin mentioned med school, it all shifted. There was somewhat of a respectful exchange of conversation. I recall Mom telling me that my father studied to be a doctor, though never really elaborated on why he changed professions.

There is, however, one rule. We're never to be alone. Andy or Ava chaperoned us on more than one occasion, but both of them would abandon us enough to spend time making out or fool around. We just never had sex, something I know Austin wants.

"I love this song," I say as the music continues to blast. "Let's dance."

We dance beside the pool, his hands never leaving my waist. He spends most of his time buried in my neck until he suggests we go somewhere quieter.

My eyes scan the area surrounding us. "Like where?"

"I thought you were a daredevil," he muses, still with his hands on my hips. "That's how your mom described you."

"Was," I reiterate. "Past tense. But seriously, we can't just disappear."

"Stop overthinking things, it's time to have some fun."

Austin leads me toward the kitchen, through a deserted hallway, and up a flight of floating stairs until we're on the second level. Opening a door, he pulls me into the room, then presses his lips against mine.

"*Austin,*" I murmur, out of breath with my hands on his

chest. "We shouldn't be up here."

He pulls away, his gaze exploring my face until he's drawn to my lips. There's a king-size bed in the room and a white sofa by the window. Taking my hand, he guides me to the sofa, where the two of us sit.

"So, did you open the envelopes?" he asks, yet much like me, we both try to avoid this topic tonight.

I nod, gently scratching the top of his hand. "I got into all of them."

"What?" His expression illuminates. "That's amazing!"

"Yeah, it is..."

"Why the face? You're not happy?"

"I'm happy I got into three excellent schools, but... well... my father doesn't exactly approve of me attending Yale. In fact, he said no."

"C'mon, Millie, you know he'll come around."

"I don't know," I mumble, still unable to process his reaction. "I guess, if he does change his mind, you're only two hours away at Harvard."

Austin pulls back, scratching the back of his neck. His body language changes, or perhaps my chaotic thoughts are reading too much into this.

"I got into Johns Hopkins."

My mouth falls open. "Johns Hopkins? I didn't realize you'd applied. I thought you wanted to go to Harvard?"

"Last-minute change." He lowers his head, avoiding my gaze.

I turn away, my heavy stare shifting toward the window. Outside is nothing but darkness. Not even the moon cares to show itself behind the thick clouds.

We talked so much about this, where we applied and what we wanted to do. Never once did he mention Johns Hopkins. Part of me feels betrayed that he held this secret from me. No matter what, I'd have been supportive. I just didn't understand why he felt the need to hide this from me.

"Baltimore," I drag, trying to make sense of this all. "That's further from Yale? Not that Yale matters if my dad has a say in the matter. Distance makes the heart grow fonder, right?"

"You know what?" His lips curve upward with hopeful eyes following. "Why do we have to worry about it right now?"

"You're right," I agree, leaning in to kiss his lips.

With a sense of urgency, he takes my mouth and kisses me deeply. His body slowly hovers above mine, pinning me down on the sofa. I let out a soft moan as his lips trail toward my neck, and his hand moves beneath my dress, skirting at the edge of my panties.

"Austin," I gasp, trying to control my urges. "Not here."

It falls on deaf ears as he moves his hands over my panties, causing me to draw a breath in sharply.

"Austin," I repeat, pushing his chest with more force. "I don't want to have sex here. Not with everyone downstairs."

Slightly offended, he draws back. "I understand, but I want you, Millie. I want you." He swallows, his tone nervous. "I want you to be my first."

We haven't exactly discussed our past to a great extent. I know he dated other girls in school, and I'd assumed he'd had sex. From the few times we've been able to be alone, he knows just what to do. Never does he appear nervous or hesitant.

"I..." I stumble on my words, distracted by the noise downstairs. "I'm not ready, I'm sorry. I know that's not what you want to hear. And yes, I am aware that I'm already eighteen, and even my sister has lost her virginity, but I just want it to be right, and this place doesn't feel right."

"I understand," he whispers, pulling away while struggling, my eyes diverting to his pants to see the reason why.

I pull him back toward me, kissing him hard and guiding him back on top of me. I may not have been ready to lose my virginity tonight, but I still want him and want to show him how much.

With fire in his eyes, his hands move back between my thighs. *"Do you want me to stop?"*

I shake my head, holding in my breath.

Slowly, he slides his fingers into my panties while deepening his kiss, brushing himself against me as I moan into his mouth. His fingers plunge deeper, the sensation causing me to buckle down as my body begins to convulse with every thrust.

"Austin," I cry, pulling him into me as I finish blissfully in his embrace.

With a satisfied smile, he kisses me softly on my nose. "I love you, Millie. I don't know what will happen in the future, but right now, I love you."

I stare into his loving eyes and gently run my hands through his bronze hair, admiring how soft it feels between my fingers.

I may have been premature with my opinions on love, but I do know this—being with Austin is something I don't want to give up. Never has anyone made me feel this way— the constant butterflies, the way we laugh together, these moments of intimacy where he makes my body come alive.

Our future may be undecided, but it doesn't stop me from gazing into the eyes of the boy who has officially stolen my heart.

"I love you, too," I whisper, then finish with a kiss to show him just how much.

FOUR

AMELIA

"*Is everything okay?*"

Andy walks up beside me, drawing his eyebrows together while eyeing Austin with his friends. They are doing shots, not sure how they snuck the bottles of tequila in or why Madison's older brother and sister haven't said a word. In fact, I don't recall seeing them at all tonight.

"I'm fine, just had a talk with Austin."

"Right," Andy chides, knowingly. "And what does he think about you and Yale now that you've officially been accepted?"

"C'mon, Andy. As if my dad will let me go."

"Uncle Lex will come around. He always does."

"I don't think so," I confess, toying with the hem of my dress. "He was cold... like nothing I've ever seen before."

"But that's just him." Andy chuckles, refusing the beer offered to him by his friend passing by. "Lex Edwards didn't become a billionaire because he plays nice. But with you, it's different. You're his daughter. Besides, Mom and Aunt Charlie will knock some sense into him, so I wouldn't worry."

Perhaps Andy has a point. Aunt Adriana never has a problem with setting Dad straight when the situation calls for it. They argue often, the normal sibling rivalry you expect. Dad just gets annoyed when Mom doesn't take his side which happens more than he cares to admit.

"Then there's me and Austin," I say softly. "What if I never find a love like him?"

"What if you find better?"

I purse my lips, quick to scold him for being such a male. "That's such a guy thing to say."

"According to what Ava has to say in our group chat, college men are different."

I shake my head at my sister's behavior. "I can't control that girl. Good luck to Dad once I'm out."

"So, Yale it is?" Andy questions with a proud smile.

I lean in to hug him tight as I've done many times when I need reassurance.

"Moving across the country will be hard, but you're only a train ride away."

"We're going to have so much fun. Just stand your ground. In the end, Uncle Lex will be proud you fought him for what matters most to you."

A scream startles us, forcing our gaze to shift toward the pool where Giselle, Andy's ex, has pushed another girl. The other girl, Seraphina, went to a movie last week with Andy. Judging by the way all eyes are on him, it's our cue to leave.

"Are you thinking what I'm thinking?" I whisper, not to draw attention.

"I'll start the engine."

Andy is out of there in a heartbeat, giving me only a few minutes to say goodbye to Austin. He holds onto me, a little too tight, and it's clear that the tequila has gotten a hold of him. Not wanting to play the nagging girlfriend, I offer him a ride home that he refuses, wanting to stay back with the boys.

Annoyed, I leave him behind and make my way toward Andy's Jeep. Andy roars the engine, speeding out of the long-winding driveway and toward home, which isn't too far away.

We pull up the front of my house. I wave goodbye to Andy, carrying my shoes since a blister is on the verge of killing me. I have no clue how Mom wears heels every day to work, making a mental note to ask her later.

I close the door behind me, tiptoeing toward the kitchen to grab some water. I switch on the light to see my father sitting at the counter with a drink in hand. The amber liquid indicates it's his usual potent choice of drink —whisky.

Great. The wrath of a father waiting up for his daughter, a daughter who just left a party where she fooled around with her boyfriend and tequila was passed around. A party that was supposed to be chaperoned, but clearly, Madison was in charge.

"Hello," I greet in monotone, avoiding his eyes and walking toward the refrigerator.

He doesn't say a word, which comes as no surprise at all. I suspect his next words will be "you'll never leave this house ever again."

"Amelia," he calls my name softly. "I apologize for what I said earlier today."

My head slowly moves out of the refrigerator. My father apologized? Has the universe gone mad? I'm unsure what to say, rarely hearing an apology ever leave my father's mouth.

I take a sip of water, closing the refrigerator. "I didn't apply to Yale to defy you if that's what you think."

"I know."

"I just wanted..." I struggle with my words, my head clouded with Austin telling me he loves me, a high which seems to disappear in my father's presence and the reminder of his behavior after doing shots. "I've always wanted to study law there. And I know Mom has only positive things to say about her experience at Yale."

"You're just like your mother," he confesses, his voice still low. I suspect the whisky in hand has everything to do with it. "I know you think I'm strict, harsh, or the so-called dictator according to what you and your sisters like to throw around, but I only want the best for you, for all of my daughters."

I place my shoes on the floor, crossing my arms in defiance. "Then why must you rule every decision of mine? I'm eighteen, Dad, and whether you like it or not, I'm an adult now. I need to make my decisions even if they're mistakes."

"I understand that—"

"And I've done nothing but prove to you I'm capable. I worked very hard to earn extra credits. All I've done is study this year. I know I'm not Ava, your favorite, but when have I ever let you down? Everything you want me to do, I do. The only thing I'm going to stand up for is going to Yale."

I see his face drop, his emotions visible, unlike his usually controlled self.

"Despite what you girls think, I don't favor Ava." His emerald-green eyes meet mine, a color identical to my own. "You'll always be my firstborn daughter, and everything you are reminds me exactly of your mother. And perhaps, what I'll admit to is that I'm scared. Your mother didn't exactly have an easy start to adulthood, largely due to my mistakes. I'm trying to protect you."

"But why can't you understand that I can protect myself? If there's anything you and Mom have taught me, it's to stand up for what I believe in. Never compromise who I am for someone else. So, this is me, Dad, standing up for my dreams, for my future.

Silence falls over the room, the same time the microwave clock flicks to exactly midnight.

"Amelia, if this is what you want, I won't stop you."

I absorb his words with a hard swallow, trying to determine whether this is a joke or real. Given that Dad rarely jokes with me of late, I'm assuming the latter.

I continue to watch him in silence until a slight smile graces his face. I'm overwhelmed at the thought of actually attending Yale at the moment, forcing me to place my bottle down on the countertop and throw my arms around him for an embrace. Inside his arms, I feel protected. I can't recall the last time I hugged him, but my tears begin to fall as I bury my face into his business shirt, accidentally smearing mascara into the white fabric.

Slowly, I pull back, sniffling. His eyes gloss over as he wipes the tear running down my cheek.

"You're going to do great things. You have the Edwards and Mason blood in you, though your argumentative side comes from your mom."

I laugh, allowing my face to rest in his hand. "Between you and Mom, I don't think failure is an option. Besides, someone has to be a good role model for Addison and Alexandra. Lord knows Ava is dying to teach them how to become the next influencer on social media."

Dad laughs, shaking his head. "Your sister will be the death of me. How much easier would it be to have all sons?"

"Maybe one day you'll be blessed with all grandsons."

"Hey..." He smirks playfully. "Don't go getting any ideas."

"I have a career to achieve, Dad. You can count on me to be studying the next seven years."

"I remember those days. I'm not as disciplined as your mom though."

Gentle footsteps echo in the distance. A few seconds later, Mom enters the room dressed in her navy-blue robe with her chocolate brown hair loose, surprised to see us laughing.

"Am I interrupting?"

"No." Dad motions for her to come over as I pull away. She moves toward him, wrapping her arms around his neck so lovingly. "We were just discussing her law degree."

Mom's eyes perk up. "So... it's official?"

"I'm going to Yale." I grin with a slight bounce.

Mom lets go of Dad, hugging me as her eyes glass over. "Gee, kid, we sure are going to miss you around here."

"You've got three more daughters to continue the headaches."

"Tell me about it. Ava will be the death of me."

"That's what Dad said." I chuckle, then slow down. "Mom, I was thinking, do you think next summer Aunt Nikki would allow me to volunteer at the Manhattan firm?"

"I'm sure she can make it happen. I'm glad she and Uncle Rocky are in the city should you get lonely. Beau is what?" She looks at Dad. "In middle school? And, of course, Will still works in the city."

"I forgot about Will," I say, barely able to remember the last time I'd seen him. "I'm sure if I get lonely, I can visit them. But Andy also got into NYU, so he's just a train ride away."

I let out a yawn, noting the time once again. There's so much to think about, plan, and do, but exhaustion from a very tiring day creeps in.

"I'm off to bed. It's been a long day. I'm sure you love-birds want to be alone." The second I say it, I cringe at myself. "You know what? Please don't answer that."

Both Mom and Dad laugh at the same time. "We shall remain quiet."

I turn back to face them one more time. "I love you guys. Thank you again for everything."

And as I watch my parents gaze lovingly upon me, I realize how blessed I am to have their unconditional love. For my years of growing up as their daughter, they have been two people so in love and never once letting me believe otherwise.

My thoughts drift to Austin. I do love him enough that I don't want to let go of what we have. Our geographical location will prove a challenge, but if we do love each other as much as we say we do, anything is possible.

I know my parents made it work despite the trials and tribulations they faced. In the end, their love was unstoppable.

As for Austin and me, only time will tell.

And for the last few months we have left together, I want to make every minute count.

I want to make memories to last me a *lifetime.*

FIVE

AMELIA

I n the blink of an eye, prom and graduation pass, and so does our summer in France.

It's been a family tradition of ours to spend the summer at our chateau in Champagne, along with my Uncle Noah and his wife Kate, who own a place next door. My cousins, Jessa, Nash, and Sienna, join us too, making it all the more fun.

The older we became, the more freedom our parents allowed. Though Alexandra and Sienna, being the youngest of us all, would often get left behind on our mischievous adventures.

This time, I savored it all—the beautiful countryside, the sunsets, the smell of the air, and dinners with my family, not knowing when I'd be able to join them next. Next summer, the plans will most likely involve working since I want to gain as much practical experience as possible. Traditionally, campuses will empty as students travel back home or to their chosen holiday destination.

All of these changes happened in the blink of an eye.

One moment I'm choosing a prom dress, the next minute the night is over, and all we have left are memories.

I also learned I've been awarded class valedictorian. An honor, and one my parents were proud of me achieving. With that came the stress of the speech, making sure my words were powerful and resonated with the audience. I practiced in front of my family numerous times, my dad giving me pointers to calm my nerves when it became a bit too much. When it comes to public speaking, he's an expert. He's spoken in auditoriums in front of thousands of people, never appearing to break a sweat.

Then all of a sudden, I'm wearing a cap and gown, standing on the stage delivering my speech, and then we are throwing our caps in the air, saying goodbye to yet another part of our lives.

Of course, Mom cried as did my Aunt Adriana. My dad watched on proudly, a dignified smile on his face as he gave me the confidence to get through the day. The day itself was emotionally draining, yet both Andy and I were ready for our next adventure—college.

It's the night before my flight to the East Coast. I run through the list of things I need to tick off. Since our return from France, I made sure to touch base with everyone I know, made plans to say goodbye or future plans to catch up in New York. Keeping myself busy takes my mind off the one thing I find the hardest to think about—leaving my family.

Mom organized a family dinner, just the six of us. All afternoon, she stayed in the kitchen cooking all my favorite dishes, making sure that everything I love will be served tonight. I appreciate the effort, but again, it makes it harder to leave.

As I sit at the table, quiet and lost in thought, my sisters remain just as silent. The food—delicious with all its aromas —doesn't erase the empty feeling sitting in the pit of my stomach. My fork aimlessly pushes the food around with my eyes fixated on the slow movements.

"I wonder if the meatloaf at Yale is still as bad as I remember," Mom says to break the silence.

"It was just as bad at USCF," Dad adds to the conversation. "It must be a universal college thing."

"All the more reason I should study local." Ava finally laughs, her smile infectious as her green eyes brighten her face. "Mom's cooking rivals the best of restaurants in LA."

"Aww, that's nice of you, honey. You still can't go to Cabo with Alyssa," Mom replies, making her final decision known.

"Drats... worth a try," Ava mumbles.

My sister, Addison, is reserved. With six years apart, a piece of me is sad to leave her during the years she'll need me the most. Ava is so carefree, always wanting to have fun, and Addison is the complete opposite, her nose usually in some book.

"You'll all visit, right?" I cheerfully ask. "Addison, you would love the Yale library. When I visited the campus, I couldn't believe how many books they had."

Addison's expression shifts, a small smile escaping. It's uncanny that Ava and Addison look so much alike, both of them a spitting image of Dad. They have the same emerald eyes we all got from him, a strong genetic trait of his. Yet, their hair color and skin tone mirror that of Dad's. Alexandra is a combination of both Mom and Dad. I'm the only one, according to everyone, who transitioned to look more like Mom.

"Daddy, when can we go visit?" Alexandra questions, tugging at his sleeve beside him.

"Soon, sweetheart. We need to get your sister settled in first. Let her get used to her new schedule and studying, then perhaps we can spend Thanksgiving in Manhattan if Mom is okay with that."

Mom beams at the idea. "That sounds perfect. Thanksgiving in the city."

We immerse ourselves in idle chit-chat, something I enjoy with my family since it's always entertaining when everyone is involved. Not long after we finish, Andy stops by with his parents to say goodbye. Andy's acceptance to NYU came as a relief to my parents since he'll only be a train ride away. I always knew he'd follow a creative career given Aunt Adriana is a designer, and his biological father used to paint as a hobby.

But it's Uncle Julian, his stepfather, who he admires the most and influenced his love of photography. The two of them have traveled all over the world, and whenever they return, I sit for hours and listen to their stories, including photos Andy captured. I may be biased, but Andy is incredibly talented and can see the beauty in almost anything.

"I'm going to miss you," Aunt Adriana confesses, struggling to compose herself. I wrap my arms around her, knowing I'll miss her just as much. She's like the big sister I never had, and it helps that she has no fear whatsoever when dealing with Dad.

"I'm going to miss you, too. You've got my email. I want to see all those designs you've been working on."

"Of course, your opinion means everything to me." She smiles before looking at Ava jokingly. "If it were up to Ava, my designs would involve midriffs and booty shorts."

My dad shakes his head in disappointment. "Did you have to go there, Adriana?"

"Why yes, dear brother," she responds in jest, then

turns her focus back to me. "Now, listen, you, I want updates on everything, including men."

"Jesus Christ, Adriana! Let the girl focus on studying. The last thing she should be thinking about is boys."

"Men, Lex," Aunt Adriana corrects him. "She'll be with men now."

And that's the other thing—I'll supposedly be surrounded by *men* now. Ava claims to be jealous, bored of high school boys and their immaturity. She turned seventeen over the summer and decided she was above the boys she circles with, including the guy she dated and lost her virginity to. At the time when she told me, I wasn't sure how to feel. Your younger sister has sex in the back of a car with some guy she's crushed on, yet here I am almost two years older than her with a steady boyfriend, and we haven't done the deed.

That's not to say we haven't moved forward. Austin and I still fool around when we can, but Dad wanted me home as soon as prom finished. He even made sure the driver greeted me at the door. The only reason I allow him to pull the so-called parental strings is because I'll soon have all the freedom in the world, and he'll have no say in the matter.

A reminder of my final goodbye with Austin comes to mind. "Oh gosh, what's the time?"

"Just after eight," Mom informs me. "You go spend time with Austin. Don't keep that lovely boy waiting."

I say goodbye to Aunt Adriana and Uncle Julian, then remind Andy we planned to catch up in two weeks for dinner in the city.

I drive over to Austin's place, though he suggests we take his car for a drive since he plans to take the vehicle off-road. After twenty minutes, we park the car and take our belongings to our favorite spot.

We sit on the picnic blanket on a hill that overlooks the city. The views are stunning at night, a light show which twinkles in the distance. The area is secluded, making it peaceful and just what we both need to calm our anxious nerves.

"Are you nervous?" I ask, staring into the distance.

"Yes," Austin admits, his trance just as deep as mine. "New school, new crowd, no parents. It's a lot to take in."

I nod, feeling just as overwhelmed as him.

"I'm just a call away, or text, or DM." I smile, offering him support. "I'll always be there for you."

Austin lowers his head. "I'd be foolish to think you'll be mine forever. Once those college boys see you, you'll be the talk of the campus."

I purse my lips, placing my hand on his knee. "That's not true. Have you seen me in study mode? I look like Chewbacca. When we were cramming for finals, I didn't wash my hair for a week."

A laugh escapes him. "Don't underestimate how beautiful you are, Millie."

"Well, I can say the same for you. I spent most of this year trying to fend off junior and senior girls from trying to dig their claws into you. College girls will fall in love with the handsome man studying to be a doctor."

"Hmm... I forgot about the doctor card. I guess it could come in handy one day."

A pang of jealousy hits me. Why does this have to be so hard? If I love him like I say I do, why am I going to a school so far away? I often look at my parents, knowing their story since Mom had shared it with me. They moved heaven and earth to be with one another. That's true love, so why am I not fighting for Austin?

And the biggest question to remain unanswered is what

if Austin is the love of my life? The man I'm supposed to grow old with and have his children. The thought of letting him go hurts, but every way I analyze the situation, it never works in our favor.

"Austin?" I say above a whisper. "I don't want us to end."

Austin closes his eyes, almost as if he's breathing a sigh of relief. He turns to face me, his finger grazing against my lip, making my heart pitter-patter like a butterfly trapped in captivity.

"Neither do I, Millie, but I don't know how to make it work. We're so far apart, and then our class load means we'll be so busy."

"Maybe," I suggest eagerly. "We don't label this or us. We don't need to say goodbye forever. Why can't we just say no words at all?"

Austin cups my chin, bringing me in for a deep kiss. I tug at his shirt, not wanting to let him go. For a moment, our eyes meet, and something passes between us. Gently, he lays me down and hovers on top of me, burying his head into my neck and lavishing me with kisses. I moan slightly, running my hands through his hair, desperate to capture his scent in my memories. His hand wanders toward my thigh, grazing up before our eyes meet again.

I want him.

"Austin," I whisper with trembling hands. "I'm ready."

His eyes widen, not with excitement as I assumed most men would feel at this moment, but of torture. "Are you sure? I don't want to pressure you."

Austin's caring nature settles my anxious thoughts. If there's any man who deserves to own this moment, one that will stay with me for a lifetime, I want it to be Austin Carter.

I take in the sight of him, bringing his lips to mine. *"You're perfect."*

And much like the last few months, this moment came and went in the blink of an eye. I gasp with each touch and wince slightly when he enters me, but soon I understand the power of intimacy. How this very moment, with the right person, can change the beat of one's heart.

With every thrust, desire overcomes us, driving our bodies to move in sync. Our kisses deepen, rushed with urgency, until the slight pain I experienced subsides, and my body begins to convulse into a beautiful finish.

I throw my head back when Austin pulls out abruptly, his body jerking forward as he spills out beside us.

"Are you okay?" I ask, barely able to catch my breath.

"Yes," he answers with a grin. *"I'm perfect."*

And as his lips find their way back to mine, we exchange our "I love you's" and promise not to map out our future on the fear of losing each other.

We'll always have this moment, and no matter what happens from now on, no one can ever take that away from us.

SIX

WILL

"**W**illiam Rockford Romano, why are you avoiding my calls?"

My mother's nagging voice barrels through the speaker. For someone who's ambitious and works long hours as a lawyer, she should understand my time during business is precious. It's not like I sit around, scratching my ass on the couch while watching football like Dad. I own a company, one that needs my attention almost every hour of each day.

"I'm not ignoring you, Mother. I've been busy, that's all."

"Oh, cut the bullshit with me. There was a photo of you with some woman at a launch party last night in Brooklyn. Busy being a playboy, I see? The apple does not fall far from the tree."

I snicker, having heard this a dozen times. "Dad would be proud."

"Yes, unfortunately, your father is quite proud of your inability to settle down," she complains, reminding me why I avoid her calls like the plague. "Now, when are you coming over for dinner? It's been too long, and your brother misses you."

My brother only misses me because I'm his saving grace from my parents. Having just turned fifteen, he has finally discovered girls. The little son of a bitch used me as an alibi on several occasions, and God knows what he did. I figured, let him make the mistakes for himself. I'm not his father, just the older brother with an empty apartment he conveniently brings "friends" back to when I'm at work. The last time he had done so, I found a fucking used condom in my bathroom he swears wasn't his. Since then, I changed my passcode to my apartment and told him to hang out somewhere else.

Closing my eyes for a brief moment, I ignore the constant ping of emails coming through, knowing I have one more meeting this afternoon, which will most likely extend into after-work drinks.

"I'll check with my assistant and get back to you."

"Is your personal assistant still the blonde with the rather bouncy ass? Or did it conflict with your working relationship, too?"

I let out an annoyed huff, wondering why on earth I have to justify my sex life to my overbearing mother. "Of course not. She has other endeavors she wishes to pursue."

There's a rustle in the background, distracting Mom until I hear, "How's my boy? Don't tell me you let her suck your dick and then fired her?"

"Rocky!" Mom shouts, the loud sound causing me to distance the phone from my ear. "How crass of you to say that to your son."

I let out a snicker. Dad has been crass for as long as I can remember. He doesn't take life seriously, something I love about him. Discipline could smack him in the face, and he still wouldn't understand the meaning of it. Unfortunately, my mother makes up for his relaxed parenting style —the complete opposite.

"Uh... no, Dad, I wouldn't quite put it that way."

"So, you fucked her, then?"

"Jesus Christ, go away. And why are you here?" The voices filter out before Mom tells him to fuck off, plain and simple. "Now listen, ignore your father, and please come to dinner. I miss you."

"I will, Mom. Promise."

We hang up the phone, my smile still lingering from Dad's blunt yet accurate calling of my sex life. Jennifer, as she shall be named, was too hard to resist. Every single goddamn time she bent over to water the plants in my office to the low-cut blouses she wore, it was too much.

Yet, I'm a gentleman. I didn't make a move until a work event last week in which she got drunk and offered to suck my cock. Of course, I warned her that she'd have to give up her nicely paid position by doing so.

She wanted cock more.

Who could blame her?

I got what I needed, and it wasn't as if she was a hard worker. Her skills were less than par. But, of course, I'm down an assistant, and these temporary women filling in have been old and undesirable.

Considering I run this company, how fucking hard is it to find someone competent?

I note the time, grabbing my phone and wandering across to the boardroom. The noise stops upon my arrival, my management team quietly waiting until Lex Edwards enters the room. The bastards all fall on their knees with his dominating presence, whereas I extend my hand, shaking his.

Unlike everyone else, I've known Lex on a personal level all my life. I have considered him an uncle, a great mentor, and one who treats me like his own son. Not only do we have personal ties, but it's also Lex who invested in my company, allowing it to launch initially, making it now a multi-million-dollar business.

He informed me of his trip to the city, and I suggested we meet as there's a chance of extending the business, though we need more capital.

"Let's get down to it," he insists, taking his spot at the table. "Show me your numbers."

By the end of the meeting, my staff scurries out like lost puppies, leaving only Lex and me. Outside the window, darkness falls, though the bright city lights never fail to shine, and just like I had predicted, we dragged well into the night.

"I'm going to agree with you. I see the potential and want the full scope of this merger by the end of the month. You deliver what I need, and the capital is yours."

I breathe a sigh of relief, confident I can do that. I only learn from the best, and there's no chance in hell that Lex will allow me to screw this up. I may have graduated with a Master's in Business, but nothing is as important as a mogul's guidance.

A tycoon, as he's often referred to.

Standing up to stretch my legs, I open the cabinet and pull out an aged whisky bottle I store in there, handing a glass to Lex. We cheer on our proposed deal, then both let out a relaxed breath.

"Change of topic," Lex says, taking another drink. "Amelia has started at Yale."

"Yale? Impressive." I nod, despite being a Harvard man myself. "What's she studying?"

The truth be told, I haven't seen her since she was a kid or maybe four years ago when she was in middle school. It would've been one of our family dinners and given our age gap of just over ten years, we had nothing in common. My memories of her are this annoying little girl who would pester me to do dangerous things in her backyard on my visits, like jumping off the roof and into the pool.

"Law, like mother like daughter," Lex professes while smiling fondly. "I wasn't exactly thrilled when we found out."

I laugh, pouring more whisky into our glasses. "Lex Edwards, billionaire tycoon with four daughters. Why am I not surprised?"

He snickers, enjoying my dig at his protective persona. "One day, you'll have kids of your own, possibly daughters, and then you'll know."

"Please..." I roll my eyes with boredom. "The last thing I want is marriage and babies. I'm quite happy being single despite what my mother believes."

"Your mother believes you can't keep your dick in your pants. Hence, why she keeps having to deal with different assistants when trying to call you."

"Hmm... gossip travels fast." I smirk playfully behind the glass. "No one understands my lifestyle. They either want on my cock or in my pocket. I'm almost thirty, too young to worry about settling down. I've got an empire to build, not pussy to chase."

Lex shakes his head with a knowing smile. "Aren't you the epitome of a young Lex Edwards? But a word of warning, one day you'll wake up and realize that being alone is a punishment, not a blessing."

"And until then, what does it matter if my bed is warm

in the morning from some chick who can get me off quickly?"

"Why do I *not* believe you allow them to stay over?"

I throw back the rest of my drink. "You have me there, old fella, just trying to paint myself as a considerate lover."

Lex points his finger at me. "You, Will Romano, are a selfish man, as was I once upon a time, but look where I ended up? If you're to follow in my footsteps, I expect some woman to own you very soon."

Laughter escapes me. "I recall the upsetting memory. You stole my favorite aunt and whisked her away to have babies in LA. I'm happy to prove you wrong. Wager, if needed."

"Now, now, don't get so cocky. Mark my words, son, it'll happen to you. And all this..." he points around my office with an arrogant grin, "... will mean nothing if you can't have her."

With a dismissive nod, I raise my glass. "The bet is on. It's time to prove Lex Edwards wrong."

SEVEN

AMELIA

We stand inside the dorm room, the last of my boxes placed on the wooden floor.

"It brings back memories," Mom confesses, her eyes wandering around the room fondly. "I stayed in this very room."

"Are you sure? They all look similar."

"There are some things you never forget," she tells me with a smile, then points to the room on the left. "By the way, that's the room where I caught your Aunt Nikki and Uncle Rocky, naked, my first day here."

I screw up my mouth, folding my arms as if it will shield me from the unwanted memory.

"Thank God I chose the other one. Though I'm sure you have stories you could tell. College years, aren't they supposed to be the best years of your life?"

Mom takes a seat on the small tan sofa. "Everyone is different. For me, I was learning how to overcome trauma. I used studying as a coping mechanism, so dating and parties were the least of my priorities."

I sit beside her, leaning my head on her shoulder, something I'll miss dearly.

"You never did explain what happened back then, aside from you and Dad spending time apart."

Mom releases a sigh, and perhaps I have pushed her too much, though I often find myself curious about what really happened.

"We were young. Well, I was young. Your dad and I started something when I was in my senior year, and he was married, just out of college. It didn't end well, and it really broke me."

"Of course, you loved him, right?"

Mom's lips curve upward, an endearing smile gracing her entire face whenever she's asked about her love for her husband. I often wonder if I give the same expression when I speak about Austin.

"I've always loved your father, but I was young and foolish with my desires and intentions. What we had, or shall I say did, wasn't sustainable. We parted ways, and years later, I guess fate chose to bring us back together."

Fate is something I've read about in romance novels, yet I'm not convinced there's such a thing. If fate is real, why didn't Austin and I end up in closer schools? What purpose is it to have us hours apart?

"I love Austin," I admit with a lowered voice. "But I know this will be hard."

"Love isn't easy, Amelia. And the stronger and deeper the love, the harder it will test you. How else will you know if that person is worth fighting for unless you put it to the test?"

"Is that what happened with you and Dad?"

"Gosh, kid, your dad and I have been tested in ways you couldn't possibly imagine."

"Mom..." I whisper, twisting my hands nervously. "I slept with Austin."

My mom sits silently beside me, only her shallow breaths heard between us. We've always been close, and Mom never makes me feel uneasy to the point that I can't be honest or ask questions whenever I'm unsure.

"I knew it would happen, it was inevitable, and Austin is a good boy."

"Are you upset with me?"

"Oh, honey." She places her arm around me, allowing me to rest my face on her chest. "Nothing you do will upset me. I love you unconditionally. You're an adult now, and having sex is part of being an adult. Just be safe, that's all I'll say. I love you, but I'm not exactly ready to be a grandmother." She chuckles softly.

"I went on the pill a few months ago," I admit, slightly apprehensive. "I just want to be a lawyer like you. I'm not here to party or sleep with random men. This is the time to focus on studying."

"Don't forget to have a little fun. It's all part of a rounded college experience."

A noise startles us at the door. We both turn our heads and see a girl with tight auburn curls thrown to the side of her face as she drags in two large pink suitcases.

"Oh, hey." She smiles, her mouth widening with two evident dimples gracing her face. "You must be my roommate. I'm Liesel."

I stand up to greet her. "I'm Amelia, and this is my mom, Charlie."

"Nice to meet you both," she says, out of breath.

"Do you need help?"

"I'm good, I think. I found some cute boys at the entrance, and they offered to bring the rest of my stuff in."

As Liesel finishes off her sentence, three guys drag boxes, a trunk, another two suitcases, and a surfboard. I turn to look at Mom for answers, but she shrugs her shoulders in confusion just like me.

"Thanks, guys, I'll catch you later tonight."

Liesel closes the door, sitting down on the trunk, letting out a long-winded breath. We wait quietly for her to catch her bearings until she raises her hand to her chest. "I'm sorry, I know I have a lot of stuff."

"It's fine, but um... why the surfboard?"

"How much time do you have? Let's just say that I left a boyfriend behind. He's from Australia, and well, this," she points to the surfboard, "... belonged to him."

"Okay, makes sense." I nod. "But wouldn't it have been easier to leave it at home?"

"My parents are moving to Hong Kong. So, it was either dump it or take it. I didn't have the heart to dump it just yet. What if Flynn is the love of my life? Maybe we'll get back together, and I'll regret my decision to discard what was supposed to be a romantic gift? I could mess with the universe."

That was a lot to take in, and beside me, I could see Mom is trying to keep a straight face.

"Well, listen, girls, I probably should let you both get settled."

My eyes fall upon my hands with an empty stare, a heavy weight on my chest soon following. This moment was bound to happen. I have to say goodbye at some point.

Liesel excuses herself to her room, leaving Mom and me to say goodbye.

"I... I um..." I stammer, unable to clear my throat. "I'll miss you, Mom."

Grabbing both my hands, Mom squeezes them tight,

her vision clouded. This is one of those moments you watch in movies but never realize the depth of emotions that play a part in such a goodbye. Leaving my sisters and even my dad has been hard. Closing the door to my bedroom, the same room which holds so many memories, is extremely difficult. Yet, above all, saying goodbye to a woman who brought me into this world and made sacrifice after sacrifice to give me the best life possible is by far the hardest of all goodbyes.

"I'm only a phone call away, okay? It doesn't matter what time, whenever you need me, I'm there for you."

I nod my head, finally blinking and letting my tears fall freely. I throw my arms around her, squeezing her tight just like I did when I was a little girl, begging our embrace to numb the sick feeling in the pit of my stomach.

"I'll be okay, Mom."

"Of course, you will be," she assures me with a smile, quick to hide her sniffle. "You have the Edwards' blood in you. Strong, born a warrior."

We hug one more time before Mom says her final good-bye, leaving the room. I take in a deep breath, the feeling of being homesick a hard slap in the face. In a matter of moments, loneliness consumes me. It's unrelenting in its pursuit, feeding off my weakened emotions and questioning my need to study so far away from home.

The walls surrounding me are bare, this room holding no memories for me to fondly reminisce in my time of need.

Just as I'm about to run outside to find Mom and tell her I can't do this, Liesel comes out of her room with a sympathetic smile.

"You know what will make you feel better? If you come to a party with me tonight."

I chuckle softly, the distraction somewhat welcoming. "A party already? I'm not sure, I should probably unpack.

Classes start in a few days, and I want to make sure I'm organized."

"There's plenty of time for that. C'mon, it'll be fun plus a good chance to meet some new people."

I pull my slumped shoulders back, improving my posture while releasing a breath. I'm an adult now. Leaving my family was bound to happen. If I am to make this work, I need to make the right decisions, not ones leading to my comfort zone.

A college party isn't such a bad idea and definitely is the distraction I need from my misery.

I nod in agreement.

"Yay! Okay, I need to find exactly where I packed my makeup. Be dressed in an hour."

With not too much time to spare, I head to my room and close the door behind me. I figure it will be a chilled party, opting to wear my jeans and a tank tonight. Throwing myself on my bed, I grab my phone and video call Austin.

"Hey, you." His handsome grin graces the screen. Behind him, a stack of boxes just like mine is beside his bed. "I'm guessing your Mom finally left?"

"Yes, and I don't want to talk about it. Can't you see my panda eyes?"

He chuckles softly. "You're still beautiful. So, did you meet your roommate?"

"I did. She's nice and really friendly. She invited me to a party tonight."

"A party?"

"Yeah, not sure where. I said yes only because she begged."

Austin lowers his gaze, his expression changing almost instantly. If I didn't know better, he's not pleased that I'm going out.

"Is something wrong?"

"It's nothing." He clears his throat, still avoiding my eyes. "Listen, I should go. I've got a lot to unpack."

"I love you, Austin," I say, missing him so much. "Please don't forget that."

Slowly, his gaze lifts to meet mine, and his face softens. "I love you, too, Millie. Call me when you get back, okay?"

"Promise." I smile before I hang up the call.

Alone, inside my dorm room, I fall back onto my bed and stare at the ceiling. It all seems too hard—moving across the country and saying goodbye to my family and the boy I love. I'm fighting hard for exactly this—Yale. But for what? What if I don't enjoy studying or change my mind about being a lawyer? I'm waiting for a sign to tell me I am on the right path, and this is exactly where I'm meant to be—that Austin and I will endure the distance and find a way to stay together.

But something warns me otherwise, a voice telling me this is all just the beginning. Just like my mom so wisely said, the stronger the love, the harder the fight.

And what terrifies me the most is that the true test is yet to come.

Heartache is just around the corner.

EIGHT

AMELIA

Nothing anyone could've said would've prepared me for my first few months of college.

It was even better.

Being surrounded by intellectual students who want to learn is vastly different from high school. Our lectures often turn into discussions I thoroughly enjoy, giving me a chance to interact with my peers on a non-social level.

I frequently find myself immersed in reading, and studying has become so much more challenging than senior year. At times, the pressure mounts, yet I quickly learned that I thrive on it. It pushes me to work harder, and if I want to make a career out of the law, I need tough skin and a strong work ethic.

Aside from Liesel, it hasn't taken too long to make friends with those who have similar interests to me. We often have lunch together and hang out for coffee, which I despised before college life. Yet now, I can't get through a day without it. It has become my staple diet when I'm unable to stop for a bite to eat. The coffee cart guy knows me on a first-name basis, and yes, he's cute.

If there's some social get-together in New Haven, we all go together, depending on our study schedule. All in all, my parents are pleased I haven't found the "bad crowd," who spends the entire time planning keg parties and getting laid.

Yes, I know who they are, and I just choose to avoid them.

But like anything, the good comes with the bad. I invariably find myself homesick, the nights being the hardest.

In times of need, I call Mom and just talk for hours about anything I can, missing the sound of her voice and needing her reassurance. Most of the time, I have questions about papers, though Dad helps me a lot with things I struggle to grasp. Surprisingly, our bond strengthened upon my departure.

Yet milestones pass like my siblings' birthdays, making it hard when I can't be there in person. I plan to head home for Thanksgiving, having not seen my family in two months, and then to add to all of that, I miss Austin.

It's Friday, a rare class-free day, and I opt to train it into the city. I take my phone out, texting Austin.

Me: *Why does the train have this odd smell?*

Austin: *It's called humans. It's what happens when you leave your dorm room after studying nonstop.*

Austin: *So... have you recovered from last night?*

A smile escapes me, the heat rising in my cheeks soon following. Thankfully, the seat beside me is empty. I stare out the window, reminiscing about last night. It started with flirtatious banter, then led to our clothes coming off and a *very* happy ending. Something we resort to of late since we were miles apart.

> **Me:** *If I weren't on a train with strangers, I'd say round two?*

> **Austin:** *You're killing me...*

> **Austin:** *Have you thought more about Thanksgiving?*

Taking a deep breath, I don't want to take too long to answer but also don't want to offend Austin, given my plans with my family, something I hope he'll understand.

> **Me:** *I have, and you know that I miss you, but I really need to see my family. Maybe you could drive here one weekend? It's only five hours away.*

I wait for a response, but it doesn't come. This separation thing has been harder than expected, and although having sex bonded us in a way, it also drives a wedge between us at times. Physically missing someone is hard, and I'd be a fool to think we can go on like this for the next seven years. Austin has needs the girls at Johns Hopkins can easily fulfill. But even then, I choose not to end things, once again letting our relationship go through the motions to stand the test of time—separation.

The train pulls up into Grand Central Station. As soon as I exit, the city's hustle and bustle greet me along with the fall breeze. Dressed in my jeans and wearing my long camel-colored coat, I chose to wear my Chucks, knowing I'll be walking around the city, and the last thing I need is blistered feet.

The familiar blond-haired boy waves at me from across the exit. I run toward him, practically throwing myself at him in desperation.

"I missed you," I mumble into his chest, holding onto him tightly.

"Missed you, too, Harley Quinn." Andy chuckles while bringing up my long-lost nickname from when we were kids. I'd forgotten all about it and how they often referred to me as Harley Quinn because of my crazy shenanigans. Thankfully, I have outgrown this reckless behavior which should warrant scrapping the nickname for good.

I peel myself away from him, placing my hands on his shoulders. "How long do I have you for?"

"Four hours, then I've got a class."

"You're such a nerd," I joke while grinning. "Have you been behaving?"

"Hmm..." He rubs his chin, and only now, I notice the slight stubble of the beard he's growing. "Let's walk and talk. Hot dogs for lunch?"

"Sure, lead the way."

We exit on 42nd Street and head toward Bryant Park, stopping briefly to grab a hot dog and soda. Andy talks about campus life, his classes, his quirky roommate, and the group he hangs out with. We both immersed ourselves into college life, realizing just how much we have changed in only this short time.

"So, tell me what's happening with the ladies?"

Andy shuffles his feet, looking uncomfortable.

"Why the face?" I ask, curious as to his change of expression. "It's not like I asked you to swallow poison."

"I... um," he stammers, scratching the back of his neck. "I've dated a few girls but nothing serious."

"Dated a few girls? That was fast. It's only been two months. Are you sure you're studying?"

"College girls are different... they are, how shall I put it?"

"Loose?"

Andy chuckles, biting into his hot dog. "I guess you could say that."

"Argh," I grunt, slumping into my chair. "Why is everyone having the time of their lives, and I'm arguing with a boyfriend over a text?"

"What's the problem now?"

"The problem is over two hundred miles between us. This is harder than I thought."

"Then break up with him. Simple."

"It's not *that* simple."

"Millie," Andy says, crossing his arms while watching me. "Do you really think Austin is just sitting there and pining for you? Have you seen the girls in college?"

"Yes," I drag, aware that beautiful women surround Austin. "But doesn't love count for something?"

"Do you love him? Or are you just saying that because you lost your virginity to him?"

My eyes widen, my head turning abruptly. *"How did you know?"*

"Ava, but in her defense, I thought it happened too."

"The two of you are a pain in my ass," I complain, frowning. "I do love him, I mean, what I feel is more than just a crush. We've been together for over a year. I can't just throw that away because it's getting hard."

Andy's attention is pulled toward a bunch of pigeons

fighting for a donut a little kid drops on the pavement. Moments later, he turns his head while creasing his brows.

"Millie, you have to be honest with yourself. Sooner or later, the two of you will grow apart. It's only natural, I mean, how many high school romances do you know that lasted?"

"Well, Mom and Dad, for starters."

Andy purses his lips. "Um... from what my mom says, they were apart for eight years, so that doesn't count."

I rack my brain trying to come up with an answer but fall short. Maybe Andy is right, but nevertheless, I don't want to give up just yet. For as long as it feels right, I'll fight for us.

"So, back to you and your dating life..."

Andy laughs beside me. "Not much to tell, Millie. It would be oddly gross if I went into detail."

I shake my head, grabbing my soda bottle to throw into the thrash. "Where to next?"

"Museum of Metropolitan Art?" Andy suggests.

"Let's go."

We head toward the subway, spending the rest of our time walking around and commenting on all the art pieces on display. We often argue when our opinions differ but forget about it minutes later when we find ourselves laughing at something trivial.

The hours pass so easily, our fun coming to an end once again. Andy hugs me goodbye as he leaves for class. We agree to catch up for my birthday in a week, dinner in the city at a restaurant of my choice.

It's a glorious day considering it is fall. The sun is out, a warm blanket on my face to cancel out the occasional cool breeze. I take my time walking through Central Park, admiring the surroundings and watching people as they go about their activities. The casual stroll is enjoyable until my legs grow tired from walking.

I stop by a small café, ordering myself a coffee and taking a seat to rest my legs. I recheck my phone, and still no message from Austin. As I'm just about to put my phone away, the phone rings with my Aunt Nikki's name appearing on the screen.

"Why, hello there, favorite aunt of mine," I greet jovially.

"If I were indeed your favorite, I'd have been visited by now," she points out while I cringe at the lecture I'm about to receive. "A birdie told me you're in the city today."

"Yes, I am. I needed a study break."

"Well, I insist you join us for dinner tonight. Rocky can take you home since there's no chance in hell you're taking a train that late."

My lips flatten, knowing I have no choice. "Of course, sounds great."

"Now, have you had a chance to visit Will?"

"Will? Uh no... I'm sure he's busy with work."

"Considering my son is a workaholic much like your dear old father, an impromptu visit wouldn't hurt. Besides, I just spoke to him to try to convince him to come to dinner, but of course, he has some woman he probably has to pursue."

I laugh at her comment. "A workaholic playboy, I'm sure Uncle Rocky is proud."

"Don't even start," she growls, jokingly. "I'll text you our address, and don't forget to go see him. Someone needs to knock some sense into that man. Perhaps it'll be you."

"I highly doubt that, but sure, I'll drop by his office in about an hour."

Not long after we end our call, my phone beeps with all

the details Aunt Nikki promised. The office building is all the way downtown, and despite my reluctance to visit Will since I haven't seen him in forever, I hop on the subway and make my way toward his office.

The large silver building is tall amongst the older and historic buildings surrounding it. Rechecking the address, I enter the building and find the elevator.

Inside the confined area, I press the button to the twentieth floor when my phone pings.

Austin: *I don't know how long I can do this for.*

Before the doors close, someone steps in, standing at the opposite end of me. My heart sinks at Austin's text, my stomach feeling sick at the thought of us ending at this moment. The conversation with Andy comes to mind. Eventually, we'll grow apart, but it's too soon. Surely, we owe it to each other to at least try for a bit longer before we completely call it quits.

Biting down on my bottom lip, I hang my head, trying to ease the unwanted hardening of my stomach. I begin to type, only to erase the message. No matter what I want to say, it feels like it comes out wrong.

This is not how we should end.

Taking a deep breath, my eyes wander to the shoes and perfectly tailored pants beside me. The gentleman's hand is tucked into his pants' pocket, his watch notable as my dad has a similar one. His scent, a rather intoxicating aftershave, makes me want to check him out, but I keep my head down for fear of being caught.

The door pings on the nineteenth floor as he steps out, allowing me only to see the back of him. His tall stature, dressed in a business suit, is quite sexy. Perhaps I've been around college boys for too long—ripped jeans and T-shirts with crude slogans seem rather unappealing.

"If you're here for an interview, which I assume you are, you may want to make sure you smile and not be caught on your phone."

I lift my head as the door closes, unable to catch his face. What an asshole! I take it all back. Men, in general, are pigs. Right now, Austin is one of them since he can't even make an effort to come see me and quite possibly is breaking up with me via text message.

When I exit the elevator, I ask the receptionist to use the restroom to freshen up. Inside the very clean and modern restroom, I stare into the mirror.

My hair has grown out this past year, the length falling past my bra strap. Running my hands through it, I tousle it to the side as I continue to glance at myself.

What the hell am I going to talk about? I haven't seen Will since forever. I was a kid, no doubt tormenting him as I always did. We have such a big age difference. I think he's close to thirty and most likely have nothing in common besides family. I can bring up his unstable love life at Aunt Nikki's request, but wouldn't that be awkward? As if he needs a nineteen-year-old girl giving him advice, well, almost nineteen in just one week.

Exiting the restroom, I wait in the reception area.

"Miss, you can wait in Mr. Romano's office. He shan't be long."

I smile politely, admiring her British accent. They always sound fancy and educated no matter what they say.

Following her into the office, the glass windows with views of the city immediately catch my attention. It reminds me a lot of Dad's office with an oversized glass desk and leather chair. Everything is strategically placed, and not a single thing looks out of place. From listening to my parents, I think he runs some tech companies and creates apps. I probably should've asked this, so I'd have something to talk about.

The sound of a voice echoes behind the door. "I don't care what it takes, either wrap up the deal or consider yourself done."

Ouch.

"You have until close of business tomorrow," the voice continues, "Uh-huh... listen, I need to call you back."

With my back toward him, I close my eyes then force a smile, spinning around. My eyes fall onto the leather shoes I saw inside the elevator, the ones that belonged to the asshole who commented somewhat prematurely on my phone behavior. Slowly, I drag my eyes upward past his navy-blue pants until I reach his belt, realizing my stare has lingered too long. I snap my head up until our eyes lock.

"Well, if it isn't Miss Edwards." His gaze is unwavering, making me slightly uncomfortable.

Will has changed so much since I last saw him, a man with very defined features and dark hair like his father's. The style is modern and polished and not lathered in product like some men I know.

I don't recall the strong jawline or how his cornflower blue eyes hold so much depth. He has aged so much, or perhaps being in the presence of a man in his thirties is vastly different to college boys I'm surrounded by all day long.

I've never seen him in a business suit, remembering the last time we saw each other, he must have still been in college, and his wardrobe consisted of jeans and tees.

"Living and breathing," I answer, eager to ignore his elevator dig. "How have you been?"

"Quite well, and you?"

"The same."

There's a silence that follows us, prompting him to close the door and take a seat behind his desk. His stare continues to make me feel paranoid, and without trying to make myself obvious, I check my hair to make sure I don't have something wrong with me. Worst yet, do I have something in my teeth? *What does it matter, anyway?* I'm sure Will's seen my many nudie runs during my toddler years.

"It's a lovely office you have here. It reminds me of my father's."

"That it is."

His closed answer leaves nothing for me to continue with.

"Have you been here long?"

"About two years," is all he answers, his annoying stare still making me self-conscious. "You know, you don't have to be so formal."

"I should hope not," I blurt out, relieved at the break of tension. "I'm almost certain you dared me to eat a worm, which I did. Surely, that should count for something."

He chuckles softly. "You always were a risktaker. And look at you now. I've heard you're studying at Yale?"

"Yes. I had a free day, so I thought I'd visit the city..." I trail off, momentarily stumbling on my thoughts as his eyes wander to my lips. My heart beats loudly, but I must be imagining all of this. He's just entertaining me because of obligation, and anyway, I should *not* be thinking about him in any other way. Austin's text still leaves me wounded. That's it.

"I don't remember you being so speechless," he follows with an arrogant smirk. "Little Miss Chatterbox from memory."

"Things change... people change."

His penetrating stare never leaves mine. "Why yes, they do..."

I glance at my phone. "Listen, I should probably go since you must have work to do." I stand up, questioning whether I should hug him since he's family. Perhaps, if I had done that at the beginning, it wouldn't have been so awkward.

"The pleasure has been all mine, Amelia."

My name rolls off his tongue with a delicious bite. *Shit! What the hell is wrong with you? He's family.*

I take a deep breath, willing my actions to gain some sort of control since my imagination has turned into some overcharged sex maniac. This isn't at all like me, it's almost as if he brings out the 'old' Amelia, the one who didn't care for consequences because she always pushed boundaries and limits. Perhaps, I can use this to my advantage. Say something to make Aunt Nikki proud that I've called her son out on his less-than-desirable behavior.

"It was nice seeing you again," I offer with a smile, turning my back on him to leave the room, "Oh, and before I forget, that assistant out there, she's quite nice. Maybe try to keep your dick in your pants, so you don't lose another one."

His expression falls, a look of anger as his eyes pierce into mine. I purposely keep walking with a satisfied smile.

One point for me.

And the best part of all of this, there's no chance of him upping me since I won't be seeing him anytime soon.

NINE

WILL

"And so, Mr. Romano, as you can see on this chart, our company has a lot to offer."

Staring blankly at the screen, I blink my eyes to break the trance I find myself in... *again.* Fuck! What the hell did he say? Not wanting to come off like an idiot, I demand a break.

"I need to make a phone call."

Without waiting for an answer, I storm out of the room and back into the solitude of my office. The glass windows surround me, a view of Brooklyn Bridge not too far in the distance. The city is busy, the usual peak-hour hustle as commuters rush home.

Pacing up and down, I clench my fists, willing to rid myself of these thoughts.

She's too young.

Immature, obviously, by her dig at my sex life.

And she's Lex and Charlie's daughter.

But the minute I stepped into that elevator, something drew me toward her. I'm used to seeing women in the building dressed in corporate wear and flashing any piece of skin they can get away with. It often ranges from younger women, interns in their twenties, to sexier, more confident women, aged yet mature in their demeanor.

Not this girl though.

She appears *different.*

I didn't catch her eyes, only the supple pink lips which often sighed when she stared at her phone. There was an innocence to her, and perhaps it was that which left me curious as to why she ended up in my building.

Assuming it was an interview, I found it highly inappropriate to wear Chucks, yet admired her fashionable choice in wardrobe on this exceptionally warm fall day. Nevertheless, I'd never allow hiring someone dressed in such attire. I pride myself in recruiting a professionally presented workforce, and Chucks aren't part of the dress code.

Then I find her in my office, and the second she spun around, those emerald-green eyes did something I can't explain. I couldn't breathe like I'd been punched in the chest, which has happened to me during several boxing matches. The exact feeling stays with you, almost as if you're close to *death* because you can't perform the simple act of breathing.

But there's nothing to do but ignore it, blame all of it on Lex after he got into my head about being alone.

And the irony—his daughter is the one consuming my head.

When we sat inside my office, she struggled to make any conversation with me worth my attention, giving me too much opportunity to examine her. My memory can't recall the last time I'd seen her, only snippets of our childhood and the way she'd taunt me with her overbearing ways.

Yet, she's turned into a beautiful woman, one I didn't

expect to see sitting on the white leather chair across from me. Amelia's face has changed, slimmed out with her features more defined, including her cheekbones. Her hair is shorter and a different color, offering a more mature style than the waist-length hair I remember she always had in pigtails.

But it was her quiet, rather introverted attitude, which puzzles me the most. As a child, she was a boisterous dare-devil, nothing at all like her sister, the Little Miss Precious, Ava. She dared me to jump out of trees and tested me in the pool with ridiculous races she'd have us compete in. And the little girl who would demand my attention on my family trips to California had soon become the bane of my existence.

Shaking my head, I push the thoughts out of my mind and send a text to Elisha—a woman who offers a great fuck whenever I need it. Within seconds, she responds eagerly with an open invitation to her place tonight.

There. Done.

This will bring me back to reality.

As the afternoon drags on, so do my rampant thoughts. By the time everyone leaves the boardroom, I've abandoned Elisha's invitation. Although I had *prompted* it, I decide to head over to my parents' place, needing a good old pep talk from Dad, who'll knock some sense into me about staying single and fucking whomever I please.

I punch the code, opening the door, and yell out to my parents.

"Will?" Mom responds, unsure, as I walk through the apartment toward the kitchen.

"Yeah, it's me, is Dad around—"

My words fall flat, stopping at the dining room as emerald-green eyes feast upon me. *Fuck.*

"I'm glad you're here, come join us. Beau is visiting your grandparents," Mom offers, opening a seat beside Amelia.

Amelia's eyes widen until she drops her face quietly, not saying a word. Huh, interesting from Miss Keep-Your-Dick-in-Check Edwards. Curiosity overcomes me as I accept my mom's offer and take a seat beside her. Her body almost stiffens, making this all the more fun.

"Amelia tells us that she visited you today?"

"Yes," I say, taking a sip of the wine Mom poured, though eyeing the beer Dad has in his hand. Would it be wrong of me to ask for something stronger? Perhaps, something hard like shots of Patrón, an excellent way to rid myself of this unwarranted feeling.

"She's a beauty, isn't she?" Dad chuckles with his ridiculous grin. "You're going to drive all the college boys crazy, just like your mother."

"I'll take that as a compliment, Uncle Rocky," she answers politely.

Mom slides the dishes over to me, and almost instantly, I recognize all the food from the Chinese restaurant across the street. Mom's hectic work schedule means she often has little time to cook. I don't blame her as I order take-out more than I care to admit. It was only Dad who complained, which always prompts an argument between them. How they're still married is beyond me. Dad can be a dick, and quite frankly, Mom can be a bitch. They are like fire and gasoline, a deadly combination.

"How are you enjoying college life?" Mom asks.

"I love it, to be honest. Homesick at times, but aside from that, I'm enjoying being in New Haven. It's a beautiful place."

"Yale had the most wicked parties." Dad whistles, digging his fork into his chicken like the caveman he is. "Do you remember that one when the cops were called, and you and I were—"

"Jesus, Dad, please don't continue that sentence."

My mom purses her lips, hiding her smile. I take it back, I know why they are still together, and lord knows I don't need any details. On more than one occasion, Dad has used the word *kinky,* and I demanded he stop talking, especially because it involves my mother.

"I hope you're enjoying the social aspects. It's good to have a well-rounded college experience. A college boyfriend isn't so bad, either."

"I'm kind of... well, seeing someone."

My ears perk up, though I keep my gaze fixated on the plate in front of me. She's beautiful. Of course, she has a boyfriend. This is what you do in college—date and fuck around.

"Oh, from Yale?"

"Actually, no, he attends Johns Hopkins."

"How did you meet?" Mom continues. "Johns Hopkins isn't exactly close."

"Back in LA, we... uh... decided to continue our relationship."

I don't know why this information bothers me. A stupid high school crush means nothing. And she's a fool to think she can keep a guy from screwing the girls knocking on his door. *What do you care, anyway?*

"Well, take it from us, young love can turn into a lifetime. I'm sure your parents can say the same."

Great, now they just contradicted my entire thought process.

The rest of the conversation revolves around college. My input is required here and there. Dad steers the conversation to work, which raises the topic of hiring a new assistant. For fuck's sake, why does everyone feel the need to entertain themselves with my goddamn business? This is beyond a joke now.

"I'm sure Amelia can handle the adult conversation," Dad says, placing his fork down. "Son, sometimes you have to think with your head and not your dick. These women, not worth the quick fuck. What you need now is someone to make your head spin. The kind of woman you can't stop thinking about."

"I hate to agree with your father." Mom grins, which is unusual for her. "When you find that woman, Will, nothing else in the world will matter."

"Okay, so thanks for the pep talk," I mumble, rolling my eyes of boredom. "This is exactly why I keep my personal life private and avoid your invitations to dinner."

"You don't want to knock up some hussy," Dad tells me.

"Jesus, Dad. Give me some fucking credit."

Beside me, Amelia has lowered her head, though from the corner of my eye, I can see a smile playing on her lips.

"Let me guess... you have something to add to this?" I question her.

"It's late," Amelia replies, checking her phone. "I should catch the train back."

"You'll do nothing of the sort. Rocky, drive her back."

"Of course." Dad wipes his mouth, pushing his chair back to find his keys.

"I'll take her," I offer, all eyes falling on me, including Amelia's, who isn't shy in hiding her annoyed expression.

"Even better." Dad winks, sitting back down and sliding the tray of chicken toward him.

Amelia says goodbye to my parents, agreeing to come back and visit soon. On the elevator ride down to the parking garage, other residents occupy the space making a conversation less than appealing.

My black Mercedes is parked in the corner, away from everyone else. As we enter the car, I expect her to say thank you or some sentiment worthy of a conversation starter, but nothing of the sort while I speed out of the city and fly down the I-95. The drive is quiet and unsure of what to say, I want to pry more into this whole boyfriend thing—the subject alone piquing my curiosity.

"So, does your dad know about your boyfriend?"

She clears her throat, avoiding my gaze. "Not exactly. He knows of him and that we dated in high school. Why do you ask?"

"Just surprised you lie to him."

Her face turns to meet mine. "I don't lie to him. I merely save that information for myself. It's not like he asked me about it, so, therefore, no lying."

"Johns Hopkins is far. What kind of a relationship is that, anyway?"

"One that's none of your business."

Her frustrated tone is obvious like she seems bothered to be in my presence.

"You better be careful," I warn her, without a smile. "If your dad finds out, all hell will break loose."

"I'm nineteen next week. I live across the country. He can say all he wants. He can't expect me to stay celibate forever," she responds with more bite than before. "And anyway, why do you care about what my dad thinks? If I have to fight my dad to be with someone I care deeply about, then so be it, I will."

I almost laugh at the notion. No one goes up against Lex.

"Why are you laughing?"

"It's like you haven't met Lex Edwards."

"As long as I'm with someone who respects me, I believe my father will be fine. Not some playboy like you who would break a girl's heart with so much joy."

"Ouch, so you think I'm a playboy?"

"Let's just say I've heard Mom and Aunt Nikki talk, plus that dinner conversation sums it up to a tee. You're no saint, which probably explains the revolving door of assistants. Mr. Bigshot, a CEO, can't commit. It's all too familiar, according to them."

"I see." I nod with a smirk. "I'm the son your father never had."

"Yes, so I've heard."

"You hear a lot of things, but hearsay isn't always the truth."

I glance over, noting her arms crossed in defiance. "My dorm is just over there. And you know what, I don't care. Fuck whoever you want. It's your life."

"Well, you seem to care since you keep bringing it up? You seem to be bothered that I like to *fuck* beautiful women."

"Trust me. I don't care. I find it entertaining, but since we're here, thanks for the ride, Will. I have no idea why you had to torture yourself by taking me home, unless, of course, you're hoping to prowl the campus looking for a damsel in distress needing to be rescued?"

"You know what?" I growl, frustrated at her assumptions. "You're just as annoying as you were when we were kids."

"Yeah, and you're just as arrogant."

I let out a huff. "Well, are you going to get out? According to you, I have someone's bed to be in."

She shakes her head with a knowing grin before exiting

the car. "Goodbye, Will, a pleasure as always. Remember to be safe... no glove, no love."

The door slams, the same time I fall back onto the seat, annoyed with the entire night.

I just have to pretend this never happened. If Lex asks me to check on her, I'll tell him I'm busy with work. Surely, he should understand that.

Yes, work, a distraction I need at this moment to ignore my bothered thoughts and rid myself of Amelia Edwards.

Once again, the bane of my existence.

TEN

AMELIA

"*Amelia, wake up. It's midnight.*"

I let out a groan with my eyes still shut. My bed moves again as a finger nudges my shoulder. One eye opens to the sight of Liesel sitting beside me with a wide grin.

"What time is it?"

"Midnight, silly. Happy birthday!"

The screech in her voice almost deafens me. I rub my face and give her my best gracious smile considering the time, not to mention my level of exhaustion.

"Thanks."

"Nineteen, we have to do something amazing tonight," Liesel suggests.

"Tonight? As in now?"

"No, not now. Some need the beauty sleep," she points out sarcastically. "Tomorrow night. Josh's older brother owns a club in the city. He can get us in."

"A club? But I have a dinner with Andy."

"So, go to the dinner, then we'll meet afterward. Where's the dinner, anyway?"

I grab my phone off the nightstand, fumbling through

my messages, with only one eye open before finding Andy's text and reading the name out loud.

"That's on the same block. How perfect is that!"

I screw my mouth, resting on my elbows. "I don't think it's such a good idea to sneak into a club. We're still underage."

"C'mon, girl. We have to live a little. Besides, what can go wrong?" she questions, crossing her arms.

"I could give you a list, but I'm tired and don't want to waste my precious birthday hours arguing with you."

"Then, it's settled. You've got the morning free, right?" Liesel hops off the bed while I nod. "Great. Let's shop for new outfits. We can't look young in the club."

"Fine," I drag, annoyed that I'm now wide awake. "Go to sleep, you need energy for tomorrow."

"I was thinking of sneaking into Josh's dorm room..." she trails off with a wicked smile. "You know, a midnight quickie."

I laugh. "I guess the date went well yesterday?"

"As good as first dates can go. He's cute, fit, plus his parents are loaded."

"Three's a charm," I note in dark amusement. "Enjoy your midnight quickie."

Liesel bounces out of the room with way too much energy. I check my phone again, reading all the early birthday messages. Both my parents already texted me plus told me they will call me in the morning. Ava's relentless with her birthday memes, all of which involve old ladies and teeth falling out. There's a text from Austin which comes through just now.

Austin: *Happy Birthday, beautiful. Are you awake?*

I hit dial, unsure of where he is. Since our argument a week ago, we have barely spoken. A few text messages, all of which avoided the topic of us.

"Happy birthday," he greets, the sound of his voice warming me instantly.

"Thank you. Am I interrupting you?"

"No, just studying. And you?"

"Liesel woke me up."

Austin's soft laugh echoes through the phone. "She's a quirky one. Can't wait to meet her one day."

"When is that?" I ask, hopefully. Suddenly missing everything about him. "My birthday is the perfect time."

There's silence following my voice. I wait, and with every second that passes, the beat of my heart begins to slow down, a persistent ache following.

"I assumed you would be busy for your birthday."

"Liesel is taking me shopping in the morning, then I have two classes. I have a dinner in the city with Andy, then Liesel's boyfriend, Josh, is taking us to some club."

"Club?" he repeats, his tone shifting.

"Yes, his brother owns it. I know what you're thinking, we're underage. But it's not like I'm going to drink. What can go wrong?"

Liesel's influence is clearly rubbing off on me as I try to convince Austin it's all in harmless fun. My hair falls over my shoulder, the blanket covering me while I give him a moment before questioning his silence.

"I should go. It's your birthday," he responds glumly.

"Okay," I say, unsure. "I guess this is it."

"Enjoy the day, Amelia. I'm sure you'll have fun."

The phone call ends. Austin rarely calls me by my full name, and that alone should've prompted me for his distaste of my upcoming plans. A wave of anger momentarily overcomes the hurt. What does he expect me to do? He doesn't want to visit me, and he didn't invite me to visit him. Maybe, in hindsight, I should've offered. It feels like I am the only one trying to hold onto us, and he no longer cares.

I toss and turn, falling in and out of restless sleep for the rest of the night.

～

"Can you send me a pic of what you're wearing?" Ava demands over the phone. "I'm so jealous you get to go to an actual club."

"Don't say anything to Dad," I warn her. "Besides, Liesel's boyfriend's older brother owns the club, which is how we're getting in. It's my birthday, and I want to celebrate."

"It's your first birthday without us," she whines into the receiver.

"Even more reason to have fun."

I soon learn that being underage in college often leads to falsifying your age to have fun. Turning twenty-one feels like a lifetime, and after my phone call with Austin, more than ever do I just want to forget and have fun.

"Um..." There's a shuffle, where I'm certain Ava shoved the phone under the pillow.

"Ava?"

"Ava?" I repeat louder. "I have to go—"

"Millie!" she snarls, catching my attention. "Dad just walked into my room. I hope he didn't hear you."

"Don't say anything," I remind her again. "Listen, I have to go."

"Send me pics, okay? I want a full update tomorrow."

I hang up the phone, quickly getting dressed into a

black body-con dress and pairing it with dark-green strappy heels. With a quick blow dry, I style my hair to the side and clasp on my gold hoop earrings. I was never one to wear too much makeup, opting for a touch of mascara and a light shade of lipstick. Aside from my first semester in junior high, my skin rarely gets blemishes. Mom has good genes, and I'll be a very lucky woman if I can look as good as her when I'm over forty.

Josh and Liesel insist we Uber into the city. They're paying, so we don't stress about parking. I keep my opinion to myself but assume Josh wants to drink, hence, his eager suggestion when he arrives at our dorm room.

The three of us met Andy at the restaurant. Thankfully, Andy is easy to get along with as we all have one thing in common—college.

Both Andy and I love Indian food. The spicier, the better. We order dish after dish until Liesel warns us of a potential stomach cramp should she try the Vindaloo. Josh loves it, digging in and ordering more. We laugh, eat to our hearts' content, and just when Andy is about to call it a night since he has to catch a red-eye to Boston to attend some important function with his Dad, the waiters come out with a chocolate mud cake with vanilla frosting. The candles burn bright while they sing their hearts out, embarrassing me as patrons of the restaurant look on.

The cake is placed on the table before Liesel cheers, "Make a wish!"

I close my eyes, unsure what to wish for—happiness, love, the well-being of my family. But deep inside, I wish to feel alive, to be consumed by passion, and to be completely in love where the air hurts to breathe if you're not buried into his chest.

I blame the fiction books I have been reading of late—

romance novels Liesel insisted I binge read because the sex was supposedly off the charts. It's as close as I can get to the real thing, and perhaps, the wish I made would make me feel all the things I read about.

"I better go, Millie." Andy stands up, and I follow, his big arms wrapping around me in a tight embrace. "Call me if things get out of control tonight."

"Hey, my reputation has been clean for a while now. Just so you know, I can be responsible."

Andy places a kiss on my forehead. "Sometimes, I actually miss my crazy cousin. She makes life interesting."

I let out a hearty chuckle. "Go now, you pest. And say hi to your dad for me."

Liesel and Josh both say goodbye to Andy before he disappears outside. Josh claps his hands, barely able to contain his excitement.

"Let's get this party started, ladies."

Getting into the club was easy. As promised, Josh's brother takes us through the back entrance and straight into the dimly-lit club, the music blaring around us with people crammed on the dance floor.

The club itself is underground. There isn't much to it— scattered bar stools, a long neon-lit bar with a back wall shelving bottle after bottle of liquor. People are dancing, some look much older, and others our age.

"Let's grab a drink," Liesel shouts into my ear. "Cosmopolitan?"

I kindly refuse the drink, not wanting to push the limits, given I'm not twenty-one.

"C'mon, Amelia. Just one?"

"How about later? Promise."

Liesel pouts her lips but doesn't push any further.

At the bar, I pull out my phone to text Ava, then

quickly hop onto Insta to see the first story from Austin's account. It's a picture of him with some friends, and more notably, a beautiful brunette beside him with her arm on his. My stomach is tied in knots, the slump of my shoulder following soon after from the image with the caption *Just another Friday night.*

Today is Saturday, so this photo was taken last night. He mentioned nothing of the sort, and in fact, I recall him mentioning he was studying. My hands clutch my stomach, the realization that he can be lying to me the only thing on my mind. Around me, the noise drowns out, and the only thing I hear is the loud beat of my heart, the thumps almost bursting out of my chest.

I stare at the photo again, examining every inch of it— the way Austin's eyes light up to the cheeky grin next to this girl who appears equally as happy. The longer my eyes focus, the deeper the hurt runs.

In the corner of my account, I see a notification for a direct message. Opening it up, I glance at the username and read the message:

> **Will R:** *Going to a club when you're only 19 is stupid. Do you know the danger you're putting yourself in?*

I shake my head in disbelief. What the hell? How does he know? And how on earth did Will find my Insta account? My momentary pain subsides as I type profusely, wondering why Will needs to act like my goddamn father.

> **Me:** *The same could be said about the number of women you sleep with.*

I see the bubble appear before his message pops up.

Will R: *I'm coming to get you.*

I let out an annoyed huff, then remember he doesn't know where I actually am. Without even thinking, I block his username. The week has been bad enough since the night he drove me home. I hate that he has crawled under my skin, and mostly, I hate the way I entertain what it might be like to kiss him when he did that thing at dinner with his lips. It came out of nowhere, watching his tongue slither on the spoon and my legs tensing at the sight. Between Will and my dying relationship with Austin, I need that drink.

"You know what? I'll take that Cosmo now."

Liesel claps her hands, ordering me one immediately. An hour later and several drinks down, I've lost count and find myself on the dance floor. Will doesn't show up, of course, all talk and no action. The guy is probably bored and wants to annoy me to serve some sort of sadistic pleasure of his.

I dance with Liesel and Josh, then with a group of women I made friends with. Our bodies sway to the beat, my eyes closing as my hair swooshes around. It becomes hot and sweaty, my skin slithering under the barely lit dance floor.

A couple of guys try to dance, and I'm happily entertained until one of them tries to wrap his hands around my waist. He smells nice and is quite masculine with toned arms. When he rubs his crotch into my ass, the nagging voice in my head tells me I need to intervene quickly, yet my motor skills are sluggish. As I am about to politely tell him to back off, I'm yanked in a different direction, almost tripping in my heels.

My chest is up against Will's, the burn in his eyes piercing me like an animal ready to attack its enemy. Deep blue eyes hold me captive until I'm finally able to break away. He's still in his work attire—dress pants with a matching dark gray jacket and a white business shirt beneath it. The top two buttons are undone and there's no formal tie as his chest is slightly exposed. *Why are you even looking, Amelia?*

"What are you doing here?"

"It seems that our conversation made me believe you weren't responsible enough to be at this club."

"Me? It shows how little you know about me."

"If you're so willing to lie to your dad…"

"Why are you so hung up on that? Surely, you have more important things to do than taunt me with matters that are still none of your business!"

I have no idea why he suddenly has to act so macho, and what's with all the *my dad* talk? It's been frustrating, to say the least. The point of me moving here was to gain some freedom, all of which seems impossible if Mr. Asshole follows me wherever I go.

"We're going," he demands, nostrils flaring.

"Let me go!" I tell him. "You're such an ass, and besides, it's my birthday."

"An ass who'll save your life tonight. And happy birthday."

"Really, save my life?" I laugh, pointing my finger into his chest. "Are you going to tattle- tale to dear old daddy? Or better yet, follow me to my bedroom. How about the shower? You want to see me there?"

His face tightens, the skin bunching around his eyes like he's suffering for being seen with me. Perhaps there's some truth to what Andy said—I played it too safe for too long now.

I grab his hand, pulling him back onto the dance floor to torment him as I dance around where he stands, swaying my body, bucking my hips, laughing as I do while he remains perfectly still.

"What's wrong?" I pout, throwing my hands around his neck. "Is it possible that Will Romano does not know how to have fun?"

He rests his hands on my hips, the sudden jolt of his touch sending this odd feeling throughout me. I've never felt this before, and quite possibly, the alcohol has everything to do with it.

"You need to calm down," he sternly warns me.

"What for? I'm an adult now. Just admit it, you're jealous because your whole life revolves around work and chasing your assistant's pussy," I blurt out, laughing. "I'm surprised you're even here, unless, of course, you're looking to get laid by someone here."

I scan the room until I realize my hands are still on him, and his are still on me. Raising my eyes to meet his, there's an odd stare as his gaze falls onto my lips. Taking a deep breath, he focuses back on my eyes. "We need to leave or else..."

"Or else what? What exactly will go wrong?"

Will shakes his head, a smirk playing on his lips. I let go of him, almost pushing him away in annoyance until he pulls me back into him and our bodies are flush. My mind is playing tricks, watching his gaze fall toward my chest, the slight flick of his tongue. I place my hands on his chest, pressing forward only to be distracted by something hard between us. *Oh fuck, that's not what I think it is because this is all types of wrong.*

He leans his head in, his breath against my ear. "You need to behave and stop rubbing yourself on my cock, or this won't end well for both of us."

I pull away, distancing myself until he latches onto my wrist, pulling me through the crowd until the cold air hits my face, and we're standing outside on the pavement.

"I'm taking you home," he grits, nostrils flaring.

"In case you've forgotten," I say, a slight hiccup escaping. "My home is in New Haven, not here."

"I'm taking you back to my place."

He doesn't say another word amid sudden anger, hailing a cab and shoving me inside. I begin to argue, though the more I argue, the more my head spins.

"Give me your phone?" Will demands without reason.

"Wh... why?"

"So I can text your friend to let her know you came home with me and you're okay. What's her name?"

"Liesel," I mumble beneath my breath. "And it's yet to be decided if I'm okay. I don't know you anymore. What if you're a knife-wielding murderer?"

"Trust me, sweetheart, the last person I'd want to deal with if that were true is you."

The sudden stop-start of the cab is making my head spin more. I shut my eyes, ignoring the sounds of beeping horns and pray for all of this to be over.

Being an adult is hard.

How much so, I'm yet to find out.

ELEVEN

AMELIA

Will yells to the cab driver to stop at some building. Having not paid attention to the directions we traveled in, I have absolutely no clue where we are. All the buildings look the same—tall and fancy—nothing out of the ordinary.

With his hand clutched around my arm, he helps me out of the cab, my feet stumbling onto the pavement. The night air is refreshing, blowing against my tired face and causing me to shiver momentarily.

"Are you okay to walk?" he questions with a frustrated stare.

I nod before my ankle gives way, and I fall into him again.

"Jesus fucking Christ," he mumbles under his breath.

Pushing me through the main door, he wraps his arm around my waist to carry me since, for some reason, everything begins to spin.

Somehow, we ride the elevator up and to God knows what floor until we're standing inside his apartment.

"So, this is your place." I look around at the bachelor

pad, noting the leather furniture which appears untouched. There's a large white sofa adjacent to an unlit fireplace. Between them, there are a glass coffee table with books on it and a plush white rug which lays on top of the dark floor-boards. I'm surprised he bothers to read. Adorning the walls is black and white artwork. I can't seem to make out the images. The only thing I can note is that the apartment lacks color. "Such a man's place."

"I highly doubt you've been in many men's places to make that judgment."

The heat rises in my cheeks—what a *dick*. "I've watched movies. It's as stereotypical as you can get."

Suddenly, the room begins to spin, and bile rises in my throat. "Where's your... your..." He points to the bathroom, and with only seconds to spare, I say goodbye to the multiple Cosmos I drank—the vile taste lingering in my mouth. Cradling the toilet, I beg for this to be over until it becomes evident that my hair and dress have been caught in the aftermath.

Stripping my clothes off, disgusted at the thought of my own vomit, I grab a towel and wrap it around me. Opening the door slowly, I call his name but beg him not to come over.

"Can I please borrow a shirt, and can you leave it at the door?"

I close the door again, my head spinning from the small movements. Pressing my head against the tiled wall, it offers some relief but only momentarily.

There's a gentle knock on the door. "It's here, and yes, you can use my shower."

Relieved, I retrieve the shirt, then hop into the shower, desperate to wash my hair. The water feels like absolute heaven, the shower alone big enough to fit my entire economics class. I relish in the warmth, allowing it to caress my body, which feels *incredibly* charged. The bar of soap glides against my skin, but I stop just shy of my thigh and take a deep breath.

Blame the Cosmos and the lingering effects of the alcohol. A small moan escapes me as I close my eyes and wash between my legs. My mind flashes to the dance floor, Will's body pressed against my mind.

Shit, this is all drunk thoughts.

Stop. Now.

Quickly, I place the bar of soap back in the holder and run my hands through my hair one more time. I finish up, drying myself and placing his shirt on. Using my fingers, I comb my hair out.

The shirt is long enough to appear like a dress—black with some rock band logo on the front.

I put my heels on, wondering if cabs will take me back to New Haven at this hour. Staying here isn't an option. I need to go back to the sanctity of my own room.

Exiting the bathroom, Will's eyes fall onto my legs. His gaze is exploring my exposed skin.

"You plan to do what exactly in my shirt and your heels?"

"I don't know, take a cab," I mumble, wincing my eyes to ignore the pulse inside my head.

"I'm taking you to bed."

"I don't want to have sex with you," I say, defeated. "Besides, you're old."

"I'm not suggesting we have *sex*. I'm ordering you to sleep in my bed because you'll thank me in the morning when hopefully, your hangover is less than vile. And besides, you're too young."

"You're not my dad."

"If I were your dad, knowing Lex, you'd be flown back to LA and confined to a nunnery. Stop being so stubborn."

He orders me to follow him to his bedroom. Opening the door, the lights turn on but not too bright. There's a king-size bed with black satin sheets, which looks so good right about now, and nothing else besides a large glass window overlooking the Hudson River.

I stand beside him until he motions for me to get in. Sitting on the edge, I remove my heels, then climb in beneath the sheets. It feels fantastic, but I wonder how many women have been in this bed and when he last had the sheets cleaned.

Will leaves the room but returns moments later with Advil and a glass of water.

"Drink this, take this, and go to sleep."

"Where are you sleeping?"

"On the couch. Why? I can sleep next to you, but sweetheart, just letting you know that sleeping with you will cause you more problems than for me."

"You're a jerk," I mutter.

He hovers next to the bed, continuing to stare at me.

"Is there something wrong? Has my dad ordered you to sit and watch me all night?"

"Happy birthday, Amelia, and good luck tomorrow morning."

I close my eyes, ignoring his scent splashed all over the pillows and how, even in my intoxicated state, I wonder what it would be like to taste his skin with my lips. The door behind him closes, and the second he leaves, that familiar ache between my legs returns. I try my best to ignore it, moving in various positions, but it begins to consume me. *Maybe if I just touch myself, it will go away.* My fingers inch toward my thighs, then slowly graze between my legs.

Instantly, my body grows hot and feverish, a fluttery sensation bouncing inside my stomach.

I graze myself again, but this time, I arch my back, and the desire is too much to ignore. My fingers move faster, the pool of wet building between my thighs putting me on the verge of combusting. I turn my head, burying my face into the pillow when all I can smell is *Will*.

A sudden flush of warmth spreads all over me, my body jerking at the sensitive touch of my fingers. The shallow breaths make it hard to swallow until I finally gain some control, my body sinking further into the bed.

I can't move a single limb, not even to reach beside me and find a tissue to wipe between my legs.

Sleep is imminent.

Slowly, my eyes begin to droop, and I can see Will's face, almost as if he were in this very room, watching me.

TWELVE

WILL

I watch her sleep despite my reluctance to do so.

Before I stepped into the room hours ago, soft moans filtered from behind the closed door. My mind began playing tricks on me—dirty tricks—and instantly, I stepped away and stood on my balcony to clear my runaway thoughts.

The chill in the night air is exactly what I need, a cold slap on my face after what has been a tumultuous night. I don't nurse the whisky I poured myself for long, downing it in close to one go and allowing the warmth to spread throughout me.

She's crawling under your skin.

Slow and steady like a creature in the wild.

When I got the call from Lex last night informing me of Amelia's Friday night adventure into a club, it took a hell of a lot of trawling through her social media, which, thank God, was an open account. She'd posted a story with a picture of a restaurant in SOHO, and I knew precisely which club was located next door.

It was the last thing I wanted to do. I'd just flown in

from Chicago after what had been an exhausting day at a business summit. I spent most of the day surrounded by every idiot and their pathetic plea for me to look at their ideas—apps that could do this or that, nothing innovative or remotely interesting, in my opinion.

And Lex is anything but patient when it comes to the so-called safety of his oldest daughter. His bark over the phone was less than pleasing, leaving me no choice but to find her and get her out of there intact.

I didn't expect to find her drunk, assuming she'd have been more responsible. Her body swayed on the dance floor, men eyeing her with thirst in their mouth-watering stares. A few tried to touch her, slide their hands to places that would've compromised her innocence. Anger ripped through me as I stormed through the crowd, unapologetically, pushing people out of the way and almost into a fist-fight with one fucker who wouldn't move.

Then she yelled at me, laughed at me, and did something I didn't expect—she placed her arms on me and rubbed herself against my body. Of course, my dick was fucking hard. What do you expect? Her tits bounced in the tight dress, and her lips looked like red candy.

Over and over again, I had to remind myself why I came to get her—Lex's voice replaying in my head, his desperation mixed with fury.

But I shouldn't have sat here staring at her all night listening to the tiny snores she releases and watching the way her body is spread out in my bed. Thoughts cross my mind, things I *should* be ashamed of. I need to control myself, act like an older sibling, and not like a man wondering what she tastes like between her legs.

Sweet, I bet.

When the morning light streams through the bedroom, I escape to the kitchen, waiting for her to wake up.

It's just after eight when I hear feet drag through the hallway.

"Good morning," I greet with an overbearing smile. "Has death found you yet?"

She sits on the stool, moaning. The shirt she wears pulls up, exposing her thigh, yet she doesn't seem bothered. I quickly shift my attention, ignoring my dick hardening at the sight. *Seriously, get a fucking grip on yourself.*

"Remind me never to drink again."

"Gladly, since you're nineteen, the law can also remind you."

"How brotherly of you..." she mumbles beneath her breath before her face cringes. "What's that smell?"

"It's called hangover food. A breakfast burrito."

"Don't say the word *burrito.*"

"Take it from an old-timer like myself, it works wonders."

A smile manages to escape her lips before she takes a bite. At first, she stops mid-chew, her face turning a slight shade of green, but soon after, she swallows and begins to look somewhat normal.

"I told you, right?"

"I do feel much better," she admits, accepting the coffee I pour for her. "You're quite the morning host."

I can see where she's going with this, but as much as I'd like to put her in her place, I take the softer approach feeling somewhat sorry for her. My first drink was in high school, some party from memory and done so as a dare. Boy, did my parents give it to me the next morning. Dad, of course, laughed, but Mom grounded me. It wasn't the best of hangovers and definitely memorable.

"Believe it or not, women don't stay here."

Her eyes draw up to meet mine with a curious gaze. "How is that even possible?"

"I'm quite particular about my routine and my bed."

Letting out a small snort, she shakes her head. "I find that hard to believe. You seem to be a man who likes his women, and I assume your interest in them goes well beyond the night and into the early morning hours."

"Did my mother, or your mother, tell you that?"

"I drew that conclusion when I forgot for a moment where I was and opened your bedside drawer to a bulk pack of condoms."

My face falls flat, but quick to save face, I tell her, "No glove, no love, right?"

"I didn't realize a safe sex talk was part of your breakfast burrito cure. Thanks, I guess. Since I'm not exactly having sex with anyone, I think it's fair to say that I'm as safe as you can get."

I cross my arms, leaning against the countertop with curiosity. "How about this boyfriend of yours?"

She bows her head. "Nothing to say."

"C'mon, Miss Edwards *always* has something to say."

A laugh, though sinister, escapes her. "There's literally nothing say. We barely talk anymore, and I'm pretty sure if you troll his Instagram account, there's someone else."

"I'm sorry."

"Hey..." Her eyes meet mine, but with a hopeful smile, she releases a breath. "It was bound to happen that one of us would find someone new."

"You're beautiful. The guys will be lining up, just like my dad pointed out." The second it leaves my mouth, I regret telling her she's beautiful even though I can't stop thinking about it. But also, the thought of her dating, let alone sleeping with other men, shoots anger through me, followed by this pang I have no idea where it comes from.

"Why... um... thank you." She clears her throat. "And you're rather handsome, so I guess it isn't long before someone actually sleeps over in your bed because you want them to."

She hops off the stool the same time my phone rings, and *Lex Edwards* flashes on the screen.

"Lex," I answer, which stops Amelia dead in her tracks. "Is everything okay?"

"I should be asking you that," his stern voice echoes over the speaker.

"If you're calling about last night, Amelia is fine."

"She's fine?"

"Yes, I stayed around, then she happily agreed to head home, so I drove her back to campus."

"You drove her back?" he repeated.

I hated lying to him, and why I feel the need to protect her, I have no clue.

"Of course, the streets are no place for a young girl at night. She's fine."

A heavy breath releases. "I'm glad you watched out for her. She hasn't picked up my calls."

"I know she had an early breakfast catch-up with a friend or something like that. She mentioned it on the ride home. I wouldn't worry. She'll probably call you once done."

"You're right..." Lex agrees. "I'm still going to have a word with her."

"I understand, but perhaps, Lex, you may want to go easy on her. Remember, you were once just like her."

She closes her eyes, listening, though I can see the worry through her expression.

"I'll try," his voice softens. "About Thanksgiving, you'll join us? We've decided to come over, though Charlotte will let Amelia know. I insist since you're part of the family and also because we have some details to iron out before the acquisition."

"Sure, I'll be there."

Lex hangs up the call as Amelia lets out a loud breath.

"Your clothes, by the way, are washed and in the bedroom."

Amelia nods quietly. "Why did you lie to my dad?"

Her question catches me off guard, mostly because I have no clue why I did it. I shrug my shoulders, unable to look her in the eye.

"Not sure, maybe because you covered for me that time I visited your place and snuck out to attend some party on Melrose. You said you wouldn't tell, and I was never got caught, so yeah..."

She nods with a knowing smirk. "I was eight. I don't remember much of it besides hearing something about Aunt Nikki chopping your balls off."

Laughter escapes me. "They're in tact, thank God."

"Good to hear." She chuckles softly. "Thank you, Will. And you were right. I shouldn't have endangered myself by going to a club and drinking myself into a stupor. I don't know what I was thinking."

"It's okay. Sometimes we do things or act on things which have no rhyme or reason."

Slowly, her eyes glaze over mine as she bites the corner of her lip. Standing just a few steps away, wearing my tee, I have this urge to reach out and scrape my thumb across her delicate lips. If she were mine, I'd lift the tee off, admire her naked form, then take her into my bed and own her.

Fuck.

Get rid of these thoughts.

"I'm going to get changed." She breaks my stance, turning away, though her cheeks are flushed. "Thank you again, Will, for not mentioning this to my dad. It's clear that he respects you."

"That he does..." I whisper as she walks away. *"That he does."*

I insist on driving her home since trains run less frequently on Sunday mornings. For most of the car ride, we talked about the past—funny anecdotes, some I remember and some I don't.

"So, tell me, when did you realize that crazy stunts could kill you?" I ask with a grin.

She purses her lips, trying to hide her smile. "When I grew boobs and jumping off things became more difficult."

My hands grip tight on the steering wheel. She has a nice set of tits, all natural and perky, the same type I jerk off to while watching porn.

Think of something else.

"Also, it just wasn't as fun. I preferred to study. Andy found other interests, and then there's Ava. We all know how that turned out."

"How is your sweet little sister?"

"Sweet?" She laughs. "Sinful. But what Daddy doesn't know, Ava gets away with."

I pull the car into a parking spot out front and exit to walk to her dorm room, slightly curious to explore the campus since I've never visited. As we head toward the building she resides in, she stops and places her hand on my arm.

"Thank you, again, for saving my ass. God knows who I could've ended up with."

I scratch my chin, watching her intently.

"You're welcome," I tell her. "But just so you know, there would've been no chance I'd have let you go home with anyone else."

Lowering her head, she grins. "You think you could've stopped me?"

My lips part, an inward gaze falling to her mouth. *Why the hell are you always drawn to them?* Like a goddamn moth to a flame. A heavy weight inside my chest restricts my movements, which, fortunately, is for the best.

I lean in, my mouth an inch away from her ear, enough that she can feel the warmth of my breath. "I could've stopped you, don't underestimate my power when there's something I want which someone else tries to steal."

Her breath hitches, the sweet sound sending a stir straight to my pants. Pulling away slowly, she turns around, and I follow her inside the foyer until she stops mid-step, and I crash into her.

"Austin?"

Leaning against the door is a younger man, though tall and athletic. He's carrying a bunch of flowers, looking pissed that she has walked in with me.

"Who's this?" he asks, with a slight grunt.

"Who? Oh, you mean Will? He's a cousin."

Cousin? This makes me sound so incestual when, in fact, we don't share the same blood.

"Oh, sorry." He cocks his head. "Thought you were someone else."

Amelia turns back around to face me, her eyes confused and riddled with guilt as if I didn't know better. "Thanks again, Will. For everything."

Stepping away, she moves toward Austin as he wraps his hands around her waist and pulls her in for a tight embrace. *Fuck.* A growl escapes my throat, and without a goodbye, I exit the building, my footsteps heavy with my fists clenched downward as I walk back to the car.

Inside the car, I lean my head back and close my eyes, ignoring the burning sensation consuming me.

You fucking idiot. What did you think would happen?

She's too young, and she's got some kid as her boyfriend.

You've got adult stuff to occupy you, pussy on-call. Why the hell is this bothering you so much?

I start the engine and slam my foot on the gas with a vengeance.

No more mind games. Just forget she even exists because you have no choice. She's everything you can't have.

And everything you want at the same time.

A deadly combination that never ends well.

THIRTEEN

AMELIA

The sight of Austin standing beside my door dressed in a pair of dark jeans, a white hoodie, and matching sneakers causes my breath to hitch as I take it all in.

His welcoming smile fades almost instantly when his eyes feast upon *Will*. The expression is one I've been privy to witness on several occasions, like when Ethan Albright sat beside me at lunch and asked me out, or even on prom night when a few of the boys from the football team serenaded me in front of the entire senior class. While it was done as a joke, Austin was less than impressed.

I'm not sure why I panicked, quick to refer to Will as a *cousin*. It wasn't so far-fetched, I guess, given that Mom treats him like a son. But then my emotions wreaked havoc, confused that I had fantasized about him inside his bed and guilty because standing in front of me is the man I love.

Austin Carter.

Without trying to draw too much attention to the situation, I thank Will and say goodbye. He doesn't appear bothered, turning his back quickly and walking at a fast pace back to the car. I figure he has some woman to *attend* to, given I cramped his style last night by crashing at his apartment drunk on Cosmos.

"You're here," I say, eyes wide as I step back to examine him again. "But how?"

"I took a train very early this morning," he responds, looking over my shoulder. "Who did you say that was?"

"And you're here for the day?"

"I leave on the last train tonight," he concludes, eyeing me oddly. "You didn't answer my question?"

I shake my head, pretending that I forgot when, in fact, I was hoping we could skirt past the topic of Will.

"He's my Aunt Nikki and Uncle Rocky's son."

"Your cousin?"

"Yes, well, sort of. We aren't actually blood-related, but my mom is his godmother and spent time raising him with my aunt and uncle."

"You've never mentioned him before."

I purse my lips, trying my best not to show anything about disinterest over this conversation. "There's not much to mention. We spent many summers together as kids, but he's older, so he got bored with my childish antics. He went off to college and then started some business. My dad's company invested in his or something like that. I'm not sure. I don't pay much attention, to be honest."

I'm well aware my ramble carries on longer than I intend. Slowly, the expression on Austin's face shifts as he wraps his hands around my waist, drawing me in closer. He tilts his head, brushing his lips against mine when the memory of his Insta photo comes back to mind.

I pull away, creating distance, taking a deep breath to rid myself momentarily from the lingering effects of his kiss to gain some perspective.

"Austin, last night," I stop mid-sentence, my head downward and staring at my shoes. "I saw a photo of you and some girl."

"Some girl?"

"Brunette, arm over you..."

"Oh, you mean Summer?"

"Well, isn't that a very seasonal name," I mumble, unable to make eye contact.

Austin lifts my chin, our eyes meeting, though I could swear with every fiber of my being that something odd passes between us. It's unlike our usual flirtatious glances or the loving eyes of the high school boy who once stood in front of me.

"You have nothing to worry about."

"I wasn't worried," I assert. "Maybe concerned because you're miles away."

"I'm here, now," he answers with a grin. "How about you show me your room?"

I swat his chest gently. "Liesel is inside, probably with the hangover from hell. Come inside while I get changed. We can go out for lunch, and I can show you around campus?"

Austin follows me in, pressing his body up against mine with a gentle brush of his lips against my ear.

"It's been months. Why don't we skip lunch for now?"

His hand glides up the side of my ribcage, then moves effortlessly toward my breasts. Everything about him feels familiar, and aside from the first time we had sex months ago, we haven't been intimate since. Video calls were exciting, but nothing compares to the real thing.

We slowly make our way to my bedroom, closing the door behind us. Austin doesn't waste time, pulling my body into his and burying his head into my neck with warm kisses. In the privacy of my room, it feels entirely different from having sex on a picnic blanket outdoors.

Our kisses become rushed, urgent with their demands as we stumble toward the bed, falling with laughter escaping us.

"I miss you, Millie."

"I miss you, too, Austin," I whisper, staring intensely into his eyes.

He runs his hands up my thighs, sliding my dress up, causing me to sit up and remove it. Wearing only my black bra and panties, his eyes wander toward the crevice of my breasts, his reflection tortured almost as if he feels pain. Slowly, his fingers move toward the clasp of my bra, the sudden snap releasing, my bra tossed onto the floor. I wiggle out of my panties at the same time he removes his clothes until he's standing beside me, completely naked.

My eyes wander down his body, past his muscular physique, and I drink in the sight of his cock standing upright. Unknowingly, I swallow the lump inside my throat, realizing that this is the first time I've seen a man completely naked.

Austin moves back onto the bed, laying on top of me with his kisses now focused on my breast. I moan in delight, arching my back as I softly beg him to enter me. Unlike our first time, he doesn't move as slow, entering me at his own pace and pressing hard as small grunts escape him.

The familiar build is itching all over my skin, moving to every inch of my body, and consuming my thoughts with pleasure. We lose ourselves in kisses, our hands exploring each other comfortably, and relish in this moment of just being ourselves without the worry of our parents.

His every move begins the spiral of pleasure, and just as

I warn him that I'm about to finish, he pulls out and spills over my stomach at the same time, leaving my orgasm to fall slightly short. My eyes spring open, the sudden loss becomes increasingly frustrating. Should I say something? He didn't have to pull out. I'm on the pill.

"I didn't forget about you," he whispers into my ear.

The palm of his hand falls between my thighs, rubbing the sensitive spot. I close my eyes again, his body shuffling down until he spreads my legs wide. Holding my breath, his tongue flicks against my swollen clit, causing me to gasp.

"*Shh,*" he whispers.

Pressing my lips together, I latch onto the headboard behind me, my body writhing while his tongue moves around my clit so effortlessly, and a warm rush spreads throughout my body.

Catching my breath, I feel him move his body back up to lay beside me and the sheets being pulled over our naked bodies.

We lay there for minutes on end. I could've sworn that if you listened carefully, you could hear our hearts beating in sync. But maybe it was my imagination, torn between how amazing it is between us and the reality that he'll leave in just a few hours.

"The perks of college life," he opens with. "No parents to bust us."

I laugh, resting my head on his chest. "So, the movies and TV shows were correct?"

"So, it seems."

Moving toward my side, I prop myself up on my elbow.

"Austin, what will become of us?"

His expression shifts, the happiness fades, and torment overcomes him.

"Why do you need answers, Millie? Why can't we just enjoy now?"

I think about his question. Maybe he's right. Why do I need answers? *Because you've bared your body and soul to this man.* I feel vulnerable, loving him so much but knowing that sometimes, the sacrifice creates a world of pain that love can't withstand on its own.

"You're right. You hungry?"

"Famished."

Austin dresses back into his clothes as I find something more appropriate to wear than my bodycon dress from last night. *Last night.* The memories of Will come racing back to mind, and how easily I had forgotten all about it in Austin's presence. When Austin excuses himself to use the bathroom, I send Will a quick DM to thank him for last night.

Me: *Thank you for getting me home safely.*

"You ready?" Austin calls from the doorway.

I nod my head, tucking my phone into my purse.

We find a local eatery, opting to sit indoors as the rain falls from the sky. We talk about classes, and I listen as Austin speaks about the new friends he made. The way he tells stories makes you feel as if you were there with him. Each one of them seems fun, and since they all are studying to become a doctor of some sort, I enjoy hearing about their lives and how they came to that decision.

"So, your friend, Henry, he's studying to become a podiatrist?"

"Yes," Austin chuckles. "We enjoy giving it to him because Zach swears he has a foot fetish."

"And Zach is the one who you think is screwing a professor?"

"Not think, I know."

"I didn't think it was possible."

"Well, in his defense, she's pretty hot."

I raise my eyes from my plate, a shot of anger sweeping through me.

"I guess if you like older women."

"What's there not to like? She's hot, wears glasses, and intelligent. A trifecta."

I nod my head, then lower my gaze, and stare at my plate. With my fork and knife in hand, I cut the green bean into pieces with a vengeance.

"Like you wouldn't say the same if there weren't a hot professor on campus?"

"I respect their authority, so no, I wouldn't feel the same."

"Right," he drags. "But older CEOs?"

My head springs up. "Excuse me?"

"Nothing. It's just you're quick to have an opinion on the matter, though I'm certain that you can't ever say you've never been attracted to an older man."

I stare into his eyes, this jealousy turning back onto him. I throw my napkin down, crossing my arms in defiance.

"What exactly is your problem? Is it Will?"

"I don't know, maybe the fact that you've never mentioned him before, but he's walking you to your dorm room when you're dressed in something so—"

I push my chair out in a fit of rage. "Don't you dare say what I think you're going to say, Austin Carter!"

His expression doesn't falter, almost as if he rolls his eyes.

"I don't know what's going on with you. I have done nothing but try to make us work. You, on the other hand, couldn't care less," I tell him brutally. "As for Will, he's close to my dad. So, him walking me home was at the request of my father and not because anything is going on."

"Right, so he's besties with your dad? A great way to fuck the little princess, huh?"

I shake my head, not willing to put up with his mood swings for any longer. One minute we're making sweet love, and the next, he's putting me down and calling me a whore.

"If you came here to fuck me and make me feel cheap, then you've succeeded," I tell him. "Goodbye, Austin. I guess fate doesn't have a chance since you decided for both of us that we're officially over."

I bow my head, ignoring the curious eyes of the other patrons. Outside, the rain is heavy, the drops falling onto the pavement furiously. I throw my hood over my head and open my umbrella, walking though still getting wet.

So, this is what heartbreak feels like, the end of something that was once wonderful. It feels like concrete drying inside my chest—hard and pressing, restricting my ability to breathe. Behind my solemn eyes, tears linger. I try my best to hold it in, but much like the rain, it falls hard and unrelenting.

And perhaps my mom was right. A love so strong can cause a mountain of grief. I'm grieving for a boy turned man who I spent the last year with, someone who shared their hopes and dreams with me, as I had done, and who I had experienced so many firsts with during a transitional time in my life.

But most importantly, someone who I chose to give my virtue to, the greatest gift of all, which can never be taken back.

I enter my dorm room and stare at my bed we made love on earlier today.

I have to finally say goodbye. I fought for too long, and for what?

To end up just as I am now.

Heartbroken.

FOURTEEN

WILL

Behind the door, inside the hotel room, she falls onto her knees at my command.

Closing my eyes, I focus on her tongue swirling around the tip of my cock, the flick of her tongue, and the build-up of her saliva around my shaft. Soft moans escape her red-stained lips as she alters between sucking me off and using her hand to get me to blow.

My entire body clenches as the grit of my teeth bite down on my jaw. Every single muscle is tense, and despite my dire need to come inside her mouth, something isn't working.

Clear your goddamn head, Romano.

It's been the week from hell, every single thing pushing me beyond my fucking limits. I fought more than I anticipated, embroiled in a legal case for a potential patent violation. Some small-time dickhead in Texas was claiming our new launch had been his original idea. The negative press followed, claiming the 'big guns' were trying to silence him.

Our company did nothing of the sort. I enlisted the help of only the best legal team, proving to him that our idea had been years in the making. The exercise itself was a waste of resources, all to prove a point to some company trying to embroil themselves in a scandal to gain press.

And then it continued. A deal almost falling through, our shares dropping, to a tech glitch in one of our major apps, forcing it to shut down and causing us to lose a hell of a lot of money.

All week, the persistent headache turned into a migraine each night. To alleviate some tension, I hit the gym even earlier, starting my days at three in the morning instead of four. Considering I go to bed at midnight and sometimes later, sleep has become close to non-existent.

Whatever the hell fucked with my mind to land myself in such a negative headspace should've disappeared when Alyssa got down on her knees and unzipped my pants. Alyssa, right? Or is it Alison? *Fuck, you can't even remember her name.*

The echo of her hollow sucks pulls me out of my thoughts. Sure, she got me hard, but as I grab her hair, hoping for a spurt of desire to drive me home, I struggle to find the familiar feeling. My smartwatch begins to beep, prompting me that I need to be at an event downstairs in less than twenty minutes.

It's time to pull out the big guns.

"Go deeper. I want to see your eyes water," I command.

She slows her movements, hesitating slightly, until she does her best to take me all in with great difficulty given my size, only to watch her throat heave. She does so again, raising her eyes to meet mine, but it proves effortless.

What the fuck is wrong with you?

I close my eyes, focusing on the sensations again, desperate for anything until a flash of an image shifts my focus—Amelia asleep in my bed. Little does she know that the bedsheet was only covering half of her body, and the t-shirt of mine she wore had risen to expose the base of her ass.

Biting down on my lip, I feel my dick harden. My mind begins to play tricks, imagining my tongue against the curve of her ass, smelling the scent of her arousal, and tasting her.

I latch onto Alyssa's head, holding her down for one more thrust before my body shudders with pleasure, and I've spilled myself out all over her face.

My heartbeat is rapid, pounding inside my chest while I try to catch my breath, panting for air. Not saying a word, I pull my pants up and quickly check the time.

"I need to go," is all I say without a thank you.

"Shall we meet later tonight?" she suggests in a seductive tone.

Do I want to fuck her? Probably. If she doesn't mind sucking me off, she probably wouldn't mind being fucked from behind either.

"Sure, come by my suite at midnight."

I leave her room and quickly take the elevator up to my room to freshen up. With the tap running, my hands press against the counter as my gaze falls upon my reflection in the mirror.

I'm just over a year off thirty, an age which should bring wisdom and experience. For years, I busted my ass in college to be exactly where I am. I was never interested in marriage, babies, or even relationships. If I needed to get off, I found a way, just like tonight.

Except for Luciana, the one who managed to get me to settle, at least, for close to a year. Something I managed to hide from my family.

I still remember her like it was yesterday, even though it was only a year ago. It was backstage at a Victoria's Secret fashion show, a last-minute event I was dragged to by a friend. Jonathan is a photographer, and he thought to introduce me to Luciana. Of course, she was gorgeous—tall, sexy, toned body with beautiful natural breasts. Her golden tan made her skin look irresistible. With dark brown hair and bright blue eyes, she caught my attention immediately.

We dated, and I broke my rule by following the course of the relationship. With both our lives busy with work, Luciana suggested we move in together to allow us to spend more time with each other. Yet, I knew she wanted more than that. She often talked about starting a family, wanting four kids in total. The whole goddamn conversation scared the shit out of me, but she was beautiful, and when it came to using her body, I so quickly fell victim to her powers.

But time passed, and I never made the next move she had so desperately craved—marriage. Jonathan couldn't understand why I wouldn't want to settle down with a supermodel. What else could I want?

I had no clue either, so I ended the relationship then and there.

Luciana was devastated, which led me to believe I had maybe acted too harshly. We tried to reconcile, but we only found ourselves in the same position—she wanted more, and I just wanted to fuck someone beautiful without the strings of commitment attached.

It ended even worse the second time, and I made the vow not to fall into that trap again.

But now what? Is there more to this thing called life? If I'm honest, I am satisfied with the way things are. Correction *was* until Amelia made her grand entrance and disturbed my peace.

Then her boyfriend rocks up at campus, only reminding me of how ridiculous this all is. I'm pretty sure that's why a week has passed, and she's gone radio silent, apart from the quick DM she sent me which I never responded to. The whole thing is a waste of time on my part, and for what? She's too young. End of story.

Yeah, so what if she comes to mind while I'm getting sucked off by another woman.

Momentary lapse, that's all.

I splash cold water on my face and dry off. Grabbing my phone off the counter, I slide it into my pocket and head downstairs to the main conference room.

This event, hosted by a leading tech giant, is designed for networking. I flew into Houston only this morning, hoping to get out of here by tomorrow.

"Will," my name is called.

Standing beside me is Lex, dressed in his suit with a drink in hand. My eyes search the bar, but almost as if Lex can sense my desperation, he calls the waiter over and requests him to bring me a drink.

"Thanks, Lex. I need a drink if I'm going to speak to Marshall. The guy is a beast when he corners you."

Lex chuckles softly. "Don't I know it. But you're going to want him on your side. His late father left his entire fortune to him, even leaving out the new wife."

"What wife number was that again?"

"I believe that was number four. This one just reached twenty-seven. The older Marshall senior became, the younger he found his wives."

"I hear they're looking to sell off part of their Asian division. What do you make of that?"

"I think it will make for an excellent investment if you play your cards right."

I purse my lips, welcoming the bourbon served to me on a silver platter. We aren't left alone for much longer. Whenever Lex is around, people swarm to him. Hours are spent talking, meetings are arranged, introductions are made to business partners nonstop until the event is almost over.

"Are you flying back home tomorrow?" I ask, exiting the room and welcoming the distance from everyone.

"I have three meetings tomorrow downtown, then fly back late tomorrow night," he informs me while waving to someone. "Charlotte is inundated with work, handling a very messy divorce of an A-lister celebrity, which leaves Ava in charge, and well, that girl is trouble."

I laugh at the thought. "She was never trouble, at least, that's what I remember."

"I never realized how responsible Amelia is until Ava was left in charge."

I slow down my movements at the mention of her name, unsure what to say until Lex continues to speak. "Charlotte's been worried because apparently, Amelia broke up with her boyfriend. Good riddance, I say. My daughter is smart. She doesn't need some boyfriend to distract her when she should be focusing on studying."

I replay the words in my head before asking the question, not wanting to say anything wrong, given that Lex is an intuitive man.

"Right, the high school boyfriend. They never last, anyway. I'm sure she'll move on."

"I should hope so," Lex responds with a stern tone. "Charlotte tells me she needs to grieve the relationship, but when I spoke to her, she was fine. She'll throw herself into studying because that's what she always does. Like mother, like daughter."

"Definitely not the girl I remember..." I mention fondly.

Lex turns his head to face me, a blank expression on his face. "You're right. Amelia is nothing like the girl you would remember. She no longer does crazy things, always thinking logically except for that stupid stunt of sneaking into some club. I blame her wild roommate for being a bad influence. And quite frankly, I sleep better at night knowing that she's left her wild ways behind."

I lower my head, hiding the smirk playing on my lips. If only Lex knew about Amelia's drunken night out or that she slept in my bed, completely passing out from Cosmos. His princess isn't that innocent, and suddenly, I relish the fact that she doesn't have her loser high school boyfriend holding her down.

The elevator pings open, both of us entering. As we are staying on different floors, I say goodbye to Lex and exit toward my room. Tapping my card, the door opens, and I step inside, quick to remove my jacket.

Shortly, a knock on the door alerts me to a visitor. I walk back over and open the door to find Alyssa standing in front of me dressed in a sexy red dress. Fuck, I forgot all about her.

Running my hands through my hair, I watch as she licks her lips, a move which doesn't stir a single movement in my still flaccid dick.

"Listen, I'm not feeling too well."

"Oh..." she mouths. "How not well?"

"Bad shrimp, I guess. It's best that we take a rain check."

Rain check to never.

"Are you sure?" she sounds disappointed. "If you need someone—"

"I don't want you to catch anything, so best you leave."

I close the door without a goodbye. Moving toward the balcony, I slide the door open and welcome the fresh night air. Removing my phone from of my pocket, I log into my

Insta account and straight to my DMs, rereading her message where she thanked me.

> **Me:** *You're welcome. Your dear old daddy tells me you've been wallowing in self-pity. I never pegged you to be so lame.*

I knew instantly this would rile a reaction from her, and a few seconds later, the message shows as read.

> **Amelia:** *Lame? And what makes you think I've been wallowing in self-pity?*

> **Me:** *Because Miss Chatterbox is quiet.*

> **Amelia:** *Maybe it's because I have nothing to say. I said thank you for rescuing me, and all I got was read. Not even an infuriating thumbs up.*

> **Me:** *Some people have work to do, just so you know.*

> **Amelia:** *Sure... work or fucking your assistant. I guess, either way, you're doing the job, right?*

> **Me:** *Someone is a little hung up with my sex life, one would think.*

> **Amelia:** *You wish. I've got better things to worry about than where your dick has been.*

> **Me:** *So crass coming from a refined young lady my*

mother makes you out to be. It's best you go back to the wallowing.

Amelia: *You know what, Mr. Smartass. I'm going to prove you wrong.*

Me: *Uh-huh... I'm waiting.*

Amelia: *Meet me in front of your apartment building next Saturday at 9 a.m.*

Me: *It sounds so exciting. I have work to do.*

Amelia: *Either meet me or don't. But if you do, be prepared because you will be proven wrong, and I am going to gloat at my accomplishment.*

Me: *I'll be there, just to watch you fail.*

Amelia: *Sweet dreams, playboy.*

With a smile on my face, I reread her last line. I have no idea what she has planned, and knowing her, it'll probably be something she thinks is fun but uneventful and mind-numbing.

Yet, a part of me can't hold back the sheer pleasure in teasing her. An easy target, that's all. And perhaps I want to prove Lex wrong and test my capabilities of how far I can push the limits with his so-called responsible daughter.

Someone has to do it, and frankly, I can't think of any better person than me.

FIFTEEN

WILL

"I'm not getting into that."

A pink Mustang convertible is parked in front of my apartment building. If you ignore the hideous shade, the car itself appears to be in mint condition. Who in God's name would do such a thing to a car?

Amelia is sitting in the driver's side, wearing a baseball cap, navy hoody, and not to mention a satisfied smile on her face.

"It's just a car. Get in."

"It's pink," I point out, my hand resting on the door. "Like really pink."

"You shouldn't discriminate based on color," she informs me. "It's very unbecoming of you."

"How about we take my car?" I plead.

"Man the fuck up and get in."

I open the door with much reluctance and take a seat, not hiding my dissatisfaction of sitting inside a girl's car. On closer inspection, the interior is pristine with white leather trim and all accessories in original condition. Whoever this belonged to must love old-time cars, though it seems a bit too feminine for Amelia's tastes.

"Is this yours?"

Amelia snorts. "Are you kidding me? I'd never own a pink car like this. It's like Barbie threw up all over it. It's my roommate, Liesel's."

She slams her foot on the gas, roaring out from the curb drawing attention to those walking on the sidewalk. I slide in my seat, embarrassed to be seen in such a car.

The wind begins to pick up as we drive out of the city and toward New Jersey. Above us, clouds cluster with gray skies warning us of an impending storm. Turning my head, I scan the back to see if the car has a roof, and thankfully, it does.

"Can you tell me where we're going?" I yell through the wind.

Amelia's lips curve upward into a smile, the same smile I remember from when she was a kid, and I asked her why we were climbing a tree in her backyard. Assuming she wanted to climb simply for fun, only to jump into the pool moments later, swallowing a gallon of water in the process.

Amelia doesn't answer my question, purposely ignoring me as she keeps her eyes on the road. I opt to enjoy the road trip, admiring the view though unsettled at being a passenger. Her driving is somewhat erratic. Others may deem her a maniac. If I want to get home in one piece, I somehow need to convince her that I'm driving back.

Our surroundings change with the view of Randall Airport just ahead. Above us, the sky is blue now, the clouds drifting away toward the ocean. The car begins to slow down as she pulls into the parking lot. When the car stops, I look around, noticing a hangar beside us.

"We're here," she announces while turning off the engine. "Are you ready?"

"What exactly should I be ready for?"

"I think it's best we get out of the car to have this conversation."

I unbuckle my seat belt, exiting the car while eyeing her dubiously. She motions for me to follow her, and as we turn the corner, it all comes into view.

There are several people dressed in parachute jump-suits, many with harnesses. An ultra- lightweight plane sits on the tarmac with gliders all around. It takes a moment for me to realize exactly why we're here.

"To clarify, you brought us here because we're going to tandem hang glide?"

Amelia nods her head with a playful smirk without a care in the world that we'll be flying thousands of feet above the ground.

"I know what you're thinking," she says, crossing her arms while we both watch some people above us detach their glider from another plane. "It's twenty-five hundred feet."

"Uh, that's one thing, not to mention the fact that we *could* die."

Amelia turns to face me, her eyes boring into me just as they had done when she was a kid, and I questioned her elaborate ideas.

"Don't give me that look," I remind her with annoyance.

"And exactly what look am I giving you?"

"The same look you've always given me before we're about to do something incredibly dangerous."

"I have no idea what you're talking about, but from memory, you said I was boring. Or was it lame? Unad-venturous?"

I purse my lips, trying to control my urge to remind her of all the things that can go wrong in the air. Number one, we free-fall to our death.

"I may have alluded to something of the sort, but what I meant was get out, live a little. This is..."

"Are you scared? Is that what you're trying to tell me?"

My eyes lift toward a hang glider soaring a few feet above us, ready to land. Moments later, the man and woman land, feet on the ground, both of them laughing while appearing exhilarated. I've done many adventurous things in my lifetime, but of late, life revolves around work. Maybe this is what I need, something crazy to break the monotonous routine of being in front of my laptop.

"Let's do this," I tell her.

We follow all the steps we need to, from practical learning to the physical side. After the instructor goes through everything, including our signing waivers, we're fitted out in the proper gear and shown how to comfortably lay inside the glider.

The crew does all their safety checks while I take one plane and Amelia the other. She yells good luck to me with a thumbs up. I didn't know whether to say the same or curse her for putting me in such a position.

I release a breath, willing the adrenaline to kick in. The engine of the plane starts at the same time my heart pumps wildly when we begin our ascent down the runway. I bite my lip as every part of my body begins to react with nausea creeping in.

The plane is in the air, the cool breeze a welcoming change. The higher we ascend and the distance from the ground we are, a smile spreads across my face replacing my momentary fear. I don't recall how long it takes us to reach our destined height, taking the time to admire just how beautiful it is from above. The instructor taps me on the shoulder, warning me we're going to detach and begin our soar. I give him the thumbs-up, and seconds later, the plane is pulling away, and we are free, soaring like birds.

My entire body feels light as a feather, a state of calm washes over me while taking in the landscape. This new feeling—a steady heartbeat—replaces the adrenaline pumping through my veins only moments ago.

Living in the moment, I realize how my life has become work, how the smallest of pleasures are never a priority. I've disconnected myself from actually living and feed myself excuses as to why money and power are my reason for existing.

And now, this on-the-whim dare to do something different has opened my eyes to something more.

Amelia has opened a part of me that has laid dormant.

I don't recall how long we soared for, but another rush overcomes me when our feet finally touch the ground. My throat is parched, my breathing erratic while I rest my hands on my knees, willing my heart to calm down. Not too far away, Amelia has also landed, and the look on her face sums it up perfectly.

She looks beautiful, grinning from ear to ear with an infectious laugh escaping her lips. The color of her cheeks is crimson, accentuating the green eyes while our gaze meets. I can't help but smile back as the instructor helps me remove the harness.

When we're both free, Amelia runs over to me, out of breath and completely exhilarated.

"How do you feel?"

"Amazing," I admit, taking a breath with a soft laugh following. "I haven't felt this good since... I can't even remember."

"Me, too." She beams, placing her cap back on. "I forgot what it was like just to act and not think."

"I take it back. Maybe you're not so lame."

She punches my arm softly. "You hungry?"

"Famished."

"There's a place not too far from here that's supposed to be the best burger joint in Jersey."

"Lead the way, daredevil."

My eyes pique with curiosity as the waitress serves all the food and places it on the table—burgers, loaded fries, hot dogs, pickles, and two sodas.

"Are you eating for two?" I ask, watching Amelia load her plate.

"Funny joke, one I'm sure you'll never make in front of my father," she says with a mouthful of fries. "A food coma is imminent."

It's somewhat refreshing to watch a woman relax in my presence, not fuss over some fad diet they're trying out to lose weight. I learned early on not to ever comment on a women's weight because even a compliment can be misconstrued as something else. Amelia, though, has an amazing body with curves in all the right places, not that I should be even thinking about that.

She raises her eyes, stopping mid-bite. "Why are you looking at me that way? Do I have mayonnaise on my face?"

I hide my smile behind the burger in my hands. "You're so paranoid."

"Well, I don't really know you anymore. You're practically a stranger."

Flattening my lips, I roll my eyes. "Don't be so dramatic."

She wipes her hands with the napkin, taking a sip of Coke before resting her elbows on the edge of the table.

"It's the truth. All I know is that you work at some company that creates apps. You're single, allegedly, and you like to fool around with your assistants."

I shake my head, letting out an annoyed huff. "My mother, or your mother, has really skewed reality. Yes, I own a company that creates apps, among many other things. Yes, I'm single. No, I don't like to fool around with my assistants. I like to fool around with women who I find attractive, despite their chosen career."

"Oh, well, that's much better," she drags, avoiding my eyes. "So, have you ever had a girlfriend?"

"That term is so juvenile," I tell her.

"So is pulling the onion out of your burger," she retorts while eyeing me. "And the pickles."

"They're disgusting."

"You're avoiding my question."

I release a breath. "I'm not avoiding your question. I was in a relationship, and it didn't work out. End of story."

Amelia's gaze fixates on me, making me uncomfortable as the silence gives her time to think of something else to ask me. Something, I'm sure I'll have no interest in answering.

"It sounds to me like you're still in love with her."

"C'mon, now you're ridiculous."

"Am I? Or am I so accurate that you're terrified I unraveled some hidden secret you've been trying to keep because your heart is so broken?"

Narrowing my eyes, I fold my arms across my chest.

"You're still as invasive as I remember you. I'm not heartbroken. In fact, I ended it. Satisfied?"

"Not really," she counters, still watching me with a curious stare. "Now it opens up a whole other conversation about your fear of commitment."

"For God's sake, you really are still a pain in my ass," I concur while grimacing. "What about you? You're a relationship person, and now you're single."

"Yes, I am," she mumbles, avoiding my gaze. "It's college, right? Perfect time to be single."

I agree in my head that no one should be tied down in college. The thought of her being single and jumping into different beds opens up another side to me I have to control, or this won't end well.

"Just focus on studying, stay single."

"Maybe, we'll see."

"What do you mean we'll see?" I question with annoyance.

"It means that a woman has needs. Read between the lines, buddy."

The waitress interrupts our conversation, clearing the table and placing the bill down. As Amelia reaches for it, I push her hand away, the same time my skin tingles with what feels like an electric shock. Pulling back, a small breath escapes her pink lips, but she covers it up with a cough.

The interruption times perfectly, this conversation potentially leading to a heated debate. After paying the bill, we exit the restaurant and walk back to the car. After an argument over who should drive back, she reluctantly hands over the keys as we make our way back to the city.

It's mid-afternoon when we get back to my apartment, and once again, the clouds have formed over the sky with the smell of rain in the air.

"Will you be okay driving home?" I ask, looking upward

at the same time a roar of thunder echoes in the distance. "Why don't you wait until the storm passes?"

"And do what exactly?"

Inside, I'm battling with the need to protect her from the unpredictable weather, which often causes erratic driving on the wet roads or to send her home. My urges jump from zero to one hundred when she does something minor like bite the corner of her lip.

You need to protect her.

That's all—it's about her safety.

"Hang?" I blurt out, distracted by my thoughts.

"Hang?" She laughs. "Hmm... I haven't heard that in a while, but okay."

And just like that, her teasing of my age only riles me up and reminds me how easily she can goad some sort of reaction from me. Out of nowhere, the rain begins to pelt from above us.

"Let's go," I mumble, heading toward the building. "If you come out of here alive, you better count your blessings.

SIXTEEN

AMELIA

The wet fabric clings to my skin uncomfortably.

Inside the apartment, the sound of the storm lashes outside the window, unapologetic with its ferocity and timing.

I remove my hoodie, and underneath my T-shirt is still dry. Will shakes his head, running his fingers through his soaked hair, attempting to dry it off. Unable to turn away, my gaze falls upon his hair, a wild mess, to the small pout on his lips while he tries to control it somewhat.

Placing his hands on the bottom of his sweater, he pulls it up above his torso, his t-shirt beneath caught in the fabric, revealing his perfectly sculpted six-pack. Biting my lip, I'm unaware of how sexy he is beneath until he notices my stare, prompting me to act quickly by diverting my eyes to the floor.

"I'm going to get changed," he informs me. "You sure you don't want to get changed, you know, since you have a knack for borrowing from my wardrobe?"

I shake my head, pressing my lips together. "I'm not that wet."

"Hmm... that's a shame," he mumbles with a smirk before walking off to his bedroom.

The second he's out of sight, I release the breath I've been holding in until my phone begins to ring inside the back pocket of my jeans. I pull it out to see Mom's name flash on the screen.

"Hey, Mom, what's up?"

"Just checking in on you. I heard about a wild storm hitting the city and knew you were visiting today."

"Oh yeah, we just..." I clear my throat, wincing at the mention of *we* and not wanting to raise any questions. "I meant, I just got caught in it but sitting inside a café now till it passes. Everyone on the sidewalk got caught, so we all panicked and just sought shelter where we could."

"I'm glad you're safe," she says, a smile evident in her tone. "So, Thanksgiving. Your father would like us to come to you. I miss the city and was thinking we could spend a few days together if you don't have any plans?"

"No plans," I tell her. "It'll be nice to have you all here. I miss you guys."

"We miss you, too, honey. And how are you? You know, after the whole Austin thing?"

I hadn't even thought about it over the last few days, preoccupied with planning this day and Will's text message to me.

"Uh, I'm fine, Mom."

"You know, it's okay not to be fine."

"I know," I say, lowering my face. "But I promise you, I'm fine. School has been busy, and I have a lot going on."

It was only partially a lie, a small one at that. And although I hate lying to her, I consider it a short extension of the truth.

The sound of footsteps draws closer as Will walks down the hallway, dressed in another pair of jeans and a black tee.

"So, listen, I was thinking—"

In a panic, my eyes widen as I point my finger toward my phone, trying to catch his attention. It takes a moment for the penny to drop, his arms folding with annoyance while he mouths for me to hurry up.

"Sorry, Mom, people are loud here in the café. Can I call you later?"

There's a slight hesitation in her voice. "Of course, honey. We'll talk later."

I hit end call fast, letting out an annoyed huff.

"That was my mom."

"I figured when you said sorry, Mom," he answers, presumably. "So, why did you lie to her? Why didn't you just say you were here?"

My smile wavers. Without even realizing it, I'm fidgeting with the ends of my hair, unsure how to answer his question.

"I didn't want her getting the wrong idea."

"The wrong idea?" He tilts his head to the side, raising his eyebrows. "Exactly what idea do you think she'd get?"

"I don't know, okay? We're not exactly of the same age, and I didn't want her reading any more into it."

Will moves closer to me, motioning for me to sit on the sofa as he plonks himself on it.

"Just because we're together, doing things, doesn't mean we're fucking each other."

The thought alone causes my eyes to widen and cheeks to burn unwillingly. There's no denying that Will is incredibly sexy, but my thoughts are wild and uncalled for. Plus, I'm sure he looks at me like some annoying kid.

"I guess you're right."

"Maybe you should call her back, let her know you're with me?" he notes with dark amusement.

Only now, I realize that he's poking fun at the situation. The devious smirk plays on his lips as he grabs the remote. Leaning forward, I punch his arm like I'd done many times before.

"Ow, what's that for?" He scowls.

"You're being a jerk."

"A jerk you want to fuck? Is that why you're upset?"

With a pinched expression, I sigh heavily. "You think very highly of yourself. Do you know that? Let's say I do need to fuck. What makes you think that you, out of all people, would even know how to satisfy me?"

Will shakes his head with a hard smile. "Sweetheart, I'd make you fall to your knees. I'm certain that ex of yours wasn't able to, hence, why you're no longer together."

The nerve of him to think that I broke up with Austin because the sex wasn't any good. The sex was great, fantastic even. Though logically, I had been with only one man, so perhaps the jerk in front of me has somewhat of a point. Is sex supposed to be even better than that?

"I think we need to watch something on TV and pretend this conversation never existed."

Still staring at the screen with a beguiled expression, we begin to argue over what to watch. Every movie he likes, I despise. Our heated debate of genre, tropes, and actors went on forever until we both agreed to settle on a documentary.

Will lights the fireplace, and between the mesmerizing flicker of the flames to the warm air inside the apartment, my eyelids begin to fall heavy. If I just close my eyes for a moment, it'll pass, and I'll be energized to drive back to New Haven.

I grab the blanket beside the sofa and throw it over me.

The screen begins to look blurry, constant yawns escaping me. It all just feels so comfortable, almost as if I'm back home.

"Hey," Will whispers beside me. "Are you still awake?"

I nod, murmuring before I move closer to him and rest my head on his shoulder. The fight to stay awake becomes too much of a battle until my eyes close to the sound of the television still playing.

~

My eyes slowly open, tired and barely able to move, the muscles of my face completely relaxed. The surroundings begin to sink in, and as my hand moves against the surface it's resting on, I realize it is the fabric of Will's sweater, and I'm lying on his chest.

Pulling away quickly, my head spins momentarily, trying to figure out what just happened. *You fell asleep on him, that's all—no need to panic.* Nothing happened. Will is fast asleep, at least, until a slight stir escapes him, causing his eyes to open, only just.

"Did we fall asleep?" he mumbles, letting out a yawn.

"Yes," I mutter, my yawn escaping. "I was so tired, and I guess you were too."

"I never nap," he states.

"Neither do I, really. I think it was the adrenaline rush, then the food coma, and then the boring documentary you put on."

A soft chuckle escapes his lips. "It was a great nap. We should be nap buddies."

"Nap buddies?" I follow with a laugh. "Sure, I'll just drive here every weekend, and we'll schedule it in. Who needs a law degree, anyway? Napping is way more important."

"Too much sass coming from you. You're ruining my Zen."

I stretch my arms above my head, tilting my head from side to side, trying to alleviate the stiff neck from laying in one position for a long time.

"What's wrong?" Will asks, shuffling into a sitting position.

"I must have slept too long in one position. Stiff neck."

"Come here."

I turn to face him with a raised brow. "Why?"

"Must you ask so many questions?"

"Fine," I answer, moving toward him as he motions for me to turn around.

Placing his hands on my shoulders, they slowly begin to squeeze shut, massaging the knot, which becomes rather uncomfortable. It feels heavy, and almost instantly, my body relaxes at his touch.

"You give a great massage. Who taught you?"

"My dad."

I burst out laughing, knowing Uncle Rocky so well.

"Do I want to know how or even why?"

Will continues to knead my shoulders. "When I was of legal age, Dad thought it would be funny to take me to one of those massage places."

"What do you mean one of *those* massage places?"

"Do I need to spell it for you?"

I recall a story Aunt Adriana once told me. I don't remember the entire thing, but the words "rub and tug" stand out.

"I think I've got it. Carry on."

"Well, I was awkward, so to stop anything going further,

I started a conversation about techniques. The masseuse, Sandra, was more than happy to give me tips. So, that's how I learned."

"Why does this not surprise me at all? I swear, your dad has lived quite some life. His stories are so wild."

Will breaks out into laughter. "Try being his son. The conversations he can carry about porn are mind-blowing. He just doesn't seem to care about creating that father-son bond through normal activities like fishing, for example."

I shake my head, unable to control my laughter. "Your dad fishing is code for 'we're hitting strip joints in Vegas.' God, I hope my dad isn't joining him on these so-called fishing trips?"

Behind me, Will falls silent, prompting me to turn around. His silence speaks volumes as does the smirk playing on his lips. I wait patiently for him to say something, but he continues to remain tight-lipped, prompting me to push my hands against his chest.

"C'mon, you know something!"

He grabs my wrists, the little rise in the corner of his mouth and amused eyes seemingly enjoying my begging.

"A gentleman never tells."

"Who said you were a gentleman?" I deadpan.

Will let's go of my wrists, digging his fingers into my ribcage and causing me to jump. I beg him to stop until I accidentally fall on top of him, out of breath.

My shallow breathing is hard to control, especially when his eyes fall upon mine, and the slight bite of his lip catches my attention. I'm drawn to the way his lips move until I find myself tracing his mouth with my finger, the touch causing me to shiver with pleasure as the ache within me begs me to explore the rest of him.

He places his hand on my shoulder, dragging it at a slow

and agonizing pace until he cups the back of the neck, allowing my hair to fall over his arm. The deep blue stare of his eyes watches me, almost pained, urging me to kiss him until the phone rings on the coffee table.

Instinctively, I climb off him to create distance between us as he takes the call. Willing my heart rate to slow to a manageable pace, Will is less than pleased with the call, arguing with whoever is on the other end and raising his voice.

When the call ends, I place my hands on my knees, unable to look at him.

"I should go. The storm has stopped."

"Yes," he croaks, then clears his throat. "Of course, you have a long drive back."

I stand up, clutching my hoodie and phone, then finally grab the keys.

"Thank you for today," is all I can say.

With a knowing smile, his stare lingers on me, but behind it lays something else, something I choose to ignore for the very reason of being able to leave this apartment with my head and heart in check.

"You know where to find me, you know, in case you want to be adventurous again."

The corners of my mouth quirk up, a small laugh escaping me.

"I think I've had enough adventure to last me for a while," I tease, cocking my head to the side. "But in case you need a nap buddy again, you know where to find me. Just a little warning, though, next time may not end as well."

And the joke, as intended, has left my mouth before I realize exactly who I'm speaking to.

"Careful, Amelia," he lowers his tone with a burning gaze. "You have no clue what you're doing."

I allow myself to bask in his longing stare, let my body feel him all over me before I walk away. Whatever just happened is dangerous.

Yet, perhaps, we allowed our weakness to get the better of us. He's a man, and I'm a woman. Neither one of us are in a relationship, and sexual urges are perfectly normal.

That is, unless your sexual desire is toward the one man you can't have.

Or shouldn't have.

Either way, I've entered forbidden territory.

The problem is, once you get a taste of it, it's almost impossible to turn back.

SEVENTEEN

AMELIA

I slam the door, throwing my bag and laptop onto our sofa in an annoyed huff.

Removing my scarf, it becomes tangled in my hair, only adding to my frustration. The temperature inside our dorm room is like a goddamn oven, causing me to swelter beneath the thousands of layers I wore.

Liesel strolls out of her room, dressed in a tank and boy shorts. Considering it's lunchtime, her attire is unusual, yet another one of her quirks.

"Okay, why the face?"

"No face," I tell her, finally removing the scarf and tossing it on top of my bag. "Can't you put clothes on and turn down the heat?"

Liesel releases a long-winded whistle. "What the hell happened to put you in such a bad mood? It's been, what? Two weeks maybe of you slamming doors, all irritable."

Pinching the bridge of my nose, I close my eyes momentarily before falling onto the sofa.

I don't even know where to begin. The workload has increased of late, many of my professors adding more assignments I need to complete in a short amount of time. That means long hours, more caffeine, and only a few hours' sleep.

My family traveling to New York only adds to the pressure of me completing all my work on time, so I can focus on them. Mom shared her itinerary—a girl's day out, a visit to some friends she wants to introduce me to who work in the legal field. Then, of course, there's Thanksgiving.

I glance at the time on the wall clock, knowing I only have an hour to pack before the car service takes me to my parents' penthouse in the city.

"There's just a lot on my mind," I inform Liesel, hoping to satisfy her with my blanket response.

"A certain someone is on your mind?" She digs further.

"No," I lie unconvincingly. "Just stuff."

Liesel pushes further, opening a cabinet and pulling a bottle of vodka out. She pours a small amount into the lid, reaching toward me. Reluctantly, I take it from her and down it in one go. The burn laces my throat, causing me to rasp before the liquor settles inside my stomach.

"That should help you clear your head, pack your clothes, and deal with your family," she continues, placing the bottle back before I stop her. I motion for her to pour me another. What harm can it do? "That's the spirit. Thanksgiving is a time to be thankful for your blessings, and I'm thankful for you and also this bottle."

I giggle then follow with a hiccup. "I'm sorry I've been a bitch. I'm not usually so moody."

"Hey, it happens to the best of us," she assures me with a warm smile. "I better go pack, too. My aunt is picking me up soon to head to the airport."

As she turns toward the room, I call her name.

"I'm grateful for you, too. I don't know what I'd do without you."

"Probably be less intoxicated," she muses. "And maybe healthier since my obsession with ordering pizza because of that cute delivery guy is out of control."

I snort, shaking my head knowingly. "It's borderline creepy."

She laughs out loud before disappearing to her room. I follow her lead, heading to my room to pack. It's been a while since I stayed at the apartment in Manhattan and have no clue what I left behind. Not wanting to risk it, I pack what I need, then check the time on my phone. Upon looking at the time, I notice no messages. Checking my socials really quickly, there's nothing needing my attention.

Annoyed, once again, I zip up my suitcase fiercely.

It's been two whole weeks since I left Will's. And in that two weeks, not a single word from him. I could've texted him myself, but after his stern warning for me to be careful, I decided against it.

I don't know what his lack of contact means, but I sure knew that men like him are easily distracted, certain that he's busied himself buried between some woman's legs. I'll admit, it got to me more than I care to admit. I never considered myself a jealous person, and why I find the sudden need to be exactly that is beyond me.

And while I didn't admit that to Liesel, the truth is I'm equally annoyed at myself for feeling this way.

Grabbing my things, I quickly say goodbye to Liesel and give her a big hug before leaving the campus behind for four days in the city.

∿

Reuniting with my family is exactly what I need. My sisters, overbearing and demanding, all want to spend time with me but for different reasons. Whenever they could tag along with Mom and me, they would.

It means that Mom and I have less time to ourselves. Throw Dad into the mix, even less time. Though, as always, he was busy with work and disappeared to his office only to return at night for dinner.

After two days staying in my parents' penthouse, I offer to help Mom prepare for Thanksgiving. Ava is nowhere to be seen, and neither are Addison and Alexandra. Still, I welcome the time with just us two women.

"With your sisters around, we haven't had much time to chat."

"I know, those chatterboxes always take the limelight," I complain, jokingly.

"So, how are you really doing?"

I continue to peel the potatoes while conversing. "Honestly, it's hard. Professors are demanding, and I'm trying to cram in some extra course work to finish earlier."

Mom nods her head knowingly. "I understand, I did the same. Just don't over-extend yourself. Your dad will kill me for saying this, but you also need to enjoy yourself, get out a little with friends."

"I just don't have the time," I admit.

"And there's no guy who has caught your interest?"

"Since Austin? No..." I hate lying, again, but don't want to raise the topic of Will, given Mom's relationship with him. She's always been honest about just how important he is from the moment he was born. I don't want to ruin their relationship, assuming she'll blame him for coercing me to hang out and given our age difference, which isn't encouraged. "I just want to be single for a while."

"Understandable. Nothing wrong with being single."

I laugh out loud. "I don't think Dad's listening, so you can tell the truth because, let's face it, Dad wants me single forever."

"Your father would be a hypocrite if he expects you to stay single. The first time he got married, he was in his early twenties."

"Oh, that's right. So, what you're trying to say is my father is no angel?"

Mom grins, cleaning the countertop before grabbing the fancy china out of the cupboard. "I shall not speak ill of your father."

"Nice call, Mom."

The doorbell rings, ending our conversation. In the other room, I hear Uncle Rocky's roar of laughter. Mom alerted me to who will attend dinner, and conveniently, Will isn't one of them.

I say hello to the Romanos, hugging all three of them. Everyone takes their seat until Mom claps her hands, and my eyes fall upon Will, standing beside my father.

The dark charcoal-colored suit is tailored to his body, and the crisp white shirt beneath his jacket is slightly unbuttoned, a vest layered over it. Dad is a very tall man, and standing beside him, Will is about the same height.

My whole body reacts to how sexy Will is. There's no surprise as to why women desperately want in his bed. Between his handsome face and incredibly muscular body, he has the whole package. Throw in that fact that he's a CEO of his own company, and there's the trifecta.

With an inward gaze, I take a deep breath and divert my attention to my sister, hoping no one notices my inability to greet him.

Just as he's about to walk over to me, Ava grabs me to pull me aside.

"I have some major goss to tell you."

"Can it wait?" I ask, distracted.

"It's about you, though."

"Me?"

"Yes, silly. And Austin."

"Austin?"

"I overheard Dad on the phone telling Will how he's glad you're single now."

"That's not gossip, Ava. We know Dad's opinion on my love life."

Dad clears his throat, pushing us along to take our seats. I take a seat next to Dad, across the table from Will. Still avoiding his gaze at all costs, our attention is called to the other end of the table. Uncle Rocky begins our meal by saying grace, as we all bow our heads in respect. Upon lifting my gaze, Will's eyes meet mine, his piercing stare anything but welcoming. What the hell is his problem? He's the one who didn't reach out to me.

Around the table, noise begins to filter out as we serve the food and immerse ourselves in conversations.

Our families reminisce about previous holidays, telling stories as laughter fills the room. Across the table, I avoid his glance on more than one occasion, trying to smile or nod when needed, though leaving the conversation to everyone else.

"How is Yale going?" Aunt Nikki directs the conversation to me. "You must be all settled in now."

"Yes," I answer, placing my fork down. "It's nice to have a break, though. It's been a difficult two weeks."

The second it leaves my mouth, Will's head flicks up, his eyes falling to mine.

"Is everything okay?" Dad asks, concerned.

"Oh yes..." I choose my words carefully as all eyes turn to me. "I'm finally used to the late nights, cramming, and idiots who like to howl in the middle of the night after a drunken party."

Uncle Rocky snickers. "I won the best howl one year. Quite the achievement."

Mom laughs as Aunt Nikki shakes her head with embarrassment. "We remember," they say in unison.

Aunt Nikki continues. "Thank God, Will has more sense than you."

Beau, Will's younger brother, smiles proudly. "I think Dad is a fine role model. If you excuse the crude remarks, belching, the way he leaves the toilet seat up..."

"Hey, kid, I'm paying for your fancy private school," Rocky reminds him, then chuckles. "At least mention the empty carton of milk in the fridge if you're going to boast about all traits."

We all laugh, my eyes meeting Will's as something passes between us. Everything at this table is a reminder of how silly my thoughts are. We're family. Granted, we don't share the same blood, but we were still raised to be one happy family. Whatever happens between us is poor judgment, a momentary lapse and silly to dwell on.

"Will, tell me what's happening with you. Keep it kid-friendly. We have young ones at the table," Mom chastises.

Mom and Will have this unique bond. When it comes to Will, she treats him like a son and always has a soft spot for him. Aside from being his godmother, she has witnessed his birth and played an important role in his life from the moment he was born.

"There's not much to tell, Aunt Charlie. We're this close to closing a deal, hopefully in the next week. Overall, business is great. It's a digital era, so as long as you've got the right idea and capital, the sky is the limit."

"Have to agree with you there," Dad concurs. "The business is exactly where it needs to be. If you continue to focus on these upcoming acquisitions, you know what's next?"

"Oh?" Mom's face brightens. "What's next?"

Will keeps a steady gaze and purposely avoids my curious stare, his shoulders straight with a confident pose. "London, actually."

"This is new?" Aunt Nikki asks with trepidation. "You're setting up an office in London?"

"Yes, if all goes to plan."

"When?" I blurt out, then try to think of something witty to say to cover up my outburst. "Aunt Kate says that summers in London are wonderful."

What a lame thing to say.

"It's true," Dad agrees with a smile. "Nothing at all like ours. We were thinking in a few months."

"*We?*" I question, my gaze darting back and forth between them.

"Yes," Will concludes, his tone rather cold. "Lex has invested capital in our London project. If it weren't for this, we wouldn't be expanding so rapidly to dominate the European market. Your father has made me quite a wealthy man."

"I saw a post saying you're the hottest billionaire under thirty," Ava adds with a smirk. "Did you overthrow Dad? Oh, wait a minute, Dad holds the title for hottest billionaire over thirty."

Mom drops her head, hiding her laugh behind her glass.

Will lowers his eyes, shaking his head playfully. "I

know, it's been brought to my attention by my college buddies. With much mocking, of course."

"My son turned billionaire." Uncle Rocky bursts with pride. "Who'd have thought?"

"Not quite yet, Dad, almost there," Will assures him. "Doesn't mean it's time to slow down. If anything, we need to move faster."

Of course, his business ties to my dad now make sense. It's why they have so much in common and perhaps why they are quite close. It makes me feel all the more stupid for feeling whatever the hell I'm feeling and attempting to kiss him at his place.

"Enough with the boring business talk. Let's talk about your women," Ava quips.

Dad and Uncle Rocky chuckle at the same time. Not wanting to hear about Will's personal life, I lower my head, aimlessly moving the peas on my plate.

"I'm not sure this is acceptable dinner conversation," Will gently scolds her.

"He's got no women," Beau blurts out, unintentionally. "He's been a broody old brother with some chip on his shoulder for the last two weeks."

"Oh," Ava mouths, unable to contain her curiosity. "Are you in love with someone?"

The second she says it, my head shoots up. *Is Will Romano in love with someone?* It makes sense, he's incredibly handsome, wealthy, and it must be someone his age. Maybe a new assistant?

He hasn't reached out to me, and that day in his apartment, he easily said goodbye, not asking me to stay.

It all makes sense now.

Will drops his head before silence falls over the table.

When he raises it back slowly, all eyes are on him, including mine.

"I'm... I am not in love with anyone," he stammers, put on the spot. "But yes, someone has caught my eye."

"I knew it!" Beau yells proudly.

"Beau Benedict Romano, will you calm down?" Aunt Nikki warns him.

As if she knew her son well, she changes topics swiftly. Soon after dessert is served, the younger ones excuse themselves from the table. I take the opportunity to retreat to the kitchen to help clean up, willing the questions to stop. It takes every part of me to resist asking him who this person is or even about London.

None of it matters.

Period.

An hour later, I exit the kitchen to find everyone but Will. According to Mom, he has an early morning business meeting with Dad and said goodbye. Annoyed he didn't even have the decency to say goodbye to me, I storm off to my room to compose myself.

The room always brings back the nostalgia of my childhood. A few stuffed toys sit on a daybed looking out the window, along with a white bookcase where I keep a few things. It isn't our primary residence, but we stay here sometimes for weeks on end.

A pale blue box catches my attention. I move toward it, lifting the lid as I pull it out. Inside sits mementos I keep, including photos from my childhood. I recall the day Mom handed me a bunch of photos and my shock to learn you could actually get them printed.

There are so many memories, all of them make me smile. Then, I stumble on a photo of Will and me. He'd have been a teen, and maybe I was about five. His eyes are shut tight as I kissed his nose. I don't remember it, but I do remember that no matter how much he taunted me or we argued over trivial matters, he always protected me.

We have this history, which is the very reason nothing can ever happen between us. But none of this erases my annoyance from him walking out tonight without a good-bye. *What's his problem, anyway?*

I decide I need to find out and clear my conscience once and for all.

I place the box back and exit my room to find my parents.

"Mom, a friend wants to catch up for a late coffee a few blocks away. Do you mind if I head out for an hour?"

"Go ahead, honey. Dad and Uncle Rocky are watching sports and drinking. You know it's going to be a long night."

Kissing her cheek, I race out of the room and exit the apartment until I'm out on the street. I hail a cab, prompting the driver to take me mid-town.

Fifteen minutes later, I'm standing at Will's, overcome by nerves. *What the hell am I doing here? Or better yet, what the hell am I going to say?*

I knock on the door, crossing my arms, only to panic from the thought of another woman being here. *Shit.*

The door swings open to Will rolling up his sleeves. The second his eyes fall on me, he appears uncomfortable, his eyes closing momentarily.

"Amelia? What are you doing here?"

I push past him, entering the apartment, not wanting to have this conversation in the foyer.

"Am I interrupting you... or anyone else for that matter?"

"Uh... no. It's just me."

"Oh, but I'm guessing she'll be here soon, the woman who has piqued your interest?"

"Amelia." He lowers his head.

"I don't even know why I'm here," I shout, pacing the space between us. "I lied to my mom and said I was going out for coffee. I just..."

"Why did you lie?" He moves closer, and highly aware of his actions, my breathing falters. "Tell me, truthfully, why did you feel compelled to lie about coming here?"

"I don't know," I answer, barely above a whisper, dropping my head to hide my shame. "I'm confused."

The graze of his finger touches my chin, and slowly, he lifts it until our eyes meet. *"We can't be together, Amelia."*

"I know," I choke, holding my breath until my lips part slightly. "Just tell me to go."

His gaze shifts, a look of torment as his eyebrows pull together, deepening the crease.

"I can't do that..."

"Why?" I beg of him. "Why can't you tell me to go?"

Slowly, his head tilts upward, the piercing gaze which has tormented me in my sleep and invaded my thoughts in my waking moments, swinging like a wrecking ball ready to destroy everything I've worked so hard to ignore.

"Because it's you, Amelia," he whispers so delicately. *"You're the one I can't stop thinking about."*

EIGHTEEN

WILL

Her mouth crashes onto mine, the warm sensation spreading throughout my body at the taste of her strawberry-flavored lips.

My hands wrap around her thighs, pulling her up while carrying her toward my bedroom. The walk is only a few feet away, yet the distance, while short, feels like miles long. Our kisses deepen, soft moans escaping her beautiful lips as we come up for air, breathless with our attention anchored on each other as if our lives depend on it.

Using my foot, I push the door open to the dimly lit bedroom. Outside, darkness has fallen, and on this cold night, frost has blanketed the large windows, the normally white-gold moon hiding behind the pillows of clouds.

Standing at the foot of the bed, I pull away, though still carrying her. Her gaze falls upon my lips, hungry and impatient while her chest rises and falls. I beg myself to think clearly, ignore whatever it is consuming me right now, and feed my body this drug it so desperately craves.

I open my mouth to speak but shut it again, conflicted by all the emotions fighting for attention at this moment.

"Tell me to stop."

Her lips crash back onto mine with urgency, almost as if she won't allow me to step away. Slowly, I place her on the bed as she sits on the edge, looking up at me, her emerald-green eyes watching me so innocently that I know this won't end well.

For her.

For me.

For our family.

But even with those thoughts, I'm distracted as she toys with my belt, her hair sliding across her shoulder, exposing her neck. Her skin, so delicate and pure, taunts me, making it hard for me to control my urges.

With the pull of my belt, my pants fall. I unbutton my shirt, leaving me only in my silk boxers. I climb on top, kissing her deeply before insisting she straddle me. Trailing my finger down her chest, she begins to undo the buttons of the maroon-colored dress she is wearing, the soft fabric falling past her shoulders, exposing her white-lace bra and panties.

Biting down, I use every muscle I have to control my fucking dick from blowing right here, right now. Every forbidden fantasy of her, all of them have become a mind fuck over the last two weeks, is happening right in front of me.

It's a blessing and a curse, the fruit and its temptation, and in this moment, my throat begins to thicken as I pinch my eyebrows together, losing all hope of resisting the one person I'm not supposed to touch.

But as our gaze locks, the silence speaks loudly between our shallow breaths, and she removes her bra—her beautiful tits beg me to devour them. My eyes widen at the sight. *They're fucking perfect.* Just as I had imagined them—

round, supple, perfectly positioned light pink nipples, fully erect and expressing how turned on she is right now.

I can't hold back, running my fingers along the curves, taking them in my mouth as she moans so carelessly, arching her back. My tongue rolls around her nipple, sucking gently with a small tug of my teeth. I knead them between my fingers, unable to control my urge to ravage her, begging her silently to let me have her completely and hoping she doesn't get scared, pulling away at a moment's notice.

Yet her moans deepen, pleasure and pain all rolled into one. Every sound, so beautiful, warns me she's close when we haven't even begun.

"If you need me to stop."

She shakes her head, quick and panicked. No words are said until she shuffles off, removing her panties and letting them fall to the ground.

Fuck.

I stare between her legs, admiring the landing strip and well-manicured bikini wax. God, how could a pussy be so fucking perfect? This isn't the first one I've seen, I've lost count. So, why in the hell does this feel all brand new?

Desperate to clear my rambling mind, my boxers come off without a second thought. She hovers back over me, but not before removing a condom from my drawer. The foil packet stills my movements.

Great, I completely forgot for the first time *ever*.

Tearing the packet between my teeth in desperation, I quickly place it on the tip of my shaft and slide it down. *What I would do to feel her bareback.*

Clutching the back of her neck, I draw her close to me, my mouth eager to kiss her deeply. I give her one more chance to walk away, knowing that whatever the hell happens tonight, it's doing things to me I've never experienced before—an out-of-body experience consuming me in unimaginable ways.

"If you tell me to stop..."

"*Will,*" she breathes, sliding herself on as her mouth parts slightly. I close my eyes, biting down as the sensation grapples my shaft and pleasures me without even the slightest of movement yet. "*Fuck me, please.*"

Her begging spurs on the beast within me. I grip her hips, watching her body ride me. Goosebumps cover every inch of her, and her nipples are hard as I pinch them softly. Her cries are mixed with moans, the sound fighting for attention with the grunts my body expels.

Shuffling my body, so I'm sitting up, it allows me to bury myself deeper within her.

Amelia's face is in line with mine, so close as we lose ourselves in the heat of the moment, and kissing her becomes an addiction I don't want ever to cure.

Pulling away while arching her back, she calls my name until I slide my hand behind her neck again and beg her to look at me.

And at this moment, our eyes connect so profoundly, my emotions run wild in fear.

This isn't just a moment, and let's say this is one time, how I do I even begin to forget how easily I'm willing to give up everything to be inside her. How desire drives me to make careless decisions because the smell of her skin is nothing like I imagined it to be. I'm lost, wandering the paths of hell because the taste of heaven is lingering on my lips.

But then she scrapes her thumb on my bottom lip, causing the feverish spell within me to intensify.

"Come with me," I demand with a rasp. "I want you to come with me."

Her lips crash onto mine, the taste so delicious. I beg my body not to release now, willing the restraint to last just a little bit longer, so we both feel the rush in sync. "I'm ready, Will."

My hands lace around her neck, our foreheads touching as I thrust inside her. She rides my cock, a rhythm building momentum until all I feel is her muscles tighten around my shaft. My body jerks forward, a shiver following as a deep grunt escapes me, and my body basks in euphoria.

My eyes blink rapidly, sweat dripping off my forehead while I try to gather my bearings and gain visibility again. The momentary flash of lights blinds me, as does the pleasure overcoming every inch of my body.

Our breaths, uneven, echo inside the room.

Slowly, she slides herself off, collapsing beside me and pulling the sheet over her. I discard the condom, tossing it on the floor, and turn to face her.

"Now what?" I ask, breathless, spreading tiny kisses on her arm.

"I don't know," she answers truthfully. "I thought you were a one-time guy."

Slightly hurt by her assumptions, I climb back on top of her to make her understand the truth. I'm held hostage to her deep stare, shades of green locking me in some sort of trance.

"We can't be together," I remind her.

"I know."

"It's forbidden."

"Completely taboo. You're like family."

"You're like a little cousin," I tell her, my eyes falling onto her lips, the stir below awakening my desire again. "Though not so little... a beautiful, sexy, gorgeous..." I kiss her shoulder until I'm on her lips, "... woman."

"Plus, I'm not *actually* related to you."

"Still off-limits."

"Completely off-limits," she agrees while running her hand in my hair before a smile plays on her lips. "But I guess one more time wouldn't hurt, right?"

My dick is already hard, and this time, I need to feel her properly, not with a fucking condom. *I can control this, just pull out before I come, and no one pays the price.*

I slide myself in, her arousal utterly wet as she moans even louder than before.

She feels perfect.

Like everything that's missing from my life.

There's just one problem.

Nothing will change the fact that she's Lex Edwards' daughter. The man who reigns over all, the ruler of his kingdom, and as of now, I'm his biggest threat.

The man about to steal his princess.

NINETEEN

AMELIA

My eyes jolt open to the sound of a siren blaring outside the building.

Releasing a groan, I struggle with the morning glare coming from the large window near my bed. *Where am I again?*

The familiar room, one I had spent much time in, begins to register—it's our townhouse on the Upper East Side.

I bury my face into the pillow, pulling my quilt above my head to drown the outside noise with the intent to fall back into a blissful sleep. With the temperature perfect, warm, and nothing like the cold outside, it's ideal for spending the morning after Thanksgiving.

You're the one I can't stop thinking about.

My body jerks up, sitting in an upright position as the memory of last night comes roaring back to my center of attention. The beat of my heart begins to quicken, and throughout my whole body, a pleasurable tingle spreads like wildfire as my mind replays the touch of Will's hand against my skin.

How his eyes did something to me, I just can't explain. They held me captive, tortured me with desire, begged me to say and do things that even my wildest of imagination never dared to explore.

But it wasn't just the weight of his stare. It was everything his body did to me. We moved so effortlessly, in sync, like a band playing in harmony to a tune. Every inch of his perfect body had me mesmerized—his toned arms, the sculpted chest, and, of course, his perfect size cock.

I gulp at the memory, knowing damn well what we did last night was wrong.

My body did things I'd never experienced, dangerous things I'd only read in romance novels. I became possessed, throwing all rationality out the door to succumb to whatever it is that makes me crumble beneath his touch.

I fall back, staring at the ceiling, trying to decipher what this all means. I'd be a fool to ignore that what happened last night was amazing, despite it being wrong.

And surely, without a doubt, he enjoyed it. We fucked twice in the space of an hour, and he had no problem finishing.

Yet, I've heard enough stories about him through Mom and Aunt Nikki to know that he enjoys his women only for one night. And why would I be any different?

As I continue to lay in bed, I toss and turn, regretting my actions, filled with remorse to then craving more. Unable to think straight, I hop out of bed, wincing as my sore muscles ache with every sudden movement. Grabbing my phone, I drag my tired self to leave my bedroom with the hope that Mom has brewed coffee because I desperately need it.

I turn the corner into the dining room, my eyes peeled to a story Andy put out about last night's dinner back home.

I smile at the caption of his turkey, missing him so much since we rarely spend time together anymore.

"Good morning, honey," Mom greets politely.

Caught up in another story of a friend, I laugh while returning the sentiment to Mom until Ava blurts out. "You look like shit. What the hell happened to you last night?"

My eyes lift, and there at the table, they fall onto the same blue eyes which devoured me last night. *Shit.* Will is sitting beside my father, dressed in navy business attire with a devious smirk on his face. He appears to be put together, freshly shaven, and sexy.

Highly aware that I'm only wearing my night shorts which barely cover my ass, long socks, and an old ratted tee, I'm pretty sure my hair is a tangled bird's nest.

"I, uh... didn't sleep well. The noise..." I swallow the giant lump inside my throat, hoping my skin doesn't flush over. "Sirens and stuff."

"Well, you look like death," Ava scoffs with a mouthful of toast.

"Thanks for the reminder, dear sister."

I quickly take a seat across from Will, though avoiding his stare as Mom asks, "Coffee?"

"God, yes..." I clear my throat. "I mean, please."

I relish the warm liquid with a cup in my hand while trying to figure out an escape plan. Avoiding eye contact is necessary, and surely, if I ignore him, my parents or sisters won't suspect anything.

"Are you heading back to campus tonight?" My father asks, placing his phone down to focus on me.

"Uh, yeah." I scratch the back of my neck. "I've got a lot of work to catch up on."

"I'll have the driver take you."

"Honestly, Dad, it's okay. I can take a train."

"I'd really like it if you would accept my offer of a car, Amelia," he almost demands.

I think about it again. Perhaps it's not such a bad thing. I could spend more time in the city, but what for? He hasn't even said two words to you.

"I'll think about it, but if I agree, nothing flashy. I don't want to be treated differently because you've gifted me a Porsche or something like that. How about something economical, good for the environment?"

"You know, Daddy," Ava goads with a wide smile. "I'll take the Porsche. I like to be treated differently and don't care for the environment."

Dad scoffs, shaking his head in amusement, then turns to Will. "Do you hear what I have to put up with? Nothing flashy. Like she expects me to walk into a used dealer to buy her some beat-up old truck."

"Now, now. Go easy on her." Mom laughs before patting my hand. "You know I'd normally defend you, but being a car enthusiast, I'd take your father's offer."

"I'll think about it," I say, wishing they would focus on anything else besides me.

"You have a bruise on your wrist," Ava points out. "What the hell are you doing in college, or *who* the hell are you doing in college?"

"Ava!" Dad almost yells. "Is it your intent to give me an early stroke?"

"Sorry, Dad." Ava snickers.

My gaze purposely focuses on the plate in front of me. It's empty and white, and I wish that I could think of anything else. It proves pointless as something forces me to look up into Will's eyes.

"I must have banged something, my dresser or desk."

"Just like when you were a kid," Will muses, lowering

his gaze. "You were always scratched up when I saw you, but you never seemed to care."

"I guess I didn't feel pain." My eyes zone in on him. "My pain threshold far outweighs a certain cry baby next to me."

"Hey!" Ava sulks. "I resent that. Besides, all I ever remembered is Amelia daring Will to do things with the high chance of hurting himself."

"Do I want to know what exactly?" Mom cringes.

"The point is—" I interrupt. "We're all alive and well."

"Speaking of being alive and well." Mom directs her stare at Dad. "What time do you expect to be back?"

"We have back-to-back meetings, so I'm not sure."

"We?" I ask, regretting it when my dad looks at me oddly.

"Me and Will. We have very important things to finalize," he states firmly.

I remain quiet as Mom lectures Dad, reminding him of other commitments. A small argument interrupts between them, though nothing out of the ordinary. When it comes to Dad working, Mom usually understands unless he committed to something else.

"Argh," Will groans, falling back on his chair while rubbing his chin.

"What's wrong?" Mom asks, worried.

"My housekeeper is sick, and I've got a delivery arriving today."

"Can your concierge let them in?" Mom suggests. "What's being delivered?"

"A new TV," Will states. "It needs to be installed and takes about an hour. I just need someone to make sure they do it right."

"I'm sorry, honey, I'm heading out to meet your mom

today. Ava is watching Addison and Alexandra, but perhaps, Amelia, you can do it?"

"Me?" I almost choke on my coffee. The liquid catches in my throat, making a gurgling sound. "You want me to go to your place and watch a man install a TV?"

"You're basically making sure they don't rob me blind."

Behind his stare, there's something I can't quite put my finger on. It takes me a moment to come up with a plan to play dumb. "Where do you live?"

"I'll text you the address." He busies himself on the phone as mine beeps.

Will: *How many times can I make you come in an hour?*

Shit! I force myself to keep a straight face, my body the first to react despite everyone watching me. Thank God they can't hear the loud thump of my heart or the butterflies inside my stomach fluttering like crazy. I have to do something quickly, terrified someone will sniff our trail.

"Fine, but you owe me. Next time, get one of your secretaries to do it," I mouth so quickly. "Oh, that's right, you don't have one because you couldn't keep your pants zipped up."

"Ouch!" Ava laughs the same time Mom shakes her head.

I could almost see the proud smile come from Dad.

"I'm going to shower," I mention casually, my eyes falling upon Ava. "Since apparently, I look like death."

I head out of the dining area, and the second I'm out of sight, I almost run upstairs to my room. Shutting the door behind me, I lean against it, heart racing as I struggle to breathe in the air. Inside my hand, my phone buzzes.

Will: *Well played, Miss Edwards. It's nice to see you're always thinking about my dick. Am I going to guess twice? Maybe three times if you don't touch yourself in the shower.*

Me: *Aren't you quite an overachiever. Let's see if you can deliver or you're all talk.*

Will: *If you're going to tease me like that, you better not complain when you've gotten no sleep. Sirens? Or perhaps you couldn't stop thinking about me fucking your sweet pussy inside my bed.*

My face turns red, praying that by the time I leave the house, he's already gone.

Me: *I strongly suggest you behave, Mr. Romano. You are with my father all day long, are you not? If you want to play dirty, don't underestimate my ability to make you suffer in your meetings.*

Will: *Always the daredevil. See you at 2.*

Throwing my phone onto my bed with a smile, I grab my things and head straight to the shower.

I enter the code as the door unlocks. The second I step inside, I smell him everywhere. The scent—intoxicating— causes my concentration to shift. I place my phone down on the hallway table, closing the door behind me. Gravitating toward the window, I stare into the Hudson River, lost in thought when I hear a noise behind me. I don't turn around, but my breathing hitches in anticipation. The footsteps move closer to me until a warm breath lingers against my neck, forcing me to close my eyes.

His lips press against my skin as I reach back to pull him into me, desperate to have him closer. The gentle kiss sends my skin into a frenzied static, tiny goosebumps forming all over.

Turning around, my body is flush with his as he lifts me, cupping his hands beneath my dress and kissing me deeply. Our tongues battle, wanting more, arousing every inch of my body. I can feel his tongue swirling in my mouth, imagining the exact thing being done between my legs. A desperate moan escapes me, no care to what's right or wrong because I need him to own me. Now.

I think he's going to take me toward the bed, but instead, he lays me on the couch and watches me with a hungry stare.

"And you so easily came back?"

"To see if you truly are a one-night-stand-type-of-guy and your reputation precedes you."

His eyes battle, almost as if I've struck a nerve. Will pulls back, momentarily, his face turning away. Then, as if something clicks, his stare swiftly moves back onto me, thirstier than before.

"We shouldn't be doing this," he reminds me.

"So you've said, yet here you are. In fact, you insisted I come here to do what exactly?" I search the room knowingly. "I'm yet to see your new TV or the hot men you promised me?"

A slight growl escapes his throat, his lips pressed flat while adopting a sullen look.

"Don't push me, Amelia."

Without a second thought, he lunges onto me, kissing me deeply as his hands explore my entire body. In a matter of seconds, he has unbuttoned the front of my dress, desperate to expose my breasts. Tugging my bra down, his mouth finds its way to my nipples, sucking hard without an apology for his ferocity.

I arch my back, welcoming his desperation but equally desperate to feel him inside me. My hands wander to his belt, fiddling with his buckle until he assists me, and his cock springs free from his boxers. I swallow at the sight—perfect and hard—eager to taste him, yet I know he just wants to bury himself inside me.

I lay on the sofa, my chest rising and falling as he enters me slowly, my mouth opening with an uncontrolled pant. Closing my eyes, I writhe in pleasure with every thrust, the quick and fast pounds to the sound of his groans. My eyes spring open, drawn to his tortured face as he begs me to come with him.

My hands clutch onto the sofa arm behind me as I warn him loudly that I'm ready. His movement picks up, the build of pleasure overwhelming me until his fingers wander to my nipples, tugging them hard and causing a sudden flush of warmth to spread throughout me. The air in the room is stifling hot and barely attainable while I try to breathe in, basking in a state of euphoric satisfaction.

Resting my hand on his cheek, willing him to calm down from his pleasurable victory, he kisses it but then pulls it away swiftly.

"Shit, I have to go."

In a frenzied panic, he jumps off me, pulling his pants back up and escaping quickly to what I assume is the bathroom. As I sit here, fixing my attire, he returns to the room.

"I need to be downtown to meet your Dad in fifteen minutes," he states, distracted by patting down his pockets. "You can let yourself out."

And with a quick kiss on the forehead, he's out of sight, though not out of mind.

I beg to hold back my questions, knowing once I start the thought process in my head, it will be a vicious cycle with no end.

But I'm weak and vulnerable, having just fucked a man who kissed me goodbye on the forehead, then walked out the door.

What now? I need to go back to campus, study for classes, and immerse myself back into college life. Are we in a relationship, or is this it? A two-day stand?

What if he sleeps with other women? Or he wants to pursue a friends-with-benefit type of relationship. Is that something I can see myself getting involved in?

I know I'm inexperienced, but is it so wrong of me to question where we stand? I let out a long-winded sigh until I realize that being in this apartment will cause more harm now than good.

The damage is done.

Just how much, I'm yet to find out.

TWENTY

AMELIA

I try my best to bury my head in studying.

Attending Yale has been my dream for as long as I can remember. I know others would've killed to get into an Ivy League college. Yet, here am I, staring blankly at the wall again and stuck in this vicious cycle I like to call *hell*.

In front of me, the glare of my laptop is the only light inside my room. The darkness from outside has crept in, and the sound of the rain tapping against the window is warning us of this cold, wintery night. It's been quite the season, and having grown up in California, I desperately miss the sunshine and palm trees.

Though the wild winter storm is perhaps a reflection of my current mood—cold, uninviting, and unpredictable with its temperament. It's what happens when a week passes with not a single call, text, or even a cheeky slide into my DMs.

My mom and sisters left last Saturday. With the girls back at school on Monday and Mom needing to be back at work, it was sad to say goodbye but part of this whole being an adult thing. Despite the distance, I manage to gain some insight as to Will's whereabouts. Mom has casually mentioned that Dad stayed back in the city to close a deal involving Will's company. According to Mom, things haven't gone as planned, and Dad was really stressed. Will, on the other hand, has been working nonstop alongside Dad. It explains the absent contact, but it doesn't erase the anger that festers as each day passes. I mean, *is* it that hard to send a text?

Once again, I find myself unable to make the first move out of fear of looking desperate.

By the following weekend, with barely any sleep and my brain wired from late-night cramming, I decide to plan a weekend of absolutely nothing but sleep.

That is, until Liesel jumps on my bed, ruining my peaceful Friday night.

"Get out of bed. We're going out."

"Out?" I stare at the window, all fogged up. "But it's cold, and I'm tired."

Liesel rips the sheets off, exposing my skin, making me shiver. "Okay, spill it. Who is it making you all broody and desperate?"

I sit up, folding my arms beneath my breasts. "I'm not broody and desperate!"

"Oh, really? You're always checking your phone, and you've been stomping around with a chip on your shoulder. Tell me who he or she is?"

"She?"

"It's college." Liesel shrugs her shoulders. "Anything is possible."

"It's not a *she*," I mumble, lowering my gaze. "And besides, have I really been that moody?"

"Well, you haven't been a ray of sunshine."

"It's nothing. Like nothing."

"Uh-huh," Liesel drags. "Well, nothing is obviously not calling you back. So, I have a plan."

"The last time you had a plan, I got drunk, and well..."

"In the *nothing's* bed?"

"Yes, but it's not what you think."

"I think you fucked him. He hasn't called back, and you're getting all clingy."

"Clingy?" I shout, followed but an incredulous laugh. "I haven't called him nor given him any reason to think I'm clingy, and I'm not."

"So then, back to my plan. There's a party a few blocks over. I say we hit it, look hot, and post stories to make our men jealous."

I roll my eyes at the ridiculous plan. "Firstly, I don't *have* a man. I'm manless. As single as you can get. Secondly, you have a man, so why do you want to make him jealous?"

Liesel motions for me to scoot over as she lays beside me, staring at the ceiling. "Because he hasn't called me back since I accidentally blurted 'I love you' in the middle of sex."

"Oh," I mouth with a scowl. "But did you mean I love you because the sex was great? Or I love you, love you?"

"Because it's great... hello, it's only been like two months. You can't love someone that quickly."

"I guess not..." I trail off. "But look, I'm tired, so a pass from me. You go, though. I'll cheer you on in my sleep."

"Fine, then," she complains in a huff, hopping out of my bed and leaving my room.

My momentary silence is interrupted by the sound of my phone buzzing beside me. I lazily pick it up, noticing Mom's caller ID.

"Hey, Mom."

"Hey, honey, just a quick hello. I'm in the city for one

night."

I sit up, pulling the blanket over my chest. "You're in the city? As in Manhattan?"

"Yes, a very last-minute thing in which your father so graciously begged me to come. Luckily, Adriana took the girls for the night."

A small laugh escapes my lips, reminiscing about my parents arguing over trivial matters because Dad would mention something last minute. It was comical watching Dad begging Mom because he doesn't want to attend certain events alone.

"Typical Dad. New outfit?"

"Of course, Ava chose it at Saks online, and I picked it up this afternoon. I was going to call you earlier but only arrived around lunch and on a red-eye tomorrow."

"You sure live an exciting life. Flying in and out for a night. Meanwhile, I'm here doing absolutely nothing."

"If it's any consolation, the weather is awful. I'd rather be in bed than out tonight. Luckily, I have Will and his date to keep me company if your father wanders off as usual."

I swallow the lump inside my throat. "Oh, that's nice he has a date. Will, the playboy, strikes again."

"Lucky you aren't on speaker." Mom chuckles softly as the noise around her heightens.

"Lucky," I grit as anger seeps through me.

"So, you're taking it easy tonight?"

"Actually, no." I hop out of bed and straight to my closet. I yank each dress aside, looking for my gray turtle-neck knitted mini dress which hugs my curves. "Liesel invited me to a party. Just a bunch of guys we know. I wasn't going to go, but why the hell not? I'm nineteen and shouldn't be in bed on a Friday night, right?"

"Sounds like fun. The number of college parties your

Uncle Rocky dragged me to... I lost count. I'll say they were fun and took my mind off things when I needed some social interaction."

"I think it's time I date." I rush, locating the dress while grabbing my knee-high boots to go with it. "I realize I've never dated before. There was Austin, and well, that's it. I'm too young to get serious, right?"

"Everyone is different, but dating isn't a bad thing," Mom says without judgment. "Just have fun and stay safe."

I hear her muffle the speaker until she says something I can't decipher. "Your father has suddenly decided to stop paying attention to an email he's typing on his phone."

"Not surprised," I retort, wondering if Will is listening at all to this conversation. Then again, why would he? He has some other pussy in the limo with him. "Tell my dear old daddy that I love him and not to worry. I don't plan to make him a grandpa anytime soon."

"If I repeat that, he'll shoot the messenger, being me," Mom confesses, followed by a small giggle. I suspect she's had wine or champagne, either one making her tipsy at this moment. "We're just about there, honey. Have fun tonight and let me know which college guy I can expect to call my son-in-law soon." There's more muffling until Mom yells out, *"Would you just relax?"*

"Thanks, Mom. Have fun, too."

I hang up the call, grabbing my gray knit dress and a black one too, barging into Liesel's room. She's standing in front of the mirror, dressed in a black-laced bodysuit and high-waisted jeans. Liesel's figure is amazing, and this outfit is a showstopper.

"The gray or black?"

Liesel's eyes perk up. "Oh yes, girl! The gray. What made you change your mind?"

"I realized I need to live life. I'm young, right? This is the prime of my life."

'Uh-huh... and Mr. Nothing is doing what tonight?"

"Out on a date with some woman," I confess with a slight growl.

"Oh, well, then." Liesel sits me down, pulling my hair out of its messy bun. "We need to make you look irresistible. Mr. Nothing is going to wish he called you back."

~

The music is blaring through the house, shoulders bumped together with barely any space for us to walk through. Liesel grabs my hand as we zig-zag through the crowd toward the kitchen, where apparently, the keg and other assorted drinks are served.

I couldn't have painted the picture any better, your typical college party, which I had seen numerous times in movies on the brink of cops breaking it up at the moment. What's the worst that could happen? It's not like we will all go to jail.

I wave hello to a few classmates, ignoring a bunch of men eyeing me from where they congregated near the billiard table.

Liesel grabs us some drinks, passing a red cup over to me that smells like punch. Tilting her head, she motions for us to join a group we know dancing in a small circle. With the cup still in my hand, I drink it in one go, willing the punch to settle and make this night more memorable.

We dance to the music, raising our hands in the air as we sway our hips to the beat of the music. It's just a bunch of us girls until Cash, a guy from my economics class, comes over.

"Hey, Miels," he greets, the sentiment not lost on me. Austin alternated between calling me that and Millie, depending on his mood.

"Hey, Cash."

"I'm surprised you came."

"A persuasive roommate." I laugh, poking Liesel in the arm. "So, what, no date? Or am I cramping your style?"

"You, gorgeous, could never cramp my style." Cash winks, a devious smirk playing on his lips.

Liesel motions something I can't seem to work out. Ignoring her sign language, which makes no sense whatsoever, Cash pulls me to the dance floor.

We dance for a while, laughing when the music turns upbeat and closing in on each other when the tunes slow. Somewhere in the middle of our dance, Liesel purposely dances beside me and whispers in my ear, "Selfie this shit and post it in your story."

I ignore her until Cash grabs my phone and puts his arm around me, posting it to his story and tagging me. I laugh, not caring anymore who sees. What does anything matter? Austin no longer speaks to me, probably busy with Winter, or was it Summer? I can't even remember her name. As for Will, he's most likely between someone else's legs right now. The thought itself burns like acid, and when my friend, Katelyn, walks past with two red cups, I grab one from her, quickly apologize, then down it in one go.

The second drink makes everything much better. I repost Cash's story, sending it to my own. We dance for a bit longer until he suggests we go somewhere quieter. I make some excuse about Liesel needing me, knowing that Cash's not-so-subtle butt grabs on the dance floor means he wants to take it further.

I want to have fun, and despite my earlier rant, I'm not ready to jump into bed with someone else.

The night begins to wear heavy with talks of the party shutting down soon. In a fit of giggles, Liesel and I hold onto each other to battle the cold as we walk back to our dorm room. At the beginning of the walk, our alcohol-fueled bodies were barely able to walk straight. But there's something to said about the cold—it sobers you up pretty quickly. It must have been all the teeth chattering or the constant talking to distract ourselves from the awful chill.

Inside the foyer of our building, we stumble and laugh until Liesel holds me back, calling my name to catch my attention.

I divert my eyes to our dorm room where Will is pacing in front of our door, dressed in a tux with an angry glare as his eyes feast upon me.

"Mr. Nothing?" Liesel whispers. "Millie, he's hot. But super angry."

"What are you doing here?"

"I need a word with you," he barks.

"I'm going to Jen's room." Liesel lets go of my arm, her gaze still fixated on Will. "Text me when you're ready."

Unsure of what to say or do, I manage to move closer and motion for him to get out of my way so I can open the door, all while trying to ignore how handsome he looks in his tuxedo.

"What could you possibly have to say to me?" I question abruptly.

I cross my arms beneath my chest as he closes the door behind him. Leaning on the door, he folds his arms just like me, but his gaze never shifts. The angered expression only appears to intensify when his eyes drop to the floor, then slowly drags them back up my body.

"So, *Cash,* is it? Is this the college guy you're fucking?" he asks, though it comes across as more of a threat. "Oh, wait a minute, dating according to what you tell your mother?"

Shocked by his jealous accusation, I refuse to break his stare. "I'm sorry, I didn't realize I had to answer to you. I'm not sure why you felt compelled to drive over here to weigh in on my personal life since, apparently, you have a date waiting for you. Let me guess, she wanted to stay the night, but you just couldn't let her ruin your streak of one-night stands?"

"Joy was my date for an event in which I couldn't exactly attend single."

"Joy?" I repeat, mocking. "Now isn't that a festive name?"

"Sounds to me like you're jealous."

"Being jealous would mean that I actually care, which I don't. I don't care who you fuck. You're the single almost billionaire, and all the women are dying to get their hands on you."

"And you're the college girl all the men want to taste."

Taken back by his comment, I pause, breaking his stare. He still hasn't given me a reason why he's here, yet I stand in front of him absolutely speechless. Nothing makes sense, nothing at all.

Slowly, he moves closer to me, my heart rate picking up with every step he takes. I try my best to ignore my body betraying me and my chest on the verge of exploding, but his scent, it's like a drug, and the closer he is to me, the more I struggle to compose myself.

"I lied to your father, told him an emergency came up with a friend. I may have jeopardized a business deal because I almost yelled at a potential client. I went over and over in my head why I even care some college kid is touching you or the fact that he's made his profile look like the two of you are together."

"Cash is just a friend..." I mumble, defending myself.

Will purses his lips, his body only inches away from mine. "And I don't understand why I want to tear apart any man who touches you in the slightest."

I beg my eyes not to look up at him, falling victim to his penetrating stare.

"I guess it's why I don't understand when I'm told you have some new woman latched onto your arm, I feel the very same."

His hands grip my face, his lips crashing onto mine. Letting out a moan, I drag him through the living room toward my room, throwing him onto my bed. Without a thought, I straddle him before he slides my dress above my hips and moves his fingers between us. I throw my head back, rubbing myself against him, ignoring everything else but the sound of his pants coming off.

Will doesn't hesitate entering me whole. My body follows, riding him fast, unapologetic with my need to come right here, right now. I don't care if I'm labeled selfish. His body is an addiction I can't seem to stop, no matter how fucked-up this all is.

He begs me again to ride it out together, and moments later, we moan in harmony, allowing our bodies to succumb to the intense orgasm we both experienced.

Our shallow breaths echo inside the room as he pulls my neck down, our foreheads touching while he still remains inside me.

"You didn't call," I state, rather than ask.

"Neither did you."

"I don't know what any of this means."

He kisses my lips, pushing deep. Undoubtedly, he's hard again. "What do you want it to mean?"

"I don't know," I falter, out of breath. "My parents can never find out. It will end badly if they do."

He stops his movements, tracing his fingers along my lips. "Then we keep us a secret. No one has to know but us."

"*A forbidden affair...*" I whisper.

With a devious smirk, he moves his hand beneath my dress and into my bra. His fingers tweak my nipple, causing me to gasp. "Our dirty little secret. No one has to know, but I do have one request."

"What is it?"

"It's only me," he mouths softly. "Only I can touch you like this."

I groan at his touch, his request to be exclusive not even a second thought. Unless, of course, he still wants to be with other women.

"But what about you?"

He pauses, his eyes tracing the tip of his finger as it glides down my body. With a steady gait, his tongue runs across his bottom lip seductively.

"Trust me, baby," he confesses with a lowered voice. "There's no one else I want to be inside of beside you."

And with the truth unveiled, I gaze at the man who has consumed me whole.

We're about to start something dangerous, something which can jeopardize everything we have.

Or maybe it's too late. The second I walked into his office, the tell-tale signs were there.

I just chose to ignore it.

And ignorance can only get you so far in life.

TWENTY-ONE

WILL

My fingers run through her soft hair as she lays against my chest.

There's nothing but silence inside the room, the sound of two lovers tangled in this intricate web we have found ourselves in.

Tonight was risky. I know very well that Lex was pissed when I had to leave, especially because I'd been in a mood all night since the phone call inside the limo. On several occasions, he tried to talk professionally, but my head wasn't in it. Nope, my head had decided to take some fucked-up ride in which every possible scenario taunted me.

Charlie knew something weighed heavily on my mind, quick to pull me aside and ask if everything was okay. She's always worried about me, just like my mother. What could I possibly say to her? Her daughter is a mindfuck, and there's no rhyme or reason to why I'm chasing someone so young when surrounding me, I can pretty much have any woman I want.

Nothing makes fucking sense.

When it comes to Lex, though, business always comes first, yet arguably, he's broken that rule several times.

"I have to go," I murmur, focusing on her lips.

Dropping her gaze, she breaks eye contact with a heavy sigh. Tilting her chin, I raise her lips to meet mine and place a gentle kiss unlike the frenzied kisses we found ourselves in only moments ago.

"Yeah, of course," she mumbles, still with a lowered gaze. "You need to sort everything out."

"I was thinking..." I stand up, buckling my pants and placing my shirt back on. "Next Saturday night. Come to my place. I'll cook dinner, and we can Netflix and chill."

She shakes her head, laughter consuming her. If only she understands just how beautiful she is—so raw, so innocent, so fucking perfect. "I didn't know you can cook dinner, too. All these secret talents of yours."

"I'm a masterpiece, according to my father."

"Your father can also burp the alphabet," she points out in jest.

I chuckle softly. "That he can."

We both reminisce about the time my dad did this incredibly stupid thing at a birthday party, embarrassing my mom as usual. The more we speak, the more it begins to sink in just how familiar it all is. How easily we just lose ourselves in memories because we have so many together.

"What time are you thinking?' she asks, toying with the ends of her hair. "I'd have to head back late."

"I was thinking you could sleep over." I wait for her reaction, praying that she wants to stay over and can read into what I'm saying without me having to spell it out.

Amelia sits quietly, not showing any emotion unlike any other woman I know. If I counted the last ten women I slept with, the same ones I had to push out the door, they would've jumped for joy at the possibility of staying over.

Instead, the reaction is less than enthused, only confusing me even more. Pulling the sheets toward her chest, her long hair falls over her shoulder, a picture-perfect showcase of all her beauty.

"You don't have to do that if you don't want to," she says stubbornly.

"Do what?"

"Invite me to stay over."

"Well, I want to." I continue to button my shirt, a smirk playing on my lips. "Besides, you've slept in my bed already and from memory, we've slept beside each other when we went camping. Granted, you told horror stories which scared everyone in the tent except me."

Amelia breaks out into laughter again. "Andy couldn't sleep for weeks. Ava would hide in Mom and Dad's bed. Their fear of clowns still reigns to this day."

"You were quite something as a kid."

"I'll take that as a compliment." She throws her pillow, goading a reaction from me. "Fine, I'll accept your invitation."

I lean in to kiss her, wishing I didn't have to leave but know I have no choice. "No need to pack any sleepwear, I expect you naked the entire time."

With a wide grin across her face, she stands on her tiptoes, wrapping her arms around my neck. "I couldn't think of anything more perfect."

The week drags on despite my exit on Saturday night. Lex said nothing more, only asking me briefly if I sorted out the issue. I assured him it was all taken care of and threw myself into business mode to close the deal, spending additional time to make sure we didn't lose this client.

I barely sleep, working all hours of the day. In between all the madness of work, I need a new assistant. Human Resources has narrowed it down to three women, and all I need to do is interview them. Like I have the fucking time. But I also know it's in my best interest, given I don't need someone who would rather suck dick than do the job they are paid to do.

And with Amelia in the picture, the last thing I need is a distraction in the office.

Yet all of my efforts during the week enable me to completely shut off on Saturday night. I want complete attention on Amelia with plans to devour every inch of her body. Although it has been a tough week, her random text messages keep me going, not to mention the dirty texting we often find ourselves in. I'm this close to abandoning everything to drive up to New Haven again but can't afford to jeopardize all the hard work I've been doing because my dick can't control itself.

Inside my apartment, the air is toasty from the fireplace roaring in the living room. Outside, the temperatures drop drastically with weather forecasts predicting a snowstorm this weekend.

Amelia sits on the bar stool with her hands resting on the countertop and a glass of red wine in front of her. Wearing a low-cut blouse and leather skirt, her crossed legs expose her thighs, making me want to run my tongue down her delicate skin.

Ignoring my hard dick beneath my pants, I continue to stir the sauce the way my nonna taught me, careful not to ruin my perfectly planned meal.

"How very Italian of you," she comments, with a knowing grin. "Who taught you how to cook?"

"My nonna," I tell her fondly. "Only when my mom wasn't arguing with her in the kitchen. I remember she told me when I was young, my Italian blood needed to pass on for generations. She would have a heart attack if I didn't procreate and give her Italian grandchildren."

"So, do you..." She clears her throat, then drinks some wine before continuing, "... date Italian women?"

I taste the sauce before leaning over and kissing her lips. "Once, in college, but I prefer the all-American emerald-green-eyed type."

"You're just saying that because I'm here, and besides, I'm quarter Cuban. What would your nonna say about that?"

"Probably disown me. Luckily, she's living it up in Boca. Can't judge me from her bingo table."

Amelia grins as I serve her food. We walk toward the table and begin to eat, talking about anything and everything. Despite our difference in age, we have plenty in common, our conversation never falling stale.

My eyes fall upon her every movement from watching her dig the fork into the pasta to swirling it around in a circular motion before bringing the fork to her pink lips. A drop of sauce falls upon her bottom lip, and slowly, her tongue rolls over the exact spot, causing my dick to almost combust on the spot.

Two more bites into her meal and I can't hold back any longer, pulling her off her seat and demand she lay on the table while I spread her legs and fuck her sweet pussy.

Watching her body convulse around me, I follow suit and collapse onto her with our breaths equally as strangled.

"*That was...*" She chokes, unable to finish her sentence.

"Not enough," I warn her. "Eat your dinner because you're going to need the stamina."

With an amused expression, she tries to hide the playing smirk but fails miserably.

"What happened to Netflix and chill?"

"Just chill," I tell her sternly. "Now eat."

In the morning, my arms wrap around hers as we both lay quietly. Despite spending the night tangled between the sheets because I'm greedy and wanted to taste every inch of her, we both fell into a blissful sleep. I can't recall the last time I slept so well, missing the warmth of a body beside me since I've lived a solitary life for a while now.

My greed continues to consume me, entering her while she sleeps and waking her up to her body completely under my spell. Her arousal is wet, making beautiful sounds as we both finish blissfully once again.

Steadying our breaths, she rests her head against my chest.

"Will, I don't know what you want from me."

I continue to run my fingers up and down her arm. "Do I need to show you again? Perhaps back door to give you a break."

She smiles in my embrace. "You're an ass."

"I'd like to be in your ass sometime soon."

My phone begins to ring. I lean over, kissing her shoulder as I lift the screen and see Lex's name. Amelia's expression falls as I answer the phone with her still beside me.

"Hey, what's up?"

"We need a game plan for Murphy. I'm heading to your place now."

I pull myself up, almost as if a splash of cold water has been thrown all over me.

"You're heading to my place?"

Amelia pulls the sheet over her, eyes wide with fear. The veins in her neck begin to pop out while she jumps out of bed, naked.

"Yeah, see you in five."

I hit "end" on the call, placing my phone on the nightstand.

"Don't panic," I tell her.

"*He just said see you in five.*" Amelia stumbles for the bathroom, kicking the door frame in the process while she shouts a string of profanities. Returning seconds later, her dress is on though her hair is a wild mess. She exits the room, returning with all her belongings in hand, including her boots.

"It looks like you've had sex all over your apartment."

"Well, we have had sex all over the apartment," I remind her while trying to put my pants on.

"Why are you not panicking?"

"Because you'll hide in my room, and all is well."

"All is not well," she cries, barely able to breathe. "My dad is coming, and you were just about to stick your dick in my ass."

"Oh, so you have thought about it?"

"Will." She places her hands on my chest with a serious expression. "I love you, but seriously, get changed because you're freaking me out."

The second the words register, a silence falls between us. The doorbell rings, leaving no time to dwell on the three words which escaped her lips in a moment of panic.

I pull on my tee, closing the bedroom door and head outside.

The living room and kitchen don't look that bad. Surely, she's overreacting as most women do.

I open the front door, motioning for Lex to come in since it would be odd to have this discussion in the hall. That, alone, would raise suspicion.

Dressed in a pair of jeans, knitted sweater, and winter jacket, it's easy to assume that coming here is out of desperation—his attire rather casual and unlike the normal business suit he wears.

"Did I interrupt anything?"

"No, not at all," I say, suddenly conscious.

"I've forgotten all about bachelor life." His eyes wander around the apartment, followed by a short chuckle. "Who sucked your dick this time? I hope it's not that new girl you hired."

I shake my head, oh the irony of the question. "No more mixing business with pleasure. Just a woman I met at a bar last night. Great set of tits."

"Nice." He smirks, removing his jacket. "You gonna call this one back?"

"Yeah, why not?" I say casually. "So, about Murphy, what's the game plan with him?"

Lex speaks for almost an hour, and while he has some great ideas, my mind is completely elsewhere. I nod on occasion, throw in a couple of suggestions not to look like an idiot, but it doesn't erase the fact that his oldest daughter is hiding inside my bathroom like a fugitive on the run.

"Listen, I'm going to head off. I've got a flight back to LA tonight but hoping to drive to New Haven to see Amelia for lunch."

"New Haven? They're predicting a storm, and the

roads are icy. Are you sure it's a good idea?"

Lex scratches his beard. "You're right, I might just call her now and let her know I might skip this one."

He dials her number, and I pray to all the gods above that her phone is on silent. *Please Please. Please.* My heart begins to palpitate, blood pressure rising to catastrophic levels. I pretend to stand here, bored, all the while freaking out that we'll get caught because of something so stupid.

"Huh, no answer," he cites, tucking his phone away. "I'm sure she'll call me back. I want to let her know that her flights are booked to return home for Christmas. We had intended to come here, but Charlotte thinks it's best for Amelia to come home."

"Yeah, sure. Why not, right?"

"Hopefully, she won't argue. If there's someone in her life, I'll pretty much know in the answer she gives me. I can bet a million dollars that if she says no to coming back home, it's because of some boy she's seeing behind our backs."

"I'm sure you'll soon find out," is all I say.

Lex says goodbye, but not before reminding me of an email I need to send today. With the door closed behind me, I head back toward my room and knock my bathroom's locked door.

"Are you alive?" I call out.

"Barely." The door opens, her face looking miserable. "You should keep food in the bathroom for emergencies such as this."

"Hopefully, that doesn't happen again. Look, it was awkward, but I believe he doesn't suspect anything."

Amelia nods silently. During the time locked inside, she styled her hair into an intricate braid. My hands itched to touch her hair, pull on it from behind as I fuck her senselessly.

"About before," she mumbles, unable to look at me. "I didn't mean it in that way. I meant..."

The I love you.

"It's okay, I get it. No need to explain."

"Right, thank you. But listen, I probably should get going before the storm hits. I've got an early class tomorrow too."

I pull her into me, caressing her lips. "Are you okay?"

"Yes, why?"

"Well, if you're okay like you say you are, I wonder how this sexy ass of yours is feeling?"

Placing her hands on my chest, a wicked smile escapes her. "I think we save it for next time, maybe against that window so everyone can see."

My dick hardens at the very thought of taking her against the glass. "You're a tease, and the only reason I'll wait is because I want it to last all night. But for now..." I guide her to the bathroom, turning on the shower and stripping her bare. "Spread your legs apart. I want to taste you."

And as her hands reach for the bottom of her blouse, pulling it over her head, she follows by removing her skirt and panties, allowing them to fall onto the floor.

Naked and completely mine to devour, I lick my lips in delight.

"Perfect," I murmur, pulling my pants down and stroking my shaft. "Maybe better if you get down on your knees and suck my cock like the good girl you are."

With passion burning in her eyes, I watch her slowly kneel. Her gaze shifts up, submissive to my demands. And just as I'm about to command her to take me all in, she runs her tongue along the tip of my cock, causing me to grunt.

"Eyes down, watch me," she demands sternly. "You're about to get the best fucking head of your life."

TWENTY-TWO

The familiar hustle of LAX is ten times worse during the holidays.

People are scurrying around, suitcases in tow. Children are running behind them, crying from being told to put their devices away with a warning that *Santa* will not deliver if they don't behave.

Airport staff are extra rude, their patience wearing thin from the panicked passengers who have connecting flights canceled due to bad weather.

I sigh heavily with annoyance, pulling my phone out of my purse to send Will a text.

Me: *People in airports are annoying. I'm this close to pulling the spoiled brat card and asking my Dad to buy a plane.*

Will: *Your dad wanted to buy a plane, but your mom said no. Something about the money going to better use like charities.*

Me: *That sounds like a fight they would have. I'll text you later... if I get out of here alive.*

Will: *You better, gorgeous.*

I smile at his text, but the smile quickly disappears when a woman's suitcase knocks on my leg. Quickly, I turn around, rubbing where she knocked it to alleviate the pain, only to notice that she has sped off to the gate without an apology.

My jaw clenches, the urge to shout profanities, although she can't hear me, becomes challenging to control. After traveling for almost the entire day, I want nothing more than to be isolated with zero people bothering me. A hot shower and proper meal wouldn't hurt either.

What you want is to be in Will's bed, naked.

I bow my head to gain some patience, reminding myself that it's Christmas, and I'm supposed to be spending time with my family. It's the season to be jolly, not fantasize about lying in a bed with my legs spread and a gorgeous man between them.

Grabbing the handle of my suitcase, I wheel it behind me and toward the exit where I'm supposed to meet Mom. I told her not to park in the parking lot nor bother trying to meet me at the gate, given the chaos.

Ten minutes later, the black Mercedes SUV pulls up to the curb, and Mom's face lights up behind the windshield.

"Hey, Mom," I greet, throwing my suitcase in the back while she jumps out of the car. Her arms wrap around me, the familiarity easing my momentary stress.

"I missed you, kid."

"Missed you, too, Mom."

We both get in the car, knowing that LAX's traffic

controllers are brutal if you linger around. Mom speeds through the traffic—peak hour, the usual pain in the ass in LA. As Mom converses, I take in the familiar sites—rows of palm trees, worn-out buildings, and bumper-to-bumper traffic—a far cry from the skyscrapers I've grown accustomed to in Manhattan and the leafy tree-lined streets in New Haven.

"Since we're stuck in this jam, tell me how school is going?"

"Hard," I respond with a yawn. "A lot of work. I mean, I knew it would be, but it's different."

"It's still early days. You need to find your groove."

"How did you find your groove?"

"Well, I had no life. So, studying was it. Rocky was relentless with parties. Nikki was a bit in between, but, of course, their world changed early on."

It's almost like I can never escape Will, even if I try. Or maybe, he was always there, but I've been oblivious. With only Mom here, I encourage the conversation involving Will, careful not to raise any suspicion.

"That must have been hard for them to welcome a child so early on. I can't even imagine it."

Mom purses her lips, letting out a small sigh. "It's one of those moments in life where you lose all hope, but in the same breath, you're blessed with unconditional love."

It was an excellent way to put it. When I think of myself, Liesel, and my fellow classmates, we all seem too young to start a family. I can't even imagine having that stress on my shoulders. And to think Aunt Nikki was only a year older than me when she had Will.

"But it worked out? Look at how amazing Will is."

The moment I say it, my lips part with adoration. *Shit.* I follow with a small cough, then play aimlessly with my hair pretending to appear bored with the topic of Will.

"It worked out," Mom agrees, knowingly. "But it wasn't without its challenges. Nikki really struggled being a working mother and so young. It was a big decision to make, and one they almost decided not to go ahead with. In the end, what a beautiful son they made."

I keep my smile fixed, not alluding to just how beautiful he really is, in and out of the bedroom.

"Tell me about you and your dating life. Anyone interesting?"

I absently fidget with my phone. "Uh, no. There's no time. Plus, these college boys are all the same. Everyone is interested in sex, and the maturity is... let's just say they lack exactly that."

The more I hear myself speak, the more I come across as some snob. Just because I'm dating someone a lot older than me doesn't make these men any less appealing. But the more I spent time with Will, the more juvenile college guys seem.

"God forbid your father ever hears this because if you could become a nun, he'd hand over every dollar of ours to make it so," Mom jokes, her smile softening. "Just be open to life. Studying is important, but so is dating. It's how you discover yourself."

"You discover yourself through dating?"

"Yes." Mom chuckles openly. "What you will or will not sacrifice. What you desire, how you enjoy spending your time... a lot can be said for dating."

"So, did you date? I mean, I know parts of your story."

"I tried," she admits, followed by a sigh, "But no one compared to your father."

"Ever?"

Mom hesitates, her lips pressing together in a slight grimace. It comes to mind what Ava told me about Uncle Julian. I wonder if Mom will take this opportunity to mention this, validating the so-called rumor.

"No one came close," she simply replies.

We gain some momentum on the freeway, and I change the topic to my sisters. According to Mom, Ava is an even bigger headache now that she's in her senior year. Addison wants to transfer to a boarding school, going through a Harry Potter phase, which my parents have said a big fat no to. Alexandra, being a sporty kid, is taking up most of their weekends with soccer games.

When we finally pull into the driveway, all the memories come flooding back, almost like I never left.

And it doesn't take long to get settled into my old home life, though this time, it feels different and not at all like I assumed it would be. My sisters are relentless in wanting my attention. It's somewhat of a good thing as it doesn't give me time to dwell on Will.

My dad is busy with work, as usual. He flew to San Jose for the day, arriving home late when we finally caught up.

The day before Christmas, I decide I must go shopping given that I haven't bought anyone presents. Ava, of course, insists she come despite my need to be alone. Going from a dorm room of just Liesel and me to a house full of family will take getting used to again. I have almost forgotten what it's like to think about somebody else's needs.

The first morning in my old bed, I woke up to the California sun seeping through my large bay window. My eyes, heavy and tired, feel like I haven't slept at all. As I continue to lay here, I recall a vivid dream I had about Will. We were at some fancy party, and everyone was dressed in cocktail attire. I entered the room to find Will in the corner with a woman. She was beautiful, wearing a sequined red dress. As I tried to walk over to him, people stopped me. I'd reach out my arms, but the closer I got, the further away he moved. Then, my dad stands in front of me, arms crossed, and demands I go home, telling me that no kids are allowed at the party.

It was all I can remember, and the dream leaves me extremely unsettled. I close my eyes again, but this time when I sleep, my dream is more pleasant. I'm lying with Will in his bed, and he's devouring my entire body. Just as I'm about to come, my eyes spring open to the sound of Ava shouting down the hallway to Addison.

The nerve of her.

Clenching my jaw, on the verge of yelling at her to shut the fuck up, I grab my phone and check the time, noting it's already ten on the East Coast. My fingers type quickly, sending Will a text.

Me: *I dreamed about you last night. It was... interesting.*

The phone begins to buzz in my hands. I answer in a low voice so no one can hear me. Turning to my side, I tuck my hand underneath my face.

"You can't just drop the word interesting and expect me to pretend like it's nothing," Will chastises, the sound of his smooth voice making me miss him more. "Was anyone naked?"

"Where are you?"

"In the office."

I laugh softly. "Yes, there was nudity amongst other things."

"Oh, do tell? I have a meeting in ten minutes but could

probably get myself off in less than thirty seconds if you continue talking."

"Lucky you," I tell him with sarcasm. "Meanwhile, I'll just continue to lie here desperate as fuck."

"You paint such a vivid picture."

"How's work?"

"How's work?" he repeats. "You can't just go from telling me you had a dream about us fucking to how's work? I pegged you for many things, but a cocktease isn't one of them."

"I'm regretting this call," I mutter jokingly.

"No, you're not. You miss me, just admit it."

A smile plays on my lips. I hate that I miss him, wishing to be back on the East Coast. After my dad made it clear to Will that if I resisted coming home, it would be evident I had a male interest, I faked rather enthusiastically how much I wanted to spend Christmas in California.

"Maybe, I've somewhat grown fond of you."

There's a muffle in the background. "Listen, I have to go."

"Of course, go work and bring in the money."

"Hey," he quips before I say goodbye. "Keep thinking the things you're thinking, and if it helps at all, I miss you, too."

My stomach begins to flutter, and with a heavy sigh, I say goodbye, sadness settling in at the thought of how far apart we are right now. I yearn to touch his face and feel his lips on mine. Everything about him just becomes so much more than my head allows it to be, all in the few simple words he said.

He misses me.

I drag myself out of bed, left with no choice when Ava bangs on my door to hurry up.

With the change in time zones and turbulent sleep, I find myself less energetic and patient. I shower, change, head down for breakfast only to argue with Addison for finishing the rest of the milk. Dad is in the kitchen, amused by this and not saying a word.

"You know, coffee works wonders, Amelia."

He was right. After my coffee, I do mellow out.

"What are your plans for today?"

"Unfortunately, shopping with Ava," I complain, pouring myself another coffee. "What about you?"

"Trying to close a deal before the end of the day. Once people are in holiday mode, it's hard to get any work out of them."

"Has it ever occurred to you to maybe go into holiday mode too?"

Dad smirks. "Nice joke, Amelia. Say that in front of your mother, and I'm cutting you off."

My shoulders fall up and down, chuckling at the thought of Mom's reaction had she heard. My laughter slows down as Dad's phone buzzes on the countertop.

"Will," he answers quickly, placing the call on speaker. "What did Duncan have to say for himself?"

"The usual, Lex. I say we cut him and let Anderson do the job," Will responds with an angered tone.

"If that's what you think, let's do it. I don't want him slowing us down."

"Agreed."

"Will, I'm here with Amelia. She's trying to convince me to take a break."

I almost spit out my coffee. This is getting awkward. I should've walked out instead of standing here like an idiot. "Hello, Will. How are things?"

"Great, actually. And you? Staying out of trouble?"

"I try," I answer as Dad smiles behind his mug. "Since Dad is here, that probably should've been a yes."

"Go easy on her, Lex. Remember what it was like when you were nineteen?"

Dad squints with a stiff smile. "I'd rather forget."

"Do you have plans to at least relax for the holidays?" I ask, pretending to act polite.

"Relax? What a foreign concept." He laughs through the speaker. "Just Christmas Eve dinner tonight at my parents' place. You know what my dad is like, he's drunk on eggnog watching *National Lampoon's Christmas Vacation.* It's his tradition."

Dad laughs loudly, knowing all too well what Uncle Rocky is like.

"I've had the unfortunate pleasure of seeing exactly that. You may want to leave before he whips out the Santa costume and asks Nikki if she's been naughty."

Both Dad and I try to hold in our laughter, though find it impossible to do.

Will groans. "Thanks for allowing me to relive the trauma."

"Merry Christmas, Will," I say, with my dad continuing to watch me. "Try not to work too hard."

"Can't promise that. But Merry Christmas, Amelia."

Dad ends the call and continues a conversation about Uncle Rocky, quick to compare him to the infamous Cousin Eddie from the National Lampoon movies. We chat a little while longer before he kisses me goodbye, leaving for work.

As soon as he's gone, my phone lights up with a text.

Will: *What I would give to bend you over for being naughty.*

Me: *I'll write a list of all the bad things I've done.*

Will: *What's number one?*

Me: *You.*

Ava strolls in the kitchen, complaining about her hair. We get into an argument over it, my patience with her wearing thin until Mom calls us both out for being petty. After we both refuse to apologize, Mom suggests we leave to avoid the rush.

The mall is the busiest I'd ever seen it, packed with people everywhere you look. There are panicked shoppers darting around and purchasing whatever they can get their hands on. I don't care for rude people, nor the lines at each checkout. The shop attendants are beyond over it, barely a customary smile on their tired faces.

Had I been proactive and organized, I could've avoided all of this by shopping online. But, of course, I have better things to focus on, which is all I can think about these days.

Exhaustion begins to creep in, my feet tired from all the walking. I get everyone a present except Ava. Given that she's following me everywhere, it makes it hard to purchase something without her knowing.

"I'm just going to go off on my own for a while."

"Why? We're almost done," Ava complains.

"Because I just want to be alone," I snap.

"God, Amelia, you're such a bitch," Ava barks, slamming the hanger back on the rack. "Ever since you got here, you've been in such a mood."

"Ava!" Mom scolds, letting out a sigh. "This isn't the place to have such a discussion."

With a pinched expression, I stare directly at Ava,

lacking any warmth toward my opinionated sister. If there's anyone testing me, Ava Edwards is at the top of the list.

"Who cares, Mom," Ava argues back. "Honestly, Amelia. Just say you don't want to be here... that you'd rather be at Yale with your friends."

Beside Ava, Mom lowers her head, remaining unusually quiet.

"You're dramatic, as usual," I retort.

"Am I?" Ava questions, placing her hand on her hip. "Because it looks to me like you left some man behind, and you'd rather be in his bed than with your family."

My eyes widen at her accusation. There's no way she could possibly know about Will unless she read my text messages. *Fuck.*

"Have you been reading my messages?"

Ava folds her arms. "No, but paranoid much? It looks like I was right."

"Think whatever you want," I sputter, momentarily beyond words. "I'll meet you at Starbucks in fifteen minutes."

I don't say another thing, abandoning them in the evening wear section, desperate to be on my own. I hate that Ava struck a nerve, and more importantly, sniffed the so-called trail I've been trying to hide. To make matters worse, I continue to lie to Mom and sense she also caught on to my behavior. Am I that obvious? The only one who seems to be treating me normally is Dad.

Trying to shop for my annoying sister proves even more difficult. I have no clue what to buy her, especially after our argument, so I end up settling for a new hair straightener since she complained about hers this morning.

By the time we get home, the air between us somewhat clears. We both help Mom with preparing our traditional

Christmas dinner and some finishing touches on the house. During the holiday season, our house looks like a picture-perfect image from a magazine. Everything is purposely placed and aesthetically pleasing from the oversized freshly-cut tree inside the living room to the twinkling lights that flicker outside the house.

We all sit down for dinner, then follow by dressing in our matching PJs Mom insists we wear to continue the Edwards' tradition. There are no complaints from us girls, just Dad, as usual.

After dinner, we settle in the den with the fire on, a cup of hot chocolate warming our hands while watching a Christmas movie. I can't help but watch my parents, the way they smile in each other's embrace to the silly jabs they taunt each other with. Even Dad is relaxed, often kissing Mom's forehead.

It makes me feel all the more alone. Even if my relationship with Will is made public, I can't seem to envision him here, beside me, without my dad's resentment. I pull out my phone, wanting to text Will, but end up putting it away. No good will come of me saying anything right now, given the questions clouding my thoughts might lead to an argument. The last thing either one of us need on Christmas Eve.

On Christmas morning, I wake to the sounds of my younger sisters running through the hallway. Grabbing my phone off the nightstand, I see a text from Will.

Will: *Merry Christmas, gorgeous.*

I grin at his text, almost as if I can hear his voice say those very words. Before my departure, we decided to ditch the Christmas presents since neither one of us are interested in material items. But that isn't without Will suggesting our present to each other should involve acts in the bedroom.

I had no idea sex could be so liberating, and how, with the right person, there are no limits. My fingers type profusely, knowing that I don't have long before one of my sisters barges in and demands we open presents.

Me: *Merry Christmas, handsome. I hope you behaved and Santa delivered.*

Will: *He will deliver, again, when you are back and naked in my bed.*

Me: *I was just thinking the same thing. Four more days, but who is counting?*

Will: *Me... I am counting.*

"Millie, get up!" Alexandra shouts behind the door.

Letting out a groan, I drag my tired ass out of my room and down the stairs. No surprises that my parents went all out with presents scattered around the Christmas tree and stockings full to the brim. Opening presents takes a solid hour with lots of oohs and ahs and a ton of jumping up and down.

I thank my parents and sisters for all the gifts—clothes, jewelry, to name a few. After the younger girls abandon the living room with their presents, I help Dad clean up while Mom prepares breakfast.

"How does it feel to be back home?" Dad asks, picking up the wrapping paper and throwing it in the trash bag in his hand. "California is very different to the East Coast."

"It's warmer," I say, touching an ornament on the tree. "It's nice."

"You've changed," he adds, his eyes fixated on me. "You've matured in the few months you've been gone."

"I guess college forces you to make better decisions. Plus, I'm nineteen now."

"You're a woman."

"Dad, you're not going to get sentimental on me, are you?"

"Hear me out." He places the bag down, taking a seat on the armchair. "You worked incredibly hard to get into Yale. You're choosing a challenging career, one that will challenge you for the rest of your life. And you've managed to make these decisions despite being raised in a wealthy family. I'm proud of you."

I drop my chin to my chest, trying not to choke up at his admission. "Thanks, Dad. It means a lot to me that you would say this."

"I was saying to Will the other day how proud I am of you. He agrees you've definitely got a strong head on your shoulders and are determined."

"You talk about me to Will?" The second it comes out, I realize my tone is panicked. Scrambling to save myself, I continue, "I'm sure he has better things to discuss than some college kid."

"You're no longer a kid." Dad smiles, though follows with a long-winded sigh. "You're a beautiful, intelligent woman, one who will break some man's heart one day."

"Oh, so you admit that I'm not a nun?"

"Quite the comedian," he notes with dark amusement. "If I could have my way—"

"I know, I know," I drag, rolling my eyes. "If you could have your way, I'd be a spinster. A virgin spinster."

"You know me well."

I cross my arms, though, with the purpose of not looking awkward when I ask the question. "So, what does Will have to say about me? Lord knows he's still traumatized by our childhood. I mean, you make someone scrape their leg once, and they'll hold it against you for the rest of your life."

"Surprisingly, he only speaks positively of you. Of course, he has his own things to worry about. We're this close to finalizing London. If all goes well, he'll be there in a few months."

My stomach hardens the moment my heartbeat slows down to what feels like a complete stop. *London.* I have no idea how many miles away but crossing over an ocean indicates very far away. It shouldn't come as a shock given the fact that it was raised at Thanksgiving. But I've deluded myself into thinking it will all change because we're together. How stupid of me. According to my dad, I may be beautiful and intelligent, but I don't have the power to stop a man from becoming the next billionaire.

"That sounds amazing for Will. I'm sure he's excited to move to London."

Dad hesitates, lost in thought. "Between you and me, I thought so too. But something has changed over the last month. He's said a couple of things, which, if I read between the lines, indicates he wants to try to make it work from Manhattan, but it's just not feasible. Not to mention costly. To make this work, he needs to be in London."

"Maybe it's just cold feet," I suggest, though wondering if I'm the reason he's hesitating. "He's lived his whole life in the States. I'm assuming that moving to another country can be daunting."

"That could be it, or he has someone here he doesn't want to leave."

I clear my throat. "C'mon, Dad. He's a player. I highly doubt it."

"You don't know him like I do, sweetie. He's changed."

This is my chance to extract anything I can about Will's so-called changed behavior. It isn't exactly like I can ask Will these very questions. He'll assume I'm clingy and desperate like most women out there.

"He looks the same to me. How do you think he's changed?"

Dad ponders on my question, a little too long for my liking.

"His head isn't clear as it was a few months ago. So much of him reminds me of my younger days, pre-marriage to your mother. I thought I was invincible, and no one could stop me. Then I saw her at a restaurant with another man. I knew then and there that nothing else mattered. Not a single cent of what I sacrificed to become this untouchable wealthy man," he pauses momentarily, then continues, "And I see that exact same thing with Will."

"Maybe it's just a phase, Dad," I tell him, desperate to make him think otherwise. "Maybe this woman he's supposedly seeing is just a phase."

"I think this one has crawled under his skin," he admits, sure of his himself. "I warned him this would happen one day, and he joked and told me never."

"Well, we all fall in love one day, right?"

Dad turns to face me with a knowing grin. "You've got time, Amelia, just focus on studying for now. All that love business will come when the time is right."

I nod, unsure of what to say.

"Is everything okay?" Dad questions, tilting his head. "You look disappointed."

"No, Dad." I give him a lopsided grin, forcing myself to

remain positive. "Everything you've said is true. I need to focus on studying. There's always time for love later."

Not long after, the rest of our family arrives for lunch. Andy and his family are the first to arrive. I don't get to chat with him much since Dad wants to catch up with him, stealing all his attention.

My Uncle Noah and Kate arrive with my cousins, then shortly after, my parents' friends. I consider Haden and Presley like family since they always attend all our family events. They have three sons, their oldest, Masen, being Ava's age.

Then Mom's bestie, Eric, arrives with his husband, Tristan. They don't have children, just two dogs they take everywhere with them—Gloria and Diana. French Bulldogs with a diva-like attitude if you get near them.

"Where's my little Gilmore Girl?" Eric calls, stretching his hands out to me.

I furrow my brows, unsure what that means. "What's a Gilmore Girl?"

"Hello! Only the most angstier TV show of all time! Rory Gilmore, the Yale graduate."

"Never heard of it," Ava and I say in unison.

"Kids these days," Eric complains before eyeing me up and down. "You're getting laid by a man."

My eyes widen at his assumption. "I... don't know what you're talking about."

"My booty call radar is never off."

"It's true," Aunt Adriana says, beside me. "It's crazy how spot on he is. Like he's a psychic of anything penis-related."

"It's one of my many talents," Eric boasts, lifting his shoulders proudly.

"How about you leave my daughter alone?" Mom

pushes on my shoulders, away from Eric. "Especially because Lex will hear you and chop your balls off."

Eric places his hands on his hips. "Your husband, after twenty years, is yet to chop my balls off. I think they're as safe as balls can get."

Aunt Adriana shakes her head. "Okay, enough ball talk, please. I'm losing my appetite."

"Oh, so you're saying that Julian doesn't like the occasional tea bagging?"

I let out an obnoxious laugh before choosing to leave this conversation. I love my aunt and uncle, but the last thing I need on my mind is their supposed sex life. Thank God Andy is nowhere around to have heard that.

The day is chaotic as it always is when everyone gets together. Yet, despite being surrounded by all my family, my talk with my dad weighs heavily on my mind.

The truth is—time is running out. According to my father, Will is destined for London.

And I'm destined for only one thing—heartbreak.

TWENTY-THREE

AMELIA

"*I need tampons.*"

Ava barges into my room without a polite knock on my door, heading straight for my bathroom to raid my cabinet.

"A please would be welcomed," I mutter under my breath.

Seconds later, Ava comes out empty-handed.

"You don't have any?"

I shrug my shoulders, trying my best to focus on the laptop screen. The assignment is due in a few weeks, but I thought to get a head start given I've lost focus of late and need to get my head back into studying mode. It doesn't help that my phone proves to be a distraction as does social media. I resort to turning my phone off entirely to focus on my paper.

"Have you checked Mom's bathroom?"

Curling her lip, Ava shakes her head with a look of disgust. "No, because the last time I tried, I stumbled on lubricant. It was strawberry-flavored. I mean, really, Mom and Dad are still having sex?"

I snort involuntarily, displaying a wide grin. "Really, Ava? Of course, they have sex. Don't ever walk past their room between midnight to six in the morning. Once you've heard Mom moan, it's permanently stuck in your head."

"Gross," Ava exclaims, wrinkling her nose while flinching. "You mean Dad can still get it up?"

"Ava!" My mouth slackens, disturbed by this conversation. "Can you not use the words 'get it up' and 'Dad' in the same sentence? Besides, he only just turned fifty-two. Mom's still in her forties. Erectile problems usually strike in the seventies, I think."

"Never say the word erectile to me ever again," Ava declares, shuddering. "This doesn't solve my tampon issue."

"I'll go to the drugstore to get you some. Happy?"

With a satisfied smile, she replies, "That's what big sisters are for."

I welcome the drive to the drugstore, stopping at a café first to grab myself a coffee. Despite the wintery season, the sun is shining, though a cool breeze warrants a sweater. It's a nice change from the godawful snowstorm hitting the East Coast right now.

Balancing my coffee in one hand, I check my phone but still no response from Will after my rather dirty text I sent him this morning. Trying my best to ignore the rejection seeping in, I think logically and assume he's busy with work even though it's the day after Christmas.

Tossing away my empty cup, I grab a red basket, throwing in a couple of things I need in there before perusing the feminine products aisle. Ava didn't even indicate what type of tampons she wants, so I send her a quick text:

Me: *How big is your vagina now that you sleep*

around? Do you need super?

Ava: *Bitch. Regular will do just fine.*

I laugh to myself before yanking a box of regulars and throwing it in my basket. As I lift my head, the familiar warm honey-colored eyes are smiling back at me.

"Austin?"

"Millie?"

My mouth falls open, and we both laugh before we find ourselves in our familiar embrace. Everything about him brings back memories—the scent of his cologne, the comfort of his arms around me. It may have been over two months, but when you've spent almost every day with this person in high school, it feels like a lifetime ago.

I give myself a moment to take him in, certain he has grown taller during our time apart. I wasn't sure if that were possible at our age to continue growing, but nevertheless, where our faces once met lost in a passionate kiss now appears unaligned.

His physique, though hidden behind a baggy sweater, still looks formed. Yet surrounding the beautiful eyes I once dreamed of every night is the face of a boy who has matured into a man. His jawline, more prominent, is shadowed by a slight beard, making him seem a hell of a lot older.

"What are you doing here?"

"Errands for my sister." He drops his gaze toward the basket. "It's that time, apparently, tomorrow."

My shoulders rise then fall, unable to hide my laughter. "Me, too. At least your sister gave you warning, mine just raided my cupboard hoping to hit the jackpot."

We both slow down our breathing, caught in a stare that feels all too familiar.

"How have you been? I mean, the last time we spoke..."

Austin places his hand on my arm. "Hey, don't get caught up on how it ended. We both were trying to adjust. It was for the best. But I shouldn't have said the things I said. I'm sorry, Millie. It was completely uncalled for."

I nod my head, glad he feels that way. "So, how have you been?"

"Busy. The class load is insane. Even coming back here, I feel like I'll falling behind or something."

"Me, too." I sigh, relieved someone else understands. "I was studying before Ava interrupted me. You know, if you need any guidance, my dad isn't working right now. I'm sure he'd chat with you, maybe give you some pointers?"

"You know what? I may take you up on that." He grins with relief, almost as if a burden has been lifted from his shoulders. "Is he free today?"

"Yes, why don't you come over? I'm sure Mom would love to say hello, too."

We agree to follow each other back to my place, paying for our purchases, then chatting while walking back to our cars. It's so good to be able to catch up without the pressure of labeling our relationship because, at the end of the day, we were friends before lovers.

"Millie, I want to be honest and tell you I'm seeing someone."

I still my movements, unsure what to say. It doesn't hurt, not one bit, but then I wonder if I need to be just as honest? There's too much at stake, so I opt to keep my personal life to myself.

"I'm happy for you, Austin. You deserve only the best."

"Thank you." He beams, letting out a huge breath. "I'll tell Summer you said that."

"Summer." I chuckle knowingly. "The name rings a

bell."

"I know what you're thinking. There wasn't anything going on until we broke up, I promise."

"I believe you," I reassure him, patting his shoulder.

"And you? Are you seeing anyone?"

I put on my best fake smile. "No one at all. I'm not good at balancing studying and the relationship thing."

Austin nods his head, keeping his mouth pursed. It's better to lie than to be honest about Will. Even I don't know what we are, so how am I supposed to define our relationship to other people? We never use the word boyfriend or girlfriend. Partner sounds like we're in some lesbian relationship. Lovers would be more appropriate, but even then, it isn't the right fit.

"So, I'll follow you home?"

"Yep, see you there."

Austin bumps my shoulder as the two of us laugh over the time in class when our teacher split his pants. The timing was uncanny, he was on the verge of sending us all to detention because of a silly prank a kid pulled yet didn't confess to. Our walk down memory lane is exactly what I need, easing my tension from the last few days.

Our laughter carries through the hallway until Ava skips down the stairs, dressed in a pair of ripped jeans and my khaki GAP sweater. *The nerve of her to borrow without asking*. With an incredulous stare, she continues to the bottom, playfully swatting Austin on the arm.

"Is this who I think it is?"

"Hey, Ava."

"We ran into each other in the drug store. Awkward,

considering I was fetching your tampons, and Austin was for his sister."

Ava blushes. "That's awkward, but I guess since you're going to be a doctor, you've got to get used to this, right?"

Austin chuckles, cocking his head to the side. "I never looked at it that way, but you have a point."

"I invited him over for coffee, plus thought he could chat with Dad. Is he around?"

"Actually..." she says, pointing in the opposite direction. "Dad is in the kitchen with Will."

My body freezes at the name, tongue-tied and unable to compute what she just said. *"Will?"*

"Yeah, apparently Mom begged him to come for two days when she found out that Uncle Rocky and Aunt Nikki decided to make a last-minute road trip to Boca."

I swallow multiple times, trying to ignore the flutter inside my stomach. With Austin standing beside me, it won't look good to Will. It didn't even occur to me that it was a bad idea to bring Austin back here because we're just friends. That is until the thought of Will and Austin inside the same room sends my body into complete panic mode.

Fuck. What the hell do I do?

Before I even have a chance to tell Austin to go, Dad and Will appear in the foyer. Dad appears surprised yet extends his hand, wishing Austin a Merry Christmas.

But then my eyes wander to the those of a man less impressed, dressed casually in a pair of jeans and a gray hoodie. With a sullen look, Will is staring at me without a single welcoming smile. His lips are pressed flat, the muscles on his face tight. Yet despite his obvious jealous expression, he still looks incredibly handsome, making me realize just how much I miss him.

This could all blow over in this very minute if Austin

even breathes to Dad about his suspicions. Austin is quick to glance at Will, then back to me. With a smile, I turn my focus to Ava, begging her to do something—anything—to bring attention to her.

Ava stares at me oddly, then almost as if it clicks, she laces her arm in Will's, distracting him momentarily.

"Dad, Austin wanted to chat to you about medical school, but if you're working with Will..."

"We can take a break." Dad offers with a heartfelt smile. "Let's go into my office, son."

They disappear, leaving Will, Ava, and me still standing in the foyer. I can practically see the steam boiling from his ears, but we both have to pretend nothing is going on with Ava present.

"Is Austin your boyfriend?" Will questions, though keeping his tone neutral.

"Ex. This is the first time I've spoken to him in months. We ran into each other in the drugstore, and we got to talking about school. He wanted to talk to Dad, and I didn't see any harm since we've known each other for a while."

"Yes," Ava adds, trying to keep it casual. "He's like family, kind of like you too."

"I need to make a business call. Excuse me."

The second he walks outside, my sister's eyes widen with shock. She covers her mouth with her palm, shaking her head in disbelief.

"Ava, not now," I beg of her. "I promise I'll tell you everything, but for now, can you cover for me while I talk to Will?"

She nods, her mouth still open. "Yeah, go. But Millie, you know if the parentals find out, you're both dead meat?"

I let out a sigh. "Yes, Ava. That's the gray cloud forever hovering over us."

TWENTY-FOUR

AMELIA

"You leave for like two minutes to do what exactly?"

"It's not what you think." I lower my voice, scanning the area to make sure no one can hear. There's a large oak tree in the middle of our circled driveway, so tall that we're able to stand behind it without anyone in the house seeing us. "I told you, I ran into him."

"And who invited him over?"

"Me, but again, it's nothing. Austin is just an old friend."

"From memory, and please correct me if I'm wrong, wasn't it only two months ago that he was in your bed?" His artic tone is anything but inviting. "And isn't this the same boyfriend who broke your heart?"

The malice rolls off his tongue so effortlessly as he bares his teeth, fuming with anger. I cross my arms beneath my breasts, annoyed he'd even suggest I'd do something. If I recall, Austin was no better, so perhaps this is a *man* thing.

"You're a dick," I blurt out, unapologetic. "You don't even tell me you're coming, blindside me in front of my dad, of all people. Now, you're accusing me of doing what?"

Will shakes his head, distracted by his phone buzzing in his pocket.

"I have to take this call," he grits, unable to look at me. "As for surprising you, I'm sorry for thinking you'd want to see me."

He takes the call, walking away from me to create distance. I don't stand around, worried we were seen, and head back inside to find Ava pacing the foyer. The second she sees me, her eyes bulge as she grabs my arm, dragging me up the staircase toward her bedroom. Closing the door behind us, she continues to yank me into her bathroom, locking the door behind us.

"You need to talk... like now."

"Ava..."

"From the beginning," she demands.

My body slides against the tiled wall until I'm sitting on the cold floor. I began with the moment I stepped into his office to my drunken mishap at the club. There's the part about Austin and his encounter with Will, and then our tandem hang gliding. When it comes time to tell her about when we first slept with each other, I hesitate, unsure how she'll react.

"You can't stop here," she complains with extremely bright eyes. "How many times have you had sex?"

I bow my head, tugging at the bottom of my sweater. "I've lost count."

"Oh my God!"

Grabbing her arm, I warn her to be quiet.

"Ava, I need you to listen to me." I squeeze her hands tight, allowing my eyes to plead with hers. "You can't tell anyone. You need to promise me this. Not Andy, not any of your friends, and especially not Mom."

Ava nods her head in agreement.

"Millie, I promise not to tell anyone. But how can you continue to lie to Mom?"

The reality of her words hit me like a ton of bricks—the deception, the secret life I've been living. I have never willingly lied to Mom and for this long. Though the more I do, the more it almost becomes second nature. And I hate myself for lying to her like she means nothing to me.

"I don't know where this is going," I stammer, my eyes falling on the floor. "This might just be a fling, so what's the point if it's over soon?"

"And what if it's love?"

"C'mon, Ava," I argue back, shaking my head. "He's a player, right? You've heard Mom and Aunt Nikki. I'm young, and men like young women."

"Yeah, I have, Millie. But I also just saw the way he turned into some jealous beast when he saw you walk in the door with Austin. If he were a player, why would he care?"

"Ego... that's it."

Ava closes the lid on the toilet, taking a seat before releasing a long-winded sigh. "Do you love him?"

"Love?" I question, raising my brows. "We sleep together, that's it. How can I love someone I've known for like two seconds?"

"But you haven't known him for two seconds," Ava points out. "You've known him your entire life. There's a photo on the wall by the staircase of him holding you the day you were born."

I hear what she's saying but refuse to entertain being in love with him. What do I know about love, anyway? I thought I loved Austin and look how that turned out. Infatuation, lust, and desire are three very accurate words to use when asked how I feel about Will.

Mom's voice echoes outside the bathroom, calling my name.

"Listen," I tell Ava softly. "I need you to help me, you know, talk to Will at the table, so it doesn't look so awkward."

"Of course, Millie," she assures me with a nod. "I've got you covered."

I unlock the door as Mom stands behind it, surprised to see the two of us inside. Her expression quickly shifts to curiosity. "There you are. Austin is looking for you, and I hope you don't mind that I asked him to stay for dinner."

Unsure of what to say, I try to keep my opinion to myself but fail miserably.

"I guess so."

"Is there a problem?"

"Well, Mom, he's her ex," Ava concedes. "How would you like it if you had dinner with your ex in front of your whole family?"

Mom's wide-eyed expression looks somewhat amused by Ava's question, yet she keeps her thoughts private. I wonder again if it has something to do with the Uncle Julian rumor.

"I understand it can be rather uncomfortable, but I gathered that everything between you guys is great because you brought him back here. I'm sorry if I misinterpreted that."

Not wanting to make Mom feel bad, I quickly jump in.

"No, Mom, it's fine," I offer with a smile. "And things between Austin and me are great. We're just friends, and whatever happened in the past is in the past. I swear I don't have any romantic feelings toward him. In fact, Ava and I were just discussing it."

"I figured you were having a conversation you didn't want your father overhearing." She smirks.

We both grin on cue, guilty as charged.

"Well, dinner will be ready soon, so why don't you go down and keep him entertained," Mom suggests, stopping just shy of the door before glancing my way. "Your father is in his office with Will. Something urgent came up. I'll be surprised if they make it to dinner."

If only luck is on my side.

I follow Mom out of the room, stopping momentarily to motion for Ava to follow us.

Downstairs, Austin is sitting in the kitchen with his phone in hand, looking just as handsome as I remember him. There's a small smile playing on his lips, and I'm wondering if he's texting his new girlfriend. It only dawns on me now that I should've mentioned that to Will, but what difference would it make? He made up his mind the moment he saw us together.

"Hey, sorry about that. Ava needed something, and I didn't want to interrupt you and Dad."

He places his phone down, turning to face me. "It's fine. Your father was very helpful until Will came in."

"To his office?"

"Yes, your father made it very clear that Will is destined to be the next billionaire."

"Dad says that about everyone."

"So..." Austin drags, tapping his fingers on the counter. "Why is Will here? Because your Dad never mentioned why?"

I shrug my shoulders. "Not sure. I only found out when you did."

"Millie..." he trails off as Mom walks into the kitchen and tells us to go sit at the table.

We both offer to help, which she kindly refuses. With Addison and Alexandra already seated, I take a seat as

Austin sits beside me. The girls are bombarding Austin with questions about being a doctor, a lot of it rather gross for dinner conversation.

Dad walks into the dining room, stopping to kiss the girls on their heads before taking a seat at the table. I glance over to him, yet he doesn't appear to be bothered by Austin sitting at the table with us, nor does it look like he suspects anything about Will and me.

I breathe a sigh of relief until Will walks in, avoiding my stare with his head down. Ava bounces behind him, pushing him along, which appears to annoy him. They take a seat across from me, and I have to give it to Ava—she's doing her best to act like she didn't just hear the biggest news of her life.

For most of the dinner, Dad is asking Austin questions, and occasionally, Mom pipes up. I shove my food around my plate, doing my best to avoid any eye contact with Will. But paranoid that my parents will notice my behavior, I throw in a few comments here or there.

"What's everyone's plans for New Years'?" Mom asks, changing the topic of conversation.

"You know mine, Mom." Ava grins.

Dad places his fork down, glancing over with a stern expression. "That's yet to be determined, Ava,"

"Aw, c'mon, Dad. It's senior year."

Mom is quick to divert attention to Austin. "How about you, Austin?"

"There are a few parties back on campus, but a few friends are thinking about staying in Manhattan."

"Oh, that would be lovely, nothing like bringing in the new year in Time's Square," Mom responds with a smile, then turns to face me. "What about you, honey?"

"Me? Maybe the city or campus. Liesel will probably drag me to something."

"You can join us," Austin suggests, a smirk playing on his lips. "Can't guarantee what will happen. Med students are a wild bunch."

Dad laughs as if it's some private joke. I try my damn hardest not to look up at Will, but like a magnetic force, my eyes move on their own accord until our gaze locks. My pulse begins to race. All my senses ignite like a fire roaring to life. The heat starts to rise in my cheeks, forcing me to drop my gaze to steady my breath.

Terrified that someone has noticed the flush in my cheeks, I drink the entire glass of water, willing myself to cool down.

"And how about you, Will?" Mom asks, glancing at him with amusement. "Rocky always likes to enjoy himself on New Year's Eve. No doubt, your mother is already planning his bail money."

Will clears his throat, turning to face Mom with a smile. "I'll be in Boston for work."

Did he just say Boston? Anger stirs within me for his lack of communication. Typical Will with his work, always first in his eyes. He's just like Dad, and the more I think about it, the more it irritates me. The same goes for London —not once has he mentioned it being a possibility real soon.

I raise my eyes again to see Ava across from me, a worried expression on her usually jovial face. As if she can read my thoughts, she begins to talk about colleges she's applied to, which, of course, warrants Dad's opinion since none of them were close to home.

"Thank you for the meal, Mr. and Mrs. Edwards," Austin says, wiping his mouth with the napkin. "It's getting late, and I should be getting home."

My parents wish him luck with school and suggest he visit any time he's back here in LA.

"I'll walk you out," I tell him, avoiding Will's gaze.

Outside the front of our home, I cross my arms to shield my chest from the cold night's air. The moon is bright tonight, full and round, a beautiful sight amongst the dark sky.

"It was great to see you, Austin."

"Millie." He lowers his gaze, only to lift it moments later. "You're playing with fire."

"What are you talking about?"

"You know what I'm talking about," he coerces with both hands in his pockets. "Are you willing to tear apart your family for some guy?"

"Austin—"

"I know you better than you think. Once upon a time, your eyes looked into mine the same way they're looking into his." I can almost hear the hurt in his voice, but he manages to ignore the stumble. "He's too old for you. Do you honestly expect him to give up his dream of becoming the next billionaire to play boyfriend to a college girl?"

And the secret comes out to the one person I didn't want to hurt. We may have been friends, and I may have been okay with his admission to dating Summer, but deep down inside, I know that Austin has figured out the depth of my feelings toward Will.

Something I can no longer hide.

"It's not that simple," I mumble.

"No, it's not that simple. Somebody is going to get hurt, and the chances are, it's all you, Millie."

"I'm an adult now," I say defensively. "I can handle this."

"You've worked hard to get where you are. Don't let this

hinder your dreams of studying law. Guys like him don't settle down, they play women, and you'll be no different."

I touch the base of my neck, unable to meet his longing stare.

"I'll be fine, I promise. Don't worry about me."

"I'll always worry about you, Millie."

Austin wraps his arms around me, a tight embrace bringing back a flood of memories. It would've been so much easier to have fallen in love entirely with Austin and continue seeing him. My parents would have approved since they've always welcomed him inside our home.

All the things that couples do together—Christmas, New Year's Eve—all of which I could've spent with him without the worry of being caught since it wouldn't be a problem.

But none of this matters, not when my heart belongs to someone else.

And I can no longer deny my feelings toward Will, however raw, consuming, and irrevocably profound my emotions may be.

I say goodbye to Austin, promising to catch up online and possibly when he's in town. Walking back toward the house, I have no idea what to do next, wanting very much to be alone right now to process tonight.

As I take steps toward the door, my gaze drifts to the window near my dad's office, and I swear eyes are watching me.

I manage to escape to my room, telling Mom I'm tired and need some sleep, avoiding Will at all costs while trying to come to terms with my admission. Ava joins me for a while, lying in bed with me and asking question after question. It isn't long before I kick her out, desperately needing solitude.

Inside my bed, I toss and turn with the urge to text Will. Every time I begin to type, I erase the message. Nothing I can say right now will calm his anger toward Austin coming here, and I'm terrified of acting differently now that my feelings have shifted.

By one o'clock, after hours of staring at the ceiling, I jump out of bed to leave my room. Dressed in my tattered Lakers tee and bed socks, I close the door to my room. The house is shadowed in complete darkness, not a single person awake.

I tiptoe toward the kitchen, open the refrigerator, and grab a bottle of water to quench my thirst. But as I continue to stand here, I toy with temptation, reminding myself exactly where the cameras are positioned.

I need to see him and clear the air between us before it tears us apart.

When I walk through the back hall, I head toward the other wing of the house with the guest bedroom, carefully avoiding where all the cameras are pointing. When it comes to security systems, my dad spared no expense. Over the years, Ava and I have learned a few tricks despite its so-called sophisticated technology.

Standing outside the bedroom door, a tightness overcomes my chest. What if he tells me he can't do this? That this was just a fling? That I'm too young and not worth the trouble? Can I handle hearing those exact words right now?

I take a deep breath. It's now or never.

Slowly, I turn the handle and gently close the door behind me. With the drapes open, I see his shadow against the large bed frame. He's resting on his back with his arm beneath his head, his sculpted chest visible under the pale moonlight. My walls begin to crumble at the sight of him. I can't hold back anymore, desperate to touch him and tell him how I feel.

Moving toward the bed, I stand beside it with hesitation. The second his hand reaches out for me, I climb under the sheets and snuggle into the side of his body, allowing his skin to envelope me with warmth. I purposely lay my head on his chest, listening to the sound of his beating heart. It's playing the most beautiful tune, and I wish for it to be only ever heard by me.

"Amelia," he breathes into my hair. "You shouldn't be here."

"I don't care," I tell him, tired of fighting how I feel. "I want you."

"I want you, too, but if we get caught, it will be over for us."

"They won't find out, I promise."

I climb on top of him as his hands softly graze my thighs. My lips find his instantly, a gentle kiss that deepens as my body aches so desperately for him. We come up for a breath, only to fall back into feverish kisses. Our soft moans, barely audible for fear of being heard, get lost in the intensity of our actions.

I remove my tee, exposing my breasts. Beneath me, Will's body tenses, his hands cupping my breast while he pushes his groin against me. The thought of being caught becomes this unknowing thrill, forcing me to strip him bare, including myself, so we're both naked.

Without warning him, I slide myself on to feel him clench beneath me. We grind softly, doing our best to keep quiet. Every inch of my body cries out to be touched. All senses heightened more than ever before. I slow down, running my hand along his jaw.

"It's only you," I murmur, slowing my movements. "Austin means nothing to me."

"I know."

"Do you know?"

He places his hands on my cheek, caressing it softly. "Amelia, my feelings for you are... I can't explain it. I've never felt this way over anyone, and it scares me. You're nineteen."

"I know. I'm young."

"You have your whole life ahead of you."

I feel vulnerable, but even at this moment, he strokes my cheek gently as my heart races, aware that he's still inside me.

"But I don't want to stop," he says with finality.

Even though our eyes barely meet in the darkness, there's something that passes between us, something so strong that neither of us can no longer deny. His lips kiss mine softly, and that connection between us deepens as we both make love, finishing in harmony.

With our breaths short, I pull myself off and continue to lay on top of him.

I don't know how long I should stay here in his arms under the roof of my parents' home.

But one thing I knew for sure is that Ava is right.

I am falling in love with him.

TWENTY-FIVE

WILL

E verything changed after that night in LA.
     The admission we both made was raw, in the moment, but nevertheless, the truth. We were fighting the same battle against our emotions and finally gave up—the force too strong.

We'd become addicted to one thing—each other.

With this came the challenge of holding together our relationship while trying to hide it from those close to us. Being in LA in the presence of Lex and Charlie was too hard.

We tried our best to remain amicable without the stolen glances, but it all became too much when Charlie insisted we spend time together as a family.

I've always respected Charlie, thought of her like my own mother, which makes the deceit harder to control. I've allowed myself to take their daughter under their roof, but resisting Amelia is futile. She has this hold over me, one that consumes me whole.

Work needs attention, and thankfully, Lex doesn't question my desire to fly back to New York. He knows the importance of closing some deals we've been trying to finalize, so I fly back the next night, eager for some normality.

Amelia follows two days later, using some excuse of trying to catch up on studying before New Year's with the hope to gain some additional class credits. Our reasons, while somewhat valid, are all in an effort to be alone.

The days when we returned, we spend most of the time in my apartment in bed because I can't get enough. I should've been working, and while I tried to pull my laptop out on several occasions, her body proves too much of a distraction.

"Do you realize we have been in bed for two days?" Amelia lazily mumbles in the pillow. "Why is there no search party for me?"

"Because you made up some pretty sweet lies," I remind her with a smirk, trying to type an email to some moron in London. "And besides, it's not like I'm holding you captive."

She snorts before shuffling her face to the side. "I quote, 'I'm holding you captive,' end quote. I believe those exact words left your lips yesterday morning when I arrived here."

Distracted once again, I slam my laptop shut and run my fingers along the curves of her spine. Her skin is smooth, flawless even. Just a simple touch, and I find myself hard, again.

"Are you complaining about the multiple orgasms you've received over the last day?"

With a wide grin, she turns around, her tits exposed, making me groan at the beautiful sight. *They're fucking perfect.*

"Now, why would I complain about that? If anything, I'd encourage you to continue to make me come as you please."

I climb on top of her, kissing her deeply before entering

her without warning. Her back arches, her chest at my complete disposal as I tug on her nipples and suck them softly. She winces slightly, only because I ravaged them last night while fucking her in the shower.

Her moans become an addiction, a beautiful sound I'm desperate to hear each time my hands touch her skin. It doesn't take us long before we both end on a complete high.

"*That was...*" she stammers, out of breath.

"Breathtaking?" I laugh, kissing the side of her neck.

"Amongst many things."

"So, listen, I have to go into the office to get some work done," I tell her, looking at the time. "You're welcome to stay here, naked."

"Nice offer. I'm going to head back to my parents' place. I need some new clothes to change into. A few friends want to catch up tonight for dinner."

I still my movements. "Which friends?"

"Girlfriends, you jealous freak. Well, tiny lie. Andy and girlfriends."

"I never said I was jealous."

"Uh-huh..." She nods with a knowing smirk. "By the way, we haven't spoken about tomorrow night. I mean, that's if you want to do something, or is the Boston thing true?"

Tomorrow night is New Year's Eve. I don't want to break it to her that Boston is, in fact, true. I'll need to leave early to make it back here before midnight.

"There's something I want to do with you," I tell her teasingly.

"Is it dirty?"

"It depends on where you're standing?"

"Huh?"

I kiss her lips, tasting her once again. "Come back here tonight, please?"

"It'll be late," she informs me.

"That's okay. You know I barely sleep."

Hopping out of bed, I find appropriate pants and a business shirt to wear. Once I'm dressed, I lean in to kiss her one more time before heading to the office.

As I sit at my desk, my fingers tap against the glass tabletop while I try to concentrate.

My mind begins to drift, and I find myself opening Insta and scrolling through Amelia's photos. With the smiles and laughter, a typical young woman is living her life. Am I selfish for holding her back? I remember all the years I spent in college, the careless behavior, and the wicked parties. For me, not being in a relationship meant I could study and party. There was no one to occupy my time or fight for attention. This gave me the ability to dream big and complete my Master's in Business.

This is her time to experience all that.

Our lives are at completely different stages, yet somehow, it almost feels like our worlds are the same, and that alone terrifies me. Whichever way I look at us, someone will have to make the ultimate sacrifice.

My phone buzzes. Lex's name appears on the screen, demanding attention.

"Lex," I greet.

"McGuire tells me he's still waiting on you to send across the proposal?"

"Yes." I clear my throat, stretching my neck to ease the tension. "I'm on it."

"Well, get on it faster. You don't want him to look elsewhere. I thought you were sending this last night?" Lex stresses with an agitated tone. "Is there something you're not telling me?"

"I'm trying to play catch-up, that's all, Lex." I strain, biting my tongue not to give anything away. "He'll have it in an hour."

Lex doesn't say another word, hanging up the phone. *Fuck.* I've riled the beast. I've witnessed Lex on the warpath, and it's not pleasant.

I tell my new secretary, Heather, to hold all my calls and bring me some coffee so I can power through this. Exactly an hour later, I'm beyond done, sending across the email to McGuire with a follow-up phone call. By the time it ends, night has fallen, and I want nothing more than to forget this day existed.

As I enter my apartment, not a single sound can be heard, the outside noise disappearing the moment I step inside. Suddenly, this apartment feels incredibly lonely. I can almost hear the echo of Amelia's laughter, only to realize she's not here.

There's nothing to do besides continue to work. I sit on the couch with my laptop, answering an email from some fucker trying to sell me something I'm not interested in. There are a few emails from Lex, some of which I answer because I can, but even he's getting on my nerves with his ridiculous demands.

I check the time, noting it's after midnight. There's no text message from Amelia. I think about sending her a text but talk myself out of it. The worry turns into jealousy once again, and I find myself stalking her stories like a fucking maniac. There are many images of food and them sitting in a restaurant with the only male being Andy.

Feeling somewhat relieved, I grab a drink from the liquor cabinet and pour myself a glass, welcoming the taste of the smoky whisky to ease the tension I've been feeling all day.

Another hour passes before the door opens, and Amelia stumbles through, dressed in a navy blue tight-fitting dress and oversized white winter jacket. Her camel-colored boots touch her knee, exposing her thighs more than I'd prefer.

There's a cheeky smile on her face, and the glassy eyes tell me she's been drinking. It only validates my concerns, but I keep my opinion to myself, not wanting to get into an argument now.

She sits on my lap, wrapping her arms around my neck. I close my eyes briefly, inhaling the smell of her perfume and burying my head in her neck, allowing her hair to fall gracefully against my face.

"*I missed you,*" I murmur.

I lean back on the sofa to get a better look at her, still in my work clothes, as she begins to unbutton my dress shirt. I graze my hand along her thigh, knowing that every touch makes it harder to pull away. She runs her hands along my chest before placing soft kisses along my collarbone.

"I love you," she utters, followed by a small hiccup. "I love you, William Rockford Romano."

My body freezes as she says the words. But slowly, her tiny snores fall between us. I shut my eyes tight, just for a moment, begging myself to ignore the three words attempting to break down all my walls.

Three words that change everything between us.

I carry her to the bedroom, laying her on the bed, removing her coat and shoes with incredible difficulty. She's dead asleep, so I place the blanket over her and head to the shower to get changed for bed.

With only three hours of sleep, the morning light hasn't even risen as I'm sitting on the edge of the bed dressed in my suit with the car service waiting downstairs.

"Amelia," I say softly. "I have to go."

She begins to stir, her eyes opening a few seconds later. "Go? Go where? What time is it?"

"Shh, sleep. It's early."

"But...what time is it?"

"Early," I state, letting out a sigh. "I need to fly to Boston today, but I'll be back tonight."

"Boston? But it's New Year's Eve."

"Yes." I kiss her lips, pulling away and ignoring the pang inside my chest for leaving her. "I'll see you tonight."

I begin to walk out of the door when she calls my name, forcing me to turn around.

"Will," she repeats, biting her lip as if she's nervous or hiding something. "Have a safe flight."

The meetings in Boston carried on longer than necessary. The boring old fuckers had nothing better to do than bring up irrelevant numbers from the past like I give a fuck. After that ended, there was a small event being held at an expensive restaurant in the city. I agreed to make a brief appearance, telling them I had plans back in the city and needed to be on the six o'clock flight back to JFK.

None of them seem to care, nor listen, offering me drink after drink until I politely tell them I have to leave.

"Mr. Romano."

My name is called, and as I turn around, it's none other than Juliette Olivier, a French woman I slept with after my break-up with Luciana.

Juliette is draped in a gold cocktail dress, a split running up her leg, stopping mid-thigh. She's just as sexy as I remember and, and most likely, just as cunning.

She kisses both my cheeks, then pulls away with a deep stare.

"It's been a while," she says, unapologetic with her flirtatious smile. "I see you're alone."

"I was just leaving," I tell her politely. "A flight back to New York."

"Well, that's a shame." She places her hand on my shoulder, then leans in and whispers, "I'd hate to be alone tonight. Perhaps, you should join me?"

I pull away, pursing my lips. "As I said, I have to go. It was nice seeing you, Juliette."

I swiftly walk out of the room and outside to catch a cab to the airport with my hands in my pocket. I quickly send Amelia a text letting her know I'm on my way home.

Me: *I'm about to board my flight. See you soon.*

Amelia: *See you soon xx*

My flight was delayed, something about mechanical failure, making it arrive at JFK just after ten. As the driver takes me home, I send Amelia another text.

Me: *I'm sorry, my flight was delayed. Be there soon.*

Amelia: *K*

Judging by the response, I suspect Amelia is less than pleased. It's just clocked over to eleven when I enter the apartment. She's sitting on the couch, dressed beautifully in an emerald- green dress accentuated with intricate beading. The garment is long, touching the floor, all of which makes her appear more mature than the short dresses she normally wears. With her legs crossed, her eyes fixate on the wall with a disappointed gleam in her eyes.

"I'm sorry for being late."

I lean in to kiss her, but she pulls back.

"Is this how it's going to be from now on?"

"Amelia," I warn her gently.

"No, Will." She raises her palm to stop me, standing up to create distance between us. "All I do is wait around for you. It's always about work."

"Of course, it's about work," I shout, tired, trying to unknot my tie. "What do you want me to do? Drop everything for you?"

She shakes her head, then lowers her eyes to the ground. "This will never change, will it?"

"I don't know how you want me to answer that."

"And on top of that, I don't know how long I can go on hiding all this. It's exhausting!"

She's out of control, but I feel her frustration. We're both caught up in this perfect storm, and it's only a matter of time before the sneaking around grows tiresome, and we crave normality.

"I have an idea." I grab her hand forcefully. "Let's go."

"Where?" she questions, annoyed at the way I grip her hand tight, refusing to let go. "And we haven't finished talking."

With her hand still in mine, I drag her from the apartment, yanking our coats from the coat rack, and run out onto the street. The cold night air is a slap in the face, unrelenting with its chill.

The sound of horns and sirens greet us as usual. Tonight, out of all nights, people are generally less patient on the streets. If we move quickly, we just might make it before midnight, only if the crowds work in our favor.

It's not uncommon for the city to be chaotic on New Year's Eve, but I've been here so often to learn a few tricks. Darting in and out of the crowds congregating at Times Square, I find us a spot to stand still.

"Will, it's so crowded," Amelia yells over the noise. "Why are we here?"

I pull her into me, tilting my head to whisper in her ear. "It's almost midnight, and this is the busiest place in the world. Everyone can see us at this moment. No hiding, it's just you and me, baby."

Slowly, she pulls away as her mouth curves to a smile. With her hands around my neck, the crowd begins to count-down as we chant along with them.

"Five, four, three, two, one..."

The ball drops as everyone shouts, "Happy New Year." A burst of light falls all around us, loud music playing. Surrounding us, people hug and kiss, but all I can do is stare into the eyes of this beautiful woman I want to call mine.

Forever.

And then, in front of thousands of people, and quite possibly the world via the lens, we passionately kiss for everyone to see. Our tongues roll softly, perfectly in sync, and as we both pull away, my heart is bursting with happiness to be able to share this moment with her.

"Last night, I know I was drunk, but I meant what I said."

"Amelia," I say softly. "Please don't feel like you need to justify drunk talk."

"No, Will. Please just let me say it, here, in front of the world."

I stare into her eyes, and with this stare, I can almost see her bare *her* soul. All her walls have broken down, and in the reflection, all I see is the two of us.

"I'm in love with you. You don't need to say anything. In fact, it would be easier if you don't."

"I don't know what to say," I admit, scared to process the very thought.

"Say nothing, please. It was just something I need to do."

I don't say anything, unsure of how much this will change us. Instead, I hold onto her tight, then follow with cupping her chin as I lay another kiss on her lips.

We walk together, holding hands, back to my building.

Inside the apartment, the air is warm unlike the harsh cold outside. I waste no time and strip her naked, kissing her shoulder before I hesitate.

My eyes are drawn to every curve, to how perfect she is in my bed, and how this is how I always want it to be. As I stare into her eyes, my whole life flashes before me. Our bond started well before she stepped into my office. It started only minutes after she entered this world.

And in so many ways, that's what terrifies me the most —she's always been the one and may possibly only ever be the one.

I can't see a future without her in it.

And to even think of one existing without her in my arms sets a knife-wielding pain like a dagger straight into my heart.

"Amelia," I breathe, caressing her cheek while watching her emerald-green eyes gaze back at me with hope.

"Yes?"

Leaning forward, my lips brush against hers, soft and gentle, intended to make our hearts beat in sync to this memorable moment. I want it to be more than just words. It's the beginning of something beautiful, something I never knew I wanted but can't live without.

I fell well before this moment, careless to admit the truth.

"I'm in love with you, Amelia Edwards," I admit, gazing into her eyes. "And no one will stop us from being together. I promise you this."

Her eyes beg me to take her, and as I lay her down on the bed about to make sweet love to her, she places her palm on my chest, directly on top of my beating heart.

"You've always been mine, Will Romano," she whispers with a smile. "Our bond is too tight for us to think we could be nothing."

I kiss the tips of her fingers, letting out a sigh. "I've got all night to show you just how much I love you."

With a soft chuckle, she positions herself perfectly, spreading her legs, ready for me to enter. "And I'm all yours, baby. However, way you want me."

I bury my head into her neck and slowly enter her. "I want you in every way possible," I murmur, relishing in her soft moans as I move at a slow and agonizing pace. "You're all mine, Miss Edwards."

And we continue to make love all night. I devour every inch of her body, switching from our soft lovemaking to our heated fucking on the countertop. We move in various positions to multiple locations within my apartment. We are creative in our efforts, and never have I ever been so aroused in my life where nothing else matters. I expect relief once I come or she comes. But then it starts all over again.

When she spreads her ass wide for me against the

window, I take the opportunity to slide into her perfect ass hole and completely own every part of her.

And then—we're done. Collapsing on the bed, I hold onto her as she rests her head on my chest.

"Happy New Year," she barely manages to get out. "They say how you bring in the new year is a reflection of the luck you'll have for the year."

I kiss the top of her head and with a small chuckle, return the sentiment.

"Happy New Year, beautiful. And I'll be a very lucky man if that's what I have to look forward to for the year."

"Or for the rest of your life," she whispers, sealing her words with a kiss.

TWENTY-SIX

AMELIA

"You go first."

Across the table, Andy twists his fingers before letting out a long-winded breath. The café we chose to meet at is located in Chelsea. It's not too busy, just a few patrons sitting around drinking hot beverages and enjoying the scrumptious pastries the café is known for.

"I'm sleeping with my professor."

I spit out the coffee, choking momentarily while I cough myself into oblivion. Andy warns me with his eyes to keep it down. Wiping the corners of my mouth, I continue to cough involuntarily.

When I finally get a hold of myself, I blurt out, "I'm sleeping with Will."

Andy's eyes widen until he breaks out into laughter, running his fingers through his hair with an amused look on his face. "Yeah, right. Good one, Millie."

"I'm sleeping with Will, and I'm in love with him."

I keep my expression to a bare minimum, showing Andy this is no joke. It takes a few moments, but when I continue to look at him seriously, his smile subsides, and his mouth falls open in shock.

"Holy shit. He's your cousin."

"He's *not* my cousin," I correct him. "Just because our parents called us that doesn't mean we technically are. We don't share the same blood as each other."

"But he's how old?" Andy does the math, his forehead wrinkling in the process. "Almost thirty?"

"Close to it."

"Age aside because let's face it, who am I to talk," Andy muses, tapping his fingers against the tabletop with an unwavering gaze. "Your dad will kill you if he finds out."

"Well, he hasn't found out."

"Yet," Andy adds.

"He won't find out. We're careful."

Andy places his hand on mine with a sympathetic glance. "Millie, you're in love with him. How do you expect to continue without your dad finding out?"

I slump into my chair, letting out a sigh. "Can we talk about you screwing your professor?"

"There's not much to say. I'm not in love with her. We just got to talking and, well, hooked up."

I fold my arms, quick to point out the obvious. "Hold on a minute. You don't just get to talk, then hook up."

"It's rather dirty, and I'd rather not repeat it in front of you because you *are* my cousin."

"Jesus, Andy. You could get into real trouble for this. What if NYU kicks you out?"

"They won't kick me out," he assures me, his head lifted high. "They'll kick her out. But look, nobody knows but you. So as long as you don't say anything, then we're all just fine."

The waitress serves us the sandwiches we ordered, but neither one of us appear to have an appetite. We both aimlessly push our food around until Andy takes a bite, then another, while I continue to sit in silence. Typical male —one minute they are expressing emotions, and the next, all seems forgotten.

"What's wrong, Millie?"

Averting my gaze, my attention is pulled to a mother and daughter sitting by the window. They are both talking animatedly, conversing one minute, then laughing the next. A tightness in my chest is followed by guilt.

"I love Will, and I love spending time with him," I say, keeping my voice low. "But lying to my parents is exhausting. And things haven't been the same with Mom."

Andy nods his head knowingly. "Maybe you need to come clean with Aunt Charlie. Out of all people, she'll understand."

"Do you think?"

"She's your best friend."

"I know," I mumble, the guilt only becoming worse.

"And, you know, your parents fought like hell to be together. If there's anyone who can offer words of wisdom, it's definitely her."

I tear a piece of the bread, bringing it to my mouth as I begin to chew slowly.

"Um, has Ava ever mentioned to you this thing about my mom, and, um..." I scratch the back of my neck. "Your dad."

Andy chuckles softly. "C'mon, it's Ava. Of course, she has."

"And?"

"My parents have never mentioned it," he tells me

honestly. "Let's say the rumor is true. What does it matter? Everyone is supposed to be exactly where they are destined to be."

He has a point, though Andy is always the rational thinker of the three of us.

"You're not the least bit curious?"

"That my dad and your mom fucked? No..." he trails off, bored.

I have to agree with him. The thought itself is somewhat disturbing. I've always loved Uncle Julian, and he's been nothing but nice to me. He isn't exactly besties with Dad, but I can't say I've witnessed any behavior to justify any animosity between them. The more I think about it, the more I think Ava has a creative imagination and thirsty for gossip.

"Listen, I'm here, Millie, if you need me. But you need to be careful. This may not end the way you're hoping it will end."

"How am I hoping this will end?"

"That everyone will accept the two of you together. Uncle Lex respects Will. When he finds out he's fucking his oldest daughter, you can bet your ass he's going to be livid."

Andy's reality check leaves me in a bad mood. I can't exactly blame him. He merely points out the truth, which I've purposely denied this entire time.

We say goodbye to each other, and I find myself wandering the streets to clear my mind. I lose track of time and directions until the buildings look familiar. A block away is Will's office. I question whether I should visit him, assuming he's busy since he hasn't texted or called me all day. I walk the block over, entering his building and up to the floor.

There's a new woman sitting at the reception desk. She's much prettier than the last, and more noticeably, has much larger breasts. With my lips pressed flat, I try to ignore the burning sensation inside my chest. Will is surrounded by beautiful, older women all the time. Even if we come out to everyone, that will never change. This jealousy consuming me is unflattering yet hard to control.

"Can I help you?" she asks, eyeing me up and down.

What a snob. I look down at my attire, admiring the leather skirt and ivory blouse I'm wearing. I despise the fact that she's questioning me all in the way her eyes move, my insecurities getting the better of me.

"Is Mr. Romano available?"

"And may I ask what your business is with him?"

My business with him is none of her fucking business, but I manage to force a polite smile before answering, "Please tell him that Miss Edwards is here to see him if he's available."

"You don't have a meeting." She raises her poorly drawn-on eyebrows with a dismissive glance. "I'm sorry, he's unavailable."

This bitch doesn't know who she is messing with. My claws come out, ready to show her who has the fucking power.

"Let me inform you of who I am. My name is Amelia Edwards. I'm Lex Edward's daughter." I see her expression shift immediately, her muscles turning slack. "I'm certain you know who my father is. Now, please ask Mr. Romano if he's free to see me."

She doesn't say another word, dialing his number and mumbling into the receiver.

"He'll see you now."

I don't say thank you. Frankly, she's undeserving.

I walk into his office as Will stands up from his chair with a grin on his face. I close the door behind me, keeping my distance for now, given we're in his office.

"To what do I owe the pleasure? I thought you had to study today?"

"Andy wanted to have lunch, so we caught up. I thought I'd drop by before heading back."

Will moves toward me. Tilting his head, he kisses my lips with urgency. I hesitate, pulling back as he steps back, watching me. I move toward the window, staring out into the city.

"What's wrong?"

"I hate all this lying."

Will remains silent, sitting on the edge of his desk. "I understand. It's not easy."

"Do you?" I turn around, frustrated. "It feels like nothing in your life has changed. In fact, you get the best of everything... me, work, but what has changed in your life?"

He narrows his eyes with a clenching jaw. "I didn't realize this is a competition of who gets it easier."

"I never said that."

"Well, let me set the record straight, Amelia. It's not easy. I have responsibilities, all of which tie into your father somehow. I deal with him more than you know, and there's a lot of pressure on me for this company to perform. Over a thousand employees rely on me to issue them a paycheck so they can put food on their table," he informs me with a controlled tone, something my father often does. "There are people on Wall Street who are watching my every business move. So, while I understand that you're tired of lying, I can guarantee you that I don't have the best of everything."

I shake my head silently, crossing my arms while lowering my gaze toward the polished concrete floor. "I'm sorry, I didn't realize... I just can't see past how many people we will hurt if we get found out."

At the exact moment, my phone begins to ring. My dad's caller ID appears on the screen. I hit reject, only for it to ring again. *Shit*. I hit the accept button.

"Hi, Dad." I turn around to face the glass window, staring out into the city.

"Amelia, will you pick up your phone when I call you, please?"

"Dad, I'm busy," I say, defeated. "What's so urgent?"

"Your mother has been trying to call you to no avail."

"I was having lunch with Andy."

"You went all the way into the city to have lunch with Andy?"

"Yes, Dad, I needed a break from studying and missed him."

"Look, Amelia, is everything okay? Your mother is worried about you."

Deep, heavy breathing sounds behind me as the hairs on my arms stand at attention while chills run down my spine. Slowly, I turn my head, my eyes meeting his. The temperature in the room becomes stifling hot, causing my breathing to pick up at an uneven pace.

"I'm fine, Dad. Just busy."

"You'll call her as soon as we get off the phone?"

Will stops just shy of where I stand, close enough for me to smell him. Reaching out, he runs his finger along my collarbone, my body tensing at his touch.

"Uh-huh, okay, Dad. I'll call Mom as soon as I'm back in New Haven."

"Amelia, I don't know what's going on with you, but I'm worried."

"You have nothing to worry about. I need to go."

"Amelia," he warns sternly. "Don't do anything to disappoint me."

"I won't, Dad. Promise."

I hang up the call, breathing out a sigh of relief.

"This was never going to be easy, Amelia," Will reminds me.

"I know that. If only my dad..." I trail off, my thoughts jumbled.

"If only your dad will approve? If I stand here and tell you he will, I'd be lying to you. I know Lex Edwards, possibly better than you. He's the ruler of his kingdom. And if he thinks his princess is in danger, he'll do everything in his power to make sure nothing happens."

He pushes my hair behind my shoulder, and leaning forward, he grazes his lips against my neck, inhaling my skin. The walls start to cave, the touch of his lips on my skin breaking them down piece by piece.

I yank his hair, pulling his mouth onto mine. His lips taste like heaven, his tongue meeting mine. Unable to stop, my tongue refuses to break from his, barely able to let go as he pulls away.

His eyes blaze with desire as he wraps his hand around my waist, carrying me toward his desk and laying me down, forcing my legs open. Letting out a moan, his eyes widen while admiring my legs, running his hands up my thigh before he forcefully pulls me toward him, then I wrap my legs around his waist.

Out of breath, with my heart running a marathon, his fingers clasp the buttons of my blouse, unbuttoning them at a slow and agonizing pace, exposing my breasts. There's no delayed gratification, no admiring my naked form. His mouth ravages my breasts, sucking hard while I arch my neck, groaning beneath his touch.

His phone begins to ring, and with scornful eyes, he presses the phone to his forehead before answering.

"Lex," he almost grunts.

There's silence, and the frustrated expression soon turns into a deliciously sinful smirk.

"I understand that you're worried." Will runs his hands along my thigh, grazing between my legs. I hold back my moan, scared of being heard. "I'll take care of her, don't worry. You know, I think of her as family. I'd never let anyone hurt her."

And with that, he plunges his fingers inside me, my back arching as the sensations ripple through me. I close my eyes, desperately trying to control myself and not combust on his desk.

"You can trust me," he says with finality. "I'll make sure no one else touches her."

He hangs up the phone, cocking his head with a wicked sneer.

"Why did you promise that?" I pant, desperate for answers.

"Well, Miss Edwards, I've been ordered to protect you. And judging by how this little pussy of yours is so wet, I don't think you're hurt. I think you want me to fuck you. Daddy says, make sure you don't get hurt. I can be very gentle if you wish."

He unzips his pants, his cock throbbing hard as it springs free and slaps against his ripped stomach. I watch him, wanting to taste it so bad.

Painfully slow, he grips my panties in his hand, sliding

them to the side as his cock glides against my swollen clit. I brace for him, my body pleading to be at his mercy and feel him whole. The torment in his expression drives my desire beyond its limits, begging to take all of me right now. He guides himself inside me, my back arching in delightful pain.

I desperately want more, his lips and hands to touch every part of me.

He flips me around, pushing my chest onto his desk. Forcefully, he uses his legs to spread mine as far apart as they'll go. His cock slides back inside and leaning over, he covers my mouth with his hand while pounding into me.

The desk is shaking, the papers flying everywhere. The screams are muffled in his hand, my body ready to combust from the intensity of his animalistic demand to own every part of me.

Quickly, he turns me back around, my hands gripping the edge of the desk.

I bite into his hand, exploding all over him, the rush consuming every inch of my body and finishing with a blissful warmth. His thrusts are desperate as he lets go of my mouth, pounding me hard one more time before his body shakes, exploding inside of me.

Our breaths, shallow and uneven, command the room with its noise. Slowly, he pulls himself out of me, collapsing on my body. I continue to lay still, trying to catch my breath as I begin to button my blouse while he rests beside me, breaking the silence between us.

"Amelia, for as long as you choose us, I'll protect what we have," he urges, running his thumb against my bottom lip.

"Do you promise, Will? This will get harder before it gets better."

"I love you, Amelia. No one will stand in our way, and that includes your father."

His deep stare, full of promises, fills me with hope. For as long as he'll protect what we have, I'll choose to fight for him.

The only man I want more than life itself.

TWENTY-SEVEN

AMELIA

F alling in love with someone can change your life entirely.

I've always observed others around me, admired my parents for their journey toward everlasting love and the trials, tribulations, and heartache they faced at times when their love for each other was tested. But no matter what, love won in the end.

Lex and Charlie Edwards are soulmates, best friends—two people with a love story to rival Romeo and Juliet.

At the beginning of senior year, I remember a time when Kate told me the story of her and Uncle Noah. They started off as friends, and throughout time, their feelings for each other developed into love. Both of them denied this, of course, which led to them ending their friendship to go their separate ways.

Uncle Noah married Morgan, Jessa's mom, until that ended unpleasantly. At the time I sought advice from Kate, I was scared to jump into a relationship with Austin because I didn't want to ruin our friendship. Kate encouraged me to take the leap, and I guess her own happily ever after came from exactly that—taking the risk on love.

It's not like I don't like Morgan. She has always been polite and is a very beautiful woman, but she's not Kate. When I'm in the presence of Uncle Noah and Kate, there's this chemistry between them. Even to this day, you can actually see how best of friends they are, and out of all the couples I know, they are always the ones to make each other laugh. They're both perfect for each other, but then again, each couple I know who has lasted the distance, has their own unique bond, a bond that has stood the test of time.

And I was naïve to think that my love for Austin could ever truly compare to how I feel about Will. It's like nothing matters when I'm with Will, yet in the same breath, nothing else matters when I'm *not* in his presence.

No matter what I do, he's on my mind and all over me as if I'm breathing him in.

Sex has become an addiction, my body falling mercy to his touch. I've never experienced intimacy to where nothing is off-limits. When we're alone, we continually raise the bar with our naughty rendezvous, and frankly, Will is insatiable.

When I stay over at his apartment, I never get any sleep. In fact, we do nothing but fuck nonstop, which neither one of us ever complains. Our differences in schedules mean we need to be creative with our efforts. I try to visit the city whenever I have no classes, and on rare occasions, Will visits me in my dorm room. A few times, we meet at restaurants and end up fucking inside the car at some abandoned parking lot.

It's only a matter of time before life pulls us in even more directions. Will's travel schedule becomes hectic. He's constantly flying in and out of New York, then to add to that, he's caught up in meetings, and our conversations become text messages more than actual voice calls.

With spring break not too far away, I try to stay on top of my schoolwork but find myself distracted and fall ill with the flu.

"God, Millie, you sound like you're dying," Liesel complains, eyeing all the medicine on my bedside table while bringing me a glass of water. "There's this weird strain of the flu going around. I read somewhere that people are worried it'll be a pandemic or something."

My insides hurt, a cold shiver spreading throughout my body. I ask her to bring me another blanket, but not long after, I break out into a cold sweat and remove everything, lying here in only my bra and panties.

"It's just a cold. I'll get over it."

My phone begins to buzz beside me, raising it to my eyes. I see Will's name and answer it, a cough escaping me.

"You sound awful," Will says, concerned. "I can't even see you. I'm in Houston again and won't be back for another week. After this, I fly to Seattle."

"I'll be okay, one more night's rest," I croak, then blow my nose into a tissue. "Besides, how exactly will you make me feel better? In case you haven't figured it out, I'm physically out of order."

Will laughs through the receiver. "My poor baby, but you do have a point. Okay, listen, I need to step into the boardroom now, but I love you. Please get better."

"Love you too."

The one night's rest I had so desperately needed turning into pure hell. I tossed and turned, coughing relentlessly. My sinuses were clogged up, followed by a fever spiking. There was no relief the next day, forcing me to stay in bed and miss classes.

Ava calls to tell me Will texted her, worried. She told Mom about me being sick. Everyone is worried, but what little does that matter when I sit here all alone. Not long after Ava told Mom, she calls me.

"Do you need me to fly over? You sound awful?"

"Mom, I have the flu. I can handle taking care of myself. I'm not a kid anymore," I say rudely, willing my head to stop spinning.

"I never said you were a kid. You're sick, and there's a strain of the flu going around sending people to the hospital. I'm worried about you."

"And I'm telling you that I'm a big girl. I'll get better."

Annoyed that she treats me like a child, I make some excuse for needing to go. If truth be told, we rarely speak these days. Between Will, schoolwork, and now this stupid flu, I try to avoid her because it eases my conscience.

But like anything in life, avoidance will only get you so far.

That afternoon, Liesel took me to the ER when my fever spiked. They placed me on an IV overnight, sending me home the next day with more antibiotics. I chose to keep my visit to the hospital hidden from my family and Will, not wanting anyone to fuss over me like some kid.

It took me a few days to feel a bit better, but the exhaustion still weighed heavily on my shoulders. I'd lost weight, only now beginning to feel a little energy as my appetite picks up. It's probably for the best that Will is still away, given that I have zero interest in sex.

"You look much better." Liesel smiles, sitting beside me on the sofa. "Enough so that you can visit your man tonight when he returns and have all the sex I wish I were having."

I chuckle softly, followed by a small cough. "As much as I'd love to do that, I have a meeting in fifteen minutes with my academic advisor. I suspect he wants to discuss the extra credits I'm working toward and maybe advancing some of my courses."

"Good luck," she calls, hopping off the couch. "If you're not here for dinner, I'll assume your vagina has other ideas."

"Miss Edwards," Professor Daniels greets as I close the door behind me. "We need to discuss your class load."

I take a seat, placing my bag beside me. "Is it about my extra credits? As you know, I'm hoping to graduate early."

Professor Daniels removes his glasses, cleaning them before putting them back on again. "I'm afraid that's not going to happen. You're falling behind with the workload."

My shoulders tense as I shake my head in confusion. "I don't understand. I've been sick this past week, but I've caught up on everything."

"Well, frankly, your grades were excellent at the beginning of the first semester, and then they began to fall. Understandably, there's an adjustment period. What I'm suggesting is that you drop some classes."

"I can't do that," I state, raising my voice unwillingly. "My mom took the same class load."

"I don't believe we can measure against what someone else does, Miss Edwards."

"I'll do anything," I plea, trying to hold back my emotions. "Just tell me what I need to do?"

Professor Daniels suggests I drop a class so I catch up, but I continue to shake my head, refusing to do so. I didn't dream of coming to Yale only to fail. What would my parents think? So, I've been distracted by Will. If I focus again, I'm certain everything will improve. All I need to do is spend more time in the library and less time in Will's bed.

I beg Professor Daniels to offer some other solutions, and we spend the next hour going through everything. The bottom line is that I need to focus on school. End of story.

Back in the dorm room, Liesel brings out the vodka—her solution to life's problems. I kindly refuse, letting out a sigh as to how exactly I'm going to juggle it all. With my planner resting in my lap, I flick the pages aimlessly. I can say goodbye to spring break, the plans to stay with Will and our weekend away at The Hamptons.

"It's just a hurdle. So, you'll study harder, and besides, you've had the flu."

"Yes, I know." I nod, though not convincingly.

It's times like this where I wish I can call Mom, desperate to hear her wisdom at a time when I feel helpless and lost. But again, I've distanced myself enough that calling her for advice would only raise suspicion.

"And so what if you've been moody?" Liesel adds, watching me cautiously. "I'd have thought all the hot sex would negate that?"

"Hot sex? It's been close to two weeks since I last saw Will."

"Hmm... that explains the mood."

"I could blame PMS?"

Liesel nods with a knowing grin. "That's right. We're flow buddies. By the way, I stole some of your tampons since I ran out."

My shoulders shake as I chuckle at her admission. Liesel is no different from Ava. "That's fine. I'll pick some up when I need them."

"Wait, you don't have them? I thought we were in sync?"

"We're in sync," I point out, eyeing the assignment to-do list written in my planner. "I'm just sick, so probably just late."

"But aren't you on the pill?"

"Yes," I drag, watching Liesel's eyebrows draw together with concern.

"You do use other protection with Will, right?"

Inside my throat, a giant lump begins to form. I scratch at my knee to distract the panic rising within me. "No, but I take the pill every day."

"Every day?"

I nod. "Every day."

"Same time?"

"Well, not always the exact same time."

Liesel lets out a heavy sigh. "How late are we talking?"

I can't believe we're having this conversation. I've been late before, it's not unusual. Though, I wasn't fucking my brains out when that occurred. I try to suppress the panic rising to the surface. Grabbing my purse, I fumble for my pill packet, retrieving it to see the white pills almost finished —the very last one sitting inside the little circled packaging.

I hold it up for Liesel to see. She bites her lip, rubbing her face with worry.

"I think you should do a pregnancy test."

I jump to my feet, pacing the area between us. "I can't do that. So, I'm four days late? Big deal."

Liesel does her best to calm me down, but the panic in her expression makes it difficult for me to ignore.

"You're right, you've been sick, so maybe your body is just going through the motions. But better to clear the thoughts and find out for sure."

The thought of this even happening numbs me to the core. I'm nineteen. I have my whole life ahead of me. I recall Mom's story about Nikki and Rocky and how they struggled for so many years. I guess, for them, they had each other, so it worked out. But I know my chances of Will staying with me are slim. He's never once mentioned starting a family or kids. From conversations I've heard from Aunt Nikki and Mom, he has zero desire for any of that.

And if he does, it will be out of obligation, not because he wants to start a family with someone who's only nineteen.

My head beings to spin, forcing me to sit down as I bury it between my legs.

"I can go get it for you. We can do it together."

I throw my hands up in the air, my chest tightening. "I don't want to know just yet... I can't do this anymore, Liesel. I can't continue to lie to my parents, fail college, and be in love with a man in which we don't have a future together. It's against all odds."

At that very moment, my phone begins to vibrate with Mom's caller ID on the screen. I hit reject, unable to speak to her.

"It's hard. I get it."

"No, Liesel, it's almost impossible to keep going. And now what, I'm supposedly pregnant too? This is so fucked up."

My breathing begins to falter as I fall sideways, curling up into a fetal position as if it'll protect me. Liesel lies beside me, holding onto me tight. "You need to talk to him. You can't go through this alone."

I shake my head. "And what? Freak him out, too. Never in his wildest dreams will he think to have a child with a nineteen-year-old. You don't understand, Will has all these amazing things happening for him. Everything he has worked for his whole life is coming to fruition. I can't be the one to ruin this for him because I was lazy in taking my pill at the same time each day."

"Yeah, but I'm sure, never in his wildest dreams did he expect to fall in love with someone who has been there all along. Will isn't a man you picked up on the street. He's family. That type of connection runs deep. He won't hurt you, Millie. Besides, he's old enough to be able to take care of you. Imagine if it were Austin? You'd both be screwed."

Maybe Liesel has a point, and maybe she doesn't. But for now, I feel alone.

And perhaps this is the trouble with love. At the best of times, it's wondrous and core-shaking. Yet, at the worst of times, it can make you feel like the loneliest person in the world.

"Millie," Liesel murmurs beside me. "You can't pretend this isn't happening. Let's get this over and done with, and chances are, we're both overreacting."

An hour later, while I continued to lay on the sofa completely numb, Liesel returns with the test. I beg her to stay with me in the bathroom, and with shaky hands, I grab the stick from her and follow her directions. I nervously pee, then hand the stick back to her as she places it on the vanity.

I flush the toilet and step away, unable to look or even breathe.

Every second that passes is painfully slow.

"Millie," Liesel breathes uneven and shaky.

Clenching my fists while hyperventilating in the small bathroom, my body tremors to the point I think I've stopped breathing.

Liesel holds up the stick, and my eyes scan to see one blue line.

That means not pregnant, right?

But there, beneath the one line I thought would be my saving grace, is another very faint blue line.

So faint but unavoidable.

"You're pregnant."

TWENTY-EIGHT

WILL

L ex insists I travel to London for three days to meet
with shareholders.

It was the last thing I wanted to do, given that I haven't
slept in my bed for close to two weeks. The pursuit to dominate the European market isn't without its challenges. The
pressure is mounting, my attention being pulled in every
direction, and sleep becoming an afterthought with
insomnia setting in once again.

I dread breaking the news to Amelia, but surprisingly,
she takes it well. We didn't fight or argue, and she simply
said she's busy with assignments since she's taking extra
credits. Her tone is off, yet I don't interrogate her given that
she's still recovering from the flu. The guilt of not seeing her
while she was sick weighs heavily on my mind, but it's
impossible to get a single moment away from work with
everything going on.

Lex is more demanding of late, assuming I'm at his beck
and call with every goddamn emergency. I sense he has his
concerns, many of them with Amelia. Yet, unlike before, he

doesn't mention it to me, and therefore, I don't ask any questions, careful not to raise suspicions.

I'm given a tour of the potential London office, all of which becomes this added stress. The topic is always part of our discussions in our executive meetings, yet I'm still unable to find a solution that allows me to stay in the States.

The more I try to play around with staff relocation and look at the costs of having someone else run London, it becomes evident that I'm the best person for the job. But the realization drives resentment throughout me. I dreamed of building this empire only for me to be the one to have sacrifice the one thing I want.

Amelia Edwards.

I fucking miss her like crazy. It almost feels like we're worlds apart, across an entire ocean. There's no way in hell that I can live in another country when I need her in my bed, with me, and only me. My jealousy is already an issue in our relationship. Any time she mentions another man's name or appears in photos with so-called 'friends,' my temper gets the better of me. I hate myself for it, but the thought of another man touching her sends me to the brink of insanity.

Just before my flight back to the States, Amelia calls me while I'm queuing to board the plane. Thank God for business class. The line for economy class with screaming children is chaos. The more I observe their behavior, the more I realize how unappealing it is to have kids.

"Hey, I'm just boarding."

"You'll be back tomorrow, right?"

"Yes, why? You miss me or something?"

Standing at a complete stop, amongst strangers, I desperately want to tell her I miss her. That it's been the longest two and half weeks of my life, and I need to be inside her more than ever.

I hear a sigh over the speaker, but her tone is soft and not the usual burst of energy she's known for. "Can we talk tomorrow when you're back?"

"Of course." I wince, remembering the forecast meeting scheduled for tomorrow. "Actually, it might have to wait until tomorrow night. I have a meeting all day tomorrow."

"We'll talk then."

She hangs up the phone without saying another word, not even a goodbye. I send her a quick text before having to shut my phone off.

Me: *Is everything okay?*

Amelia: *It will be.*

Me: *I love you.*

Amelia: *I love you, too, Will.*

I couldn't shake off the feeling that something else is troubling her, but there's nothing I can do right now until I get back on home soil.

"Gentlemen, let's wrap this meeting up," I suggest, irritable from the jetlag. "We've gone through what we need to go through. We're just going around in circles now."

"What about Edwards? Won't he want to make a decision?"

"Considering this is my company, I'll consider Lex's opinion but will ultimately make my own decision."

I stand up, stretching my arms before exiting the room and going back to my office. Ending that meeting early means I have three extra hours to spend as I please. Upon my walk back to my office, my personal assistant, Heather, motions for me to look at the guest area. My eyes are drawn to the long, lean, tanned legs crossed on the white leather lounge to the black straps wrapped around her ankles.

There's a familiarity to the legs until I draw up her body and meet the eyes of a gorgeous woman. The same woman I had bedded for close to a year.

"Luciana?" I say, stunned to see her. "What are you doing here?"

Standing up, her eyes implore me while her lips curve up into a smile. She walks toward me wearing a soft V-neck dress, tight and hugging her curves in all the right places. I purse my lips, remembering how sexy of a woman she is.

"I'm in town and wanted to drop by to say hello." Luciana extends her arms, prompting an embrace which I feel pressured to do. With her arms wrapped around my neck, I hold her tight for just a moment, then pull back, uncomfortable with how intimate a simple hug feels.

"Is now a bad time?"

"Of course not, please come into my office."

We enter the office, and I motion for her to take a seat as Heather offers her a beverage. She kindly accepts a glass of water before switching her attention back onto me.

"How have you been?" I ask, resting back in my chair. "Are you still modeling for Victoria's Secret?"

"Yes. I've just signed another contract which is why I came here."

"Oh?"

"It's for a television show to be filmed in the city. My contract is for the next five years."

"Congratulations," I offer with a genuine smile. "That's exciting for you."

"It's exciting." Her gaze fixates on mine, twinkling under the fluorescent light. "I don't like where we ended, Will."

I should've seen it coming, the not-so-subtle glances, the crossing of her legs exposing her thighs purposely—all of Luciana's signature moves. Avoiding her persistent stare, I fidget with my cufflinks.

"It ended the way it needed to end. I wasn't ready for the life you wanted."

"And now?"

"Now?" With a slow and steady gait, I raise my eyes to meet hers. "I'm seeing someone."

Luciana grimaces, narrowing her eyes, looking less than pleased with my admission.

"Who is she?"

"Does it matter?" I question rudely.

"Of course, it matters," she sneers, toying with the gold necklace around her neck. I recognize it from when we were together. A birthday present from me if my memory serves correct. "I want to know who means more to you than me."

Her arrogance amuses me. "My private life is exactly that, private. If this is what you came for, then I'm sorry."

She leans over the table, purposely showcasing her cleavage. I divert my eyes, not wanting to encourage her in any way. Sure, she has naturally big tits which fit perfectly in the expensive lingerie Victoria's Secret is known for, but everything in front of me isn't the person I'm in love with.

"We were good together," she reminds me, her eyes

fixated on my mouth. "And we were especially good together in the bedroom. Do you remember, Will?"

I bite my tongue, trying my best to think of the appropriate words to let her down. Yes, we were great in the bedroom because she was a good fuck at a time of my life when I knew no better.

And now, the only body I want to devour is Amelia's. My addiction and obsession, the only touch I want to feel all over me.

"I remember, and yes, it was good... at the time," I tell her, quick to continue. "I'm with someone, and that person is important to me. So, again, if this is what you've come for, I'm sorry, Luciana, but we ended a long time ago."

Dropping her shoulders, she ducks her chin before letting out a breath and standing up. I follow her lead, eager to usher her out and avoid any further conversation on the past.

"I guess I should congratulate you or something."

"It was nice seeing you again, Luciana."

She leans in for a hug, then pulls away, caressing my face with her hand. "Make her happy, okay?"

I let out a soft chuckle. "I'm trying."

A loud noise enters the room as the two of us turn toward the door. Amelia is standing there with her hand on the doorknob. Heather runs up behind her, panic-stricken.

I barely recognize Amelia. It's been weeks since I last saw her, and only now I realize how the flu really affected her. Her usually rosy cheeks look pale and gaunt. There are dark circles under her eyes. Everything about her appears worn out.

"Amelia, what are you doing here?"

"I need to talk to you," she stammers, her breathing shallow. "But I can see you're busy."

Her eyes dart back and forth to Luciana. Quick to realize our friendly goodbye looks suspicious, I pull away and create distance between us.

"Luciana, this is Amelia, a family friend of mine."

I use my words cautiously, aware that Heather is present. The last thing I need is for her to gossip with her co-workers, and it leaks to Lex.

"Amelia, Luciana."

"How do you know each other?" Amelia blurts out rudely.

I lower my gaze but choose to be honest to avoid deception on my account.

"We dated."

Luciana tilts her head with an overbearing smile. "We lived together a year ago."

"You never said you lived with someone?" Amelia questions, folding her arms beneath her chest, angered by the truth.

"It slipped my mind," I say, watching her expression shift from anger to pure rage.

Amelia storms out, the hurt evident on her face. I call her name, following through the office doors until we're in the lobby. She presses the elevator repeatedly, desperate to get away from me. I grab her arm, willing she stop.

"Fucking hell, Amelia. What's wrong with you? Someone could've seen that outburst."

Amelia turns to me swiftly, nostrils flaring with widened eyes. "I thought you had a meeting all day?"

"I did. It ended early."

"And you didn't think to call me? I told you I needed to speak to you."

"And I told you tonight."

"But you have free time to do whatever it is you were

doing with your ex-girlfriend in your office?" she accuses, raising her tone. "The girlfriend who you lived with, according to her. Must have been serious for playboy Will to commit to someone being in his bed every night."

"Amelia, don't start..."

"Don't start what?" she yells, almost a cry. "I get it, okay? I'm not her. I am not a woman with my own career and money. I don't have the freedom to do whatever the hell I want. I can't just walk holding your hand without being questioned about our age. I'm everything that you don't need, and everything you do need is standing inside your office, no doubt wishing you guys get back together."

I lower my head, unsure what to say.

Just as I'm about to open my mouth to tell her how much I love her and that while some of that may be true, in the end, I only want her, the doors ping open.

We both glance at the opened elevator, and the familiar emerald-green eyes are staring directly at us.

Lex Edwards.

In the flesh.

TWENTY-NINE

AMELIA

My father's eyes dart back and forth. The normally vibrant emerald-green pupils turning a darker shade as the three of us stand here inside the lobby.

"Amelia," he demands, his tone deepening. *"What are you doing here?"*

"I...I..." I stumble on my words, thinking of anything, trying to rid myself of the hurt from moments ago when I caught Will and his ex-girlfriend in an overly friendly embrace. "I lost my wallet and didn't know where to go. I had no cash on me."

"You lost your wallet?"

"Yes, and I was upset," I continue to lie, clearing my throat to sound more believable. "I was a few blocks over ready to meet a friend when I realized it. It must have been on the subway. I didn't know who to turn to, so I came here."

Dad's expression remains blank, unreadable. If he does, in fact, suspect anything, he's doing a great job at disguising it.

"And Will and I got into a fight because he called me

irresponsible. I was meeting a boy, Dad, and I should be studying."

"You should be studying," he grits, clenching his jaw while staring at me oddly. "I got a call from your academic advisor saying that you're falling behind. Who is this boy you're meeting?"

"It doesn't matter, Dad."

Will continues to remain quiet, then excuses himself, leaving me to fend for myself. I'm hurt he'd do such a thing when all along he promised me he would fight for us. And here I am, fighting for us and this so-called baby I'm carrying, only for him to walk away.

Swallowing the lump inside my throat, my chest begins to hitch, making it harder to breathe.

"It does matter, Amelia!" Dad yells, the echo bouncing off the glass walls. "I knew you going to Yale was a bad idea. You aren't mature enough to handle being on your own."

I raise my eyes with a pinched mouth, devoid of any emotion as his words anger me.

"So, all that talk about me being responsible was to do what exactly?"

Holding his elbows wide from his body, he lowers his head to control his breathing. His expensive suit looks tight on his overly tensed muscles, the veins on his neck visible next to his white-collared shirt.

"Right, excellent parenting," I mouth, placing my hands on my hips. "This is all your fault."

"My fault?"

"Yes! You and your stupid rules, the way you control my life. If it weren't for you, my life would be much better."

"Watch your words, young lady."

"I don't give a fuck who you are," I bellow, staring at

him with contempt. "Cut me off, disown me. I'm done with being Lex Edwards's daughter."

I run into the elevator, closing the door with urgency to leave my father standing there with his head down. The second I'm alone, my body begins to shake, the urge to violently throw up teetering on the edge.

I exit the elevator, walking fast to distract my sick stomach, only to feel an uncomfortable gush between my legs. I rush to the bathroom, closing the stall behind me, yanking my jeans down to see a pool of blood between my legs.

Panicked, I wipe between my legs to clean myself up, but the sight of the blood makes me dry heave. My head falls into the bowl, the barely-there contents of my stomach exiting my body brutally.

My body continues to shake, my tears falling against my cheek turning into sobs. I peer between my legs, certain that the stains are a sign that I've gotten my period despite the positive pregnancy test.

With no one to turn to and my dorm room so far away, I grab my phone and call the only man I can rely on.

"Andy?" I cry, choking on my sobs. "It's me. I need you."

My eyes open, only to fall back to sleep again. The dreams become nightmares, tormenting my sleep then forcing me to wake up, my body covered in sweat. Darkness engulfs the room but sitting beside me is Andy. He smiles softly, caressing my cheek before tucking me in tighter. My eyes fall heavy again, sleep the only thing my body so desperately craves.

The next time I wake up, daylight has entered the room.

The sun is shining, a sign of spring with summer not too far away. I take in my surroundings, noticing the scattered desk in the corner to the familiar photos on the wall.

"Andy?" I croak, trying to open my eyes, a familiar touch stroking my cheek. It feels like home, my entire *world*. The simple touch brings only fond memories, an unconditional love like a warm blanket on a cold winter's day.

With difficulty, my heavy lids begin to open to see Mom staring at me, concerned.

"*Mom?*" I cry, the tears choking me.

"*Oh, baby.*"

Mom's arms wrap around me as I pull her toward me, clutching onto her for life. The knitted sweater she wears smells of her perfume. I bury my face into her, desperate to be smothered in her love again. I miss her like crazy, and everything I've been trying to avoid is no longer worth the pain of losing my best friend.

"I'm so sorry, Mom," I stutter, holding onto her still. "For everything."

"Amelia, honey, just breathe, please."

"You must hate me."

"I don't hate you. That's not possible."

Andy crouches down on his knees to kiss my forehead. "Millie, I called your Mom because I was terrified. Do you remember what happened?"

I try to even my breaths, my heading spinning with a migraine persisting.

"Have some water. You're dehydrated." Mom opens the bottle of water for me, urging me to drink.

"I...I..." I turn to look at Mom, pleading with her to understand.

"Andy?" Mom says softly, touching his arm. "Would you mind giving us some time?"

"Of course, Aunt Charlie. I'll be in the library. Just text me when you're done."

Andy grabs his things, closing the door behind him. The second he's gone, Mom squeezes my hand.

"Before you say anything, I want you to know something." She struggles with her words, pausing to gain some composure. "Nothing you can say to me will make me love you any less. I've been through my share of troubled times, and I always felt alone. I never want you to feel that way."

I wipe the tear falling down my cheek. "I... I don't know where to start."

"You're in love with Will, aren't you, honey?"

My eyes search hers for judgment, yet I come up with nothing.

I nod my head. "How did you know?"

"You're my daughter, my best friend. I'd like to think I know enough about love to know when someone is deeply experiencing it."

"Don't hate him, Mom."

She smiles softly. "I can never hate Will. He'll always own a piece of me. I love him like I would if he were my son. Our bond goes way back before you were even born."

"I'm sorry I lied to you. I was so caught up in it all, and I just didn't think straight."

"Love will do that to you."

"Mom," I choke out her name, allowing the sobs to consume me. "I thought I was pregnant, but I just got my period."

Mom lets out a huge breath, wrapping her arms around me tight as her tear falls onto my face. We hold onto each other before I pull away, trying to calm myself down. My gaze falls upon the distant stare on her face, almost as if she's reliving an unpleasant memory.

"Okay, honey," she says, wiping her tears away. "Let's talk seriously for a moment. Have you done a test?"

Unable to speak the words, I nod.

"And it came out positive?"

I nod again.

"How late were you?"

"Close to ten days, but Mom, before I came here, I bled out after I..."

I choose not to continue with that sentence, not knowing if she's spoken to Dad after my outburst.

Mom's face falls, her lips trembling as she squeezes my hand tight. "Honey, we need to get you to the doctor. There's a chance you may have miscarried. I need for you to get checked out."

Without another word, I hop out of bed slowly, only noticing now that I'm dressed in Andy's sweatpants and sweater. As Mom busily types a text on her phone, I'm wondering if she's telling Dad.

"I'm texting the car service, not your father if that's what you're thinking."

"I'm sorry, Mom, I did think that." I pause, tugging on the sleeve of the sweater I'm wearing. "I said things to Dad. I know I've hurt him. He knows, doesn't he?"

Mom holds my hand, trying her best to assure me. "Your father will always love you. But for now, we need to make sure you're okay."

"Mom, you didn't answer my question?"

With heavy eyes, she raises them to meet mine with a simple nod.

The doctor assumes I miscarried but requests I perform a

test to see if it comes back negative. Mom suggests I stay at the penthouse for a few days before heading back to campus, worried over my well-being and concerned with how gaunt I look after my bout with the flu.

I climb into bed, the exhaustion weighing heavy. I still haven't spoken to Will, avoiding his calls and text messages on my phone. Andy texted me, telling me he spoke to Will, suggesting he give me time to rest. Since then, the phone calls and text messages have stopped.

Inside my bed, I feel safe and comforted as Mom strokes my hair, watching me rest.

"Mom?" I murmur, the tears springing to my eyes again. "How did I get myself in this mess?"

"You fell in love," she simply states. "I never told you this, Amelia, but after your Dad and I broke up the first time, I spent eight years apart from him. And then I met this man, this amazing man."

My tears stop momentarily, almost as if someone turned off the tap controlling my tears.

"It was the first time in a long time when I truly felt something. We dated, went away on holiday, and when we came back, he proposed marriage."

"Marriage?"

Mom nods her head. "I said yes. What was I waiting for? This perfect man proposes marriage, and I loved him. Everyone loved him."

"But what happened?"

"Fate," she responds wistfully. "The day after we got engaged, we went to lunch, and sitting inside that restaurant at a business meeting was your father. Out of all places, after eight years, and a day after I get engaged, fate delivers this."

My mouth falls open, shocked at the very thought,

certain that it isn't a coincidence but the universe intervening.

"Your father was relentless in his pursuit to win me back, but I was so hurt. We had this history, and I felt abandoned by him. That trust isn't so easy to repair, you know."

"But Mom, who was the guy?" I ask, my curiosity getting the better of me. "I mean, what happened to him."

Mom glances at her wedding band, toying with it while lost in thought.

"It was your Uncle Julian."

Everything Ava said was right, well, not everything, but close to it. I should be surprised, but the more I think about it, the more it makes sense. Uncle Julian is wonderful, at least, with Aunt Adriana he is. Far be it for me to admit that he's quite attractive for his age, he's just such a genuine and loving guy. Andy dotes on him as if he were the same man who brought him into the world.

"As you can see, life has a funny way of working out. It's all about timing."

"So, you and Dad, you had an affair behind Uncle Julian's back?"

Mom nods, keeping her mouth shut.

I let out the breath I've been holding in. "But Dad is so protective over you. I mean, I still remember a time when we went to some function and some guy tried to pick you up, he was so jealous. The whole car ride home he didn't talk to you."

"I've lost count of your father's jealous outbursts. After a while, I just learned to ignore it." She lays beside me, allowing me to rest my head against her shoulder. We both stare at the ceiling, deep in thought.

"And then what happened? Uncle Julian came back and fell in love with Aunt Adriana?"

"It's a little more complicated than that. They both were seeking help for their mental health and just formed a friendship while navigating through the trauma they had experienced."

It all begins to make sense—the timelines, the connections.

"They're so right for each other. I've always thought that, you know. I see how he treats her, and it's so respectful. I mean, I'm not saying Dad doesn't treat you with respect, but you do butt heads a lot."

"That we do." She chuckles softly. "Your dad can be a real asshole at times."

"But you love him," I state, rather than pose the question.

"My life is him and you girls, of course." She strokes my hair as I turn to my side, clutching onto her arm. "When I found out I was pregnant with you, I was terrified. Amelia, I was eighteen when I first fell pregnant with your father. He was married, he just left me, and I was devastated. I moved away to live with my grandmother and lost the baby at six months. I blamed myself and thought about taking my own life."

"Mom," I choke, caressing her hand. "You were that young?"

She nods, her lips pressing flat before continuing, "I was in love, foolish, and I paid the price. So, when I ran into your father, I was terrified of getting hurt again."

"But you were older, wiser?"

"Yes," she admits. "I was forced to grow up early. But your father had his own battles, and he didn't know about the pregnancy. I can't blame him when both of us had our faults."

"Mom," I say, lowering my head. "I don't want Will to know."

"That's your decision, honey. But in the end, everything always comes out."

There's a loud bang at the front door, and my mother gives me a knowing look. She removes a set of keys from her pocket, placing it on my dresser.

"My car, here in the city. I want you to have it."

"But you love your car, Mom?"

"It's just a car, honey."

She kisses my forehead and suggests I try to get some rest. My eyes grow weary until a text message appears on my screen.

Will: *I tried to stay away but I can't. Talk to me, please.*

Amelia: *I have nothing to say.*

Will: *Don't give me that bullshit. Is that how you want it to end? Over some immature presumption that I'm trying to fuck my ex?*

Me: *I can't do this right now. I need to be alone.*

Will: *So, this is it, you're choosing to end us? Am I not even worth fighting for?*

I don't respond, wiping the tears from my face. Before I turn my phone off, I see a voicemail sitting at the bottom righthand corner. I listen to the message, a call from Doctor

Waltham. According to him, my HCG levels are too low, indicating I've lost the baby.

Hanging up the phone, I place it against my chest. For the last few days since I found out I was pregnant, I didn't allow myself to think about the future. I distracted myself in whichever way I could until I spoke to Will.

But now, it's all over.

My imagination wonders what the child would've looked like—Will or me? Was it a girl or boy? All these unwarranted thoughts consume me at this moment. I didn't even have time to process everything, only to lose the baby. The doctor assures me that miscarrying isn't uncommon, yet why do I feel like it's my fault, and I somehow caused this to happen?

Turning my phone off, I close my eyes again and fall asleep only to wake up again to the sound of sirens blaring through the night.

I slowly get out of bed in the dark and walk down the hall toward my dad's office. With my bare feet, the faintest of glows radiate from the room as I move toward the door, standing still, watching him drink straight from the bottle of scotch. His laptop is open, his phone in front of him on the woodgrain desk.

My memories play a reel like a movie at a theater. The time he took me to the zoo, and we fed the animals, organizing a private session, to the times he'd read me a story, using his superhero voices because I had an obsession with Batman. There was the time I got my learner's permit, and he yelled at me when I almost scratched his expensive Mercedes against a street pole. To our father-daughter dances where he'd proudly dance in front of everyone, dressed in his fancy tuxedo.

I wrap my arms around myself, willing to shield myself from the pain.

No matter what I decide, someone will get hurt. And as I continue to stare at the man who has loved me unconditionally my entire life, all I can see now is the shadow of my father breaking down.

Followed by the bottle of scotch smashing against the concrete wall.

THIRTY

LEX EDWARDS

"*C'mon, Edwards. At least think about it.*" This goddamn idiot is getting on my last nerve. The last time Zuckerman tried to close a deal, it fell through, losing millions. I've been one step ahead of him, and frankly, I want him out.

"I'm not repeating myself. What you're proposing isn't viable."

Zuckerman shakes his head in disbelief, tapping his pen against the table, annoyed I have declined his proposal.

"Let me get this straight? You're telling me what I'm proposing isn't viable, yet what Romano proposes is?"

My patience is wearing thin. How dare he question my decision.

"Romano did his homework," I emphasize, holding my head high. "Your numbers are sloppy. Do I need to remind you of what happened with the Chicago project?"

Zuckerman pinches his lips together, rising from his chair with a clenched jaw. He paces the area near the window, stopping abruptly to face me with an incredulous stare.

"So, Romano fucks your daughter, and he gets what he wants? Is that how it works?"

What did he just say to me?

His callous words begin to register. *Did he just say what I think he said?* My chest begins to harden. My hands clench into a fist beneath the long boardroom table. I keep my gaze on him fixed, careful not to express anything but a blank stare.

"I think you should leave this room." I try to keep my tone controlled, refusing to show him any emotion. "The next time you want to question me or bring my family into our business discussions, you can consider yourself done."

Zuckerman shakes his head, exiting the room while slamming the door. Alone, in the boardroom, his words repeat in my head, *"Romano fucks your daughter, and he gets what he wants?"*

It can't be true. A preposterous accusation from a man pissed off because he didn't get what he wanted. To think he could come up with such an elaborate notion as if anything could happen between Will and Amelia. For starters, there's an age gap. Amelia dates boys her age.

Will doesn't believe in relationships, admitting to me multiple times his distaste for settling down. They would never lie to me. I trust them both.

But then Zuckerman's vengeful remark plays again, *"Romano fucks your daughter."*

The dickhead doesn't know what he's saying, and on further thought, the guy is done. If he wants to accuse Will of touching my daughter, he can kiss his high-paying role goodbye.

Unsettled by our heated exchange, I leave my office with a meeting two blocks over at Will's building. I decide to walk to try to clear my head. I've had my fair share of dealings with assholes, but Zuckerman is high up there for his unwarranted behavior.

Standing on the sidewalk, waiting to cross, I run my hand through my hair, willing this overwhelming feeling to rid itself. Things of late had been stressful. I'm barking orders more than I care to admit and wasting time on idiots like Zuckerman.

Amelia's academic coordinator's call created more stress for Charlotte and me, given that it blindsided us. According to Amelia, everything was fine. I understand she fell ill with the flu, but her coordinator is convinced Amelia is no longer focused as she was at the beginning of the school year. Given her usually straight A's, I don't understand how this happened.

Charlotte insists we give Amelia a week to open up to us about her struggles rather than confront her. Considering that Amelia has barely spoken to Charlotte and seemingly avoids her calls, there appears to be a more significant issue at hand. My patience with this matter is wearing thin as each day passes. I need a goddamn holiday, preferably with Charlotte minus the cockblockers otherwise known as our daughters.

Stepping into the building, I nod my head at a few people who walk by. I enter the elevator, willing my shoulders to relax before I reach the twentieth floor. My phone pings repeatedly in my pocket, but I ignore it, granting myself a moment of solitude.

The second the doors open, Will and Amelia are standing in front of me. The two of them appear to be arguing. Will is running his hands through his hair, frustrated with their argument as Amelia is breathing heavily.

But then they turn to face me—eyes wide in shock.

My eyes dart back and forth, listening to Amelia spin

some story about losing her wallet. The more she rambles, the shakier her voice becomes. I flick my gaze to Will, noticing his body language stiffening before he excuses himself to leave us behind.

Why the fuck is she in the city with friends when she should be at Yale studying?

Baring my teeth, I raise my voice, questioning her failed marks and the call from her academic advisor. It becomes all the more evident as I stare into my oldest daughter's eyes that someone else is behind this behavior of hers.

Someone is pulling her away from everything she worked hard for.

And away from her *family*.

Then, she raises her voice back, disrespecting me with her angered words until she basically tells me to fuck right off. The second she disappears into the elevator, Zuckerman's words replay, *"Romano fucks your daughter."*

The voices are unable to shut off, scenario after scenario playing in my head—Will's decline in his performance of late and his head elsewhere in meetings. Before Christmas, we attended the gala, where he claimed he had an emergency, almost costing him a client.

His quick acceptance to visit LA and stay in my home.

Then there's Amelia's unusual behavior. The constant visits to the city, schoolwork falling behind, and the break-up with Austin, to name another thing.

Zuckerman can't be correct.

But then, I remember their argument as the elevator pinged open. This was more than a lost wallet at hand. And then she blamed me for controlling her life, her outburst completely disrespectful and uncalled for. This isn't the daughter I raised. This is a woman who's consumed by a man, a man who should be off-limits, who took advantage of our family ties, used me to get close to her, and then did what?

Don't say it. Don't repeat what Zuckerman said.

I turn back to enter the elevator, fury springing to life when the doors close, trapping me in my personal hell. My pulse begins to race, muscles quivering, the beat of my heart loud as a drum with an urge to smash my fist against the mirror inside the confined space.

Each passing second feels like an hour. Then the door opens up to the ground floor. With sweaty palms, I yank my phone out of my pocket to call Charlotte.

"Lex," Charlotte huffs over the receiver. "I need to step into a meeting with a client. I'll call you back in an hour?"

I can't speak. My chest so tight then even words are trapped, unable to form a coherent sentence.

"Lex? Hello, are you still there?"

"*I'm here*," I bellow.

"What's wrong?"

"Did you know that Will and our daughter are an item?"

"Lex, what are you talking about? Listen, I don't have time for your assumptions."

My nostrils begin to flare like a wild animal staring at its prey.

"Did you know, Charlotte?"

Charlotte releases a breath. "Lex, Amelia is going through something, I'll admit. But a relationship with Will? That's ridiculous. He's family."

"Will you just listen to me, Charlotte!" I demand, anger pouring through me like molten hot lava. "They've both been lying to us. Amelia is falling behind in her school-work, spending all her time in the city, and Will is distracted at work. Every time they've been in a room together, there was this odd behavior, yet I passed it off as nothing."

"So, what, Lex? That doesn't mean anything is going on."

"No, Charlotte," I beg of her to listen. "You don't understand. I just saw them."

"Doing what?"

"They were..." I clear my throat, closing my eyes momentarily. "They were arguing. She was here, in this building. She lied to my face about why she was here, and I could see it in her eyes. Don't you see? She's been pushing you away because she knew we'd figure it out."

"Lex," her voice wavers, "She's pushing me away because she no longer needs me. She's an adult, now."

"No, Charlotte. You're wrong. She's pushing you away because it's easier to do that than lie to your face," I tell her brutally.

The line goes quiet, and all but Charlotte's heavy breathing can be heard.

"They want me inside. I don't know what to say. I'll call you the minute I'm out but promise me you won't do anything stupid, please?"

"Charlotte..."

"Lex, please?" she pleads in desperation.

"I promise."

The call ends, and I'm no closer to feeling any better after my talk with Charlotte. I need her, right now, to calm my flaring temper. As minutes pass while standing on the busy street, I head toward a bar a few blocks over, avoiding work, eager to numb the pain.

Inside the bar, I begin to drink myself into a stupor, time lost on me as I toy aimlessly with the peanuts in the bowl.

There are a dozen messages on my phone and missed calls, but the only one that mattered is Charlotte's.

Charlotte: *Our daughter needs us. I'm on the next flight to JFK.*

"Bartender, pour me another," I call, then lower my head.

"Look, buddy, you've had a few."

"What the fuck do you care? Do you know who I am?"

The young guy rolls his eyes, disrespecting my authority. My thoughts travel back to Will and all the times I demanded he sort Amelia out for her reckless behavior. Her underage clubbing and the countless conversations I've had privately with him over my concerns with her well-being. All of this was acted with trust, trust in which he broke without a single thought.

"This is the last drink."

The final glass of scotch is served to me.

But I don't care. I'll find a way to continue numbing the pain because I have no choice.

My little girl is gone.

I know Amelia is staying in our penthouse, Charlotte warned me earlier. She doesn't say another word, the two of them inseparable since the moment she arrived. I purposely keep my distance, drowning my sorrows inside my office with another bottle of scotch.

The liquor turns into a vicious seed, and when my temper flares beyond my imagination, I smash the bottle against the wall in a fit of rage. Everywhere I turn, all I hear are Zuckerman's words torturing me with its truth.

In the darkness of the night, I crawl into bed, lying beside my wife. Her scent feels like home, my fingers itching to touch her, yet I restrain.

The bed shuffles, and almost as if she feels my pain, knowing exactly what I need at this moment, she strokes my cheek with a gentle touch.

"We'll get through this," she whispers beside me. "She needs us, Lex."

"You didn't see the way she looked at me," I choke, closing my eyes to rid myself of the memory. "With so much contempt."

"She's young, and she's in love," Charlotte murmurs, moving her body close to me, blanketing me in warmth. "We were just as foolish as she is. If anything, we were worse. We had more at stake. You were married. I was a teen. Amelia is an adult now, and mistakes will be made. We just need to love her, guide her in the best way possible."

Love? There was no mention of love. I thought they were supposedly *fucking.* None of it matters anyway, each thing just as bad as the other.

"Promise me, Lex, you'll let her get through this in her own way."

"You want me to sit back and do nothing?"

"I want you to step out of the equation for just a moment. She's at a crossroad in her life, don't push her to make a decision because you think it's right."

I don't say another word, closing my eyes shut to allow sleep to numb me. What only feels like minutes later, a cough expels violently like I've swallowed a bunch of razor blades. Beside me, Charlotte is fast asleep, undisturbed by my noise.

My eyes are shut tight, and I'm unable to ignore the fire clawing up my throat. Water, I need water. Crawling out of bed, I stumble to the bathroom to drink a glass of water, attempting to clear the burn inside my throat.

It all comes back to me like a recurring nightmare.

I grab my phone on the bedside table and send Jeff, our lawyer, a text message. A few minutes later, the phone buzzes in my hand as I answer it quietly.

"Edwards, it's four in the morning?"

"Make it happen, or your job is on the line."

"But I thought we were waiting until Anton and his group confirmed the merger?"

"You listen to me, Jeff," I lower my voice, careful not to wake Charlotte. "I want Romano in London effectively immediately. Either you make that happen this morning, or it's over for you. Your wife wouldn't be too pleased that your stepdaughter is sucking your dick every day when she drops off your lunch, now would she?"

Silence falls between us until he releases a sigh. "I'll draw up the papers."

I hang up the phone and turn to look at Charlotte, who's still fast asleep. The street glow filters in the room, enough so that I can admire her silhouette. She's just as beautiful as the day I fell in love with her, maybe even more so. Charlotte doesn't deserve this either. I hate seeing my wife so troubled, and for the last few weeks with Amelia ignoring her, I know she was hurt, though she tried to hide it.

But all of this, every emotion we've experienced is only because of our love for our daughter.

I stumble out of bed again, wincing as my head spins.

With small footsteps, I walk toward Amelia's room. Slowly, I push the door open and see her asleep in bed.

She looks so innocent and pure like Daddy's little girl. Memories of her as a child flood my thoughts—her first steps, her first word, and the time she got her driver's license, just like we always talk about. I was so excited for her, but little did I know that my oldest daughter was growing up.

Then, she got a boyfriend, and Austin was a good kid. He had a steady head on his shoulders and respected my authority.

He's not a man who fucks women for pleasure, nor uses them as a conquest.

How dare he touch her.

Betray my trust.

Will Romano has no clue who he's messing with, and in just over a day, he'll be away from my daughter, out of her life for at least five years.

I'm going to make damn sure it happens, even if it costs me every cent I own.

THIRTY-ONE

WILL

The board called an impromptu meeting, the request coming through to my phone at five in the morning.

I didn't catch a moment of sleep. The last two days have been pure *hell*.

The moment I left Lex and Amelia in the lobby, I did so to distract Lex from thinking something is going on between Amelia and me. I went back to my office, only to have to deal with Luciana, who witnessed it all. I half expected her to lecture me on dating someone younger, but she simply expressed her sympathy, then left me alone.

Lex never showed up for our meeting, and Amelia disappeared. I tried calling Ava, but she had no clue what was going on. After attempting to call Amelia repeatedly, the calls end up going to voicemail. I sounded like a goddamn maniac.

Andy finally texts me, telling me she's safe with Charlie but needs some time alone.

Fuck. Charlie came to the city.

Deep inside, I know we're in troubled waters, that our relationship is about to be tested, and we aren't the only ones involved. Amelia finally texted me and made it clear that she needed a break from us.

The anger and pain soared through me, even more so because she didn't respond when I asked her if I was worth the fight.

With only my phone in hand, unshaven with no sleep, I slip into the boardroom to see my entire executive team at the table. I sit at my usual spot before everyone straightens their posture when the king himself walks in.

I lower my head, refusing to give him any respect, directing my attention to Jeff, who calls the meeting to begin.

"Let's make this quick since this meeting wasn't planned for today," he begins, sliding a piece of paper in front of me. "We need you in London, now. All shareholders in our newly purchased European division have signed on the proviso that you're stationed in London effective Monday of next week. You'll need to leave tomorrow."

My jaw begins to ache, my teeth pressing down hard, causing a shooting pain up the side of my face. The conditions on the contract jumble my mind, not able to comprehend. All I can compute is the five-year lease on the building and penthouse in which I'm expected to reside.

The silver tip of the pen hovers above the piece of paper in front of me.

My lips press together in a slight grimace as all eyes inside the boardroom fall upon my every move.

All I have to do is sign my name—a simple task I've done many times.

Yet, the repercussion of such an easy action will onset tremendous suffering. I felt it the moment I stepped into the room only ten minutes ago, to last night when I lay wide awake unable to shut down my thoughts. Everywhere I turn, and every breath I take isn't without a constant ache that has long buried itself inside me.

This pain, unbearable and consuming, is what *we* have become.

"Is there a problem, Mr. Romano?"

My gaze lifts, the head of our legal team, Jeff, quizzing me with a frustrated stare. His team worked non-stop to make this deal happen. Our company was against all odds, yet we persisted and won the final bid. Purchasing this other company will expand our name in the tech industry and officially make us a billion-dollar empire.

This is everything I've worked hard for in my career— the long hours, non-existent social life, constant travel, and stress associated with starting up a new company. All of it has come to fruition.

Then she walks back into my life.

Amelia Edwards.

She's no longer the annoying kid who would torment me with her childish games, and I'm no longer the teenage boy who would entertain her to avoid the wrath of my mother and aunt.

Our families have ties, strong ties, something neither of our mothers let us forget over the years. Unlike many other families, we're bonded by the timing of the past and not connected through sharing the same blood or gene pool.

Perhaps, in the chaos of what we have become, it's our way of justifying our actions.

The biggest surprise I never expected to take my breath away that afternoon several months ago is how Amelia turned into this beautiful woman. The very reason why my emotions fucked with my head, causing me to hesitate in front of our executive team.

Her body isn't supposed to be so irresistible to the point

that I crave her every goddamn moment. I've been with many women, but no one has ever owned me like she does when we're alone. And maybe I shouldn't have succumbed to my desires and taken her selfishly to satisfy my craving her innocence.

But in return, she did something which rendered me speechless. Something a man, older and more experienced, should've known better.

She made me fall in *love* with her.

"I repeat Jeff's question since perhaps you didn't hear it," Lex voices coldly, unforgiving with his tone. *"Is there a problem?"*

Across the room, the most powerful man I know watches me with an uninviting stare. His fingertips drum against the woodgrain table. The shade of his usually vibrant green eyes has turned almost black.

Anyone else caught in his unrelenting stare would've recoiled and signed the contract. But as the sick feeling in the pit of my stomach begins to alleviate, it's instantly replaced with resentment.

He left me no choice.

My company's future is in his hands. We need him to invest to complete this purchase, and all I have to do is sign this contract and move to London.

Away from Manhattan and away from his oldest daughter.

Beside me, my phone vibrates with a text appearing on the screen. Slowly, my eyes shift across to the notification. I keep my expression flat as the words tear through me like bullets ricocheting from a loaded gun.

Amelia: *I will always choose him.*

With these five words end everything between us. I'm left with no choice. Even if I give this all up for her, she'll never be happy unless her father approves.

And I know for a fact he doesn't want a man like me to be in a relationship with his daughter. We've been friends well before this, and for many years, he's been a mentor and a father figure and treated me like his own son.

He knows I never cared for women unless it was for my own selfish physical needs. We often joked about my inability to settle down with anyone since all I care about is work. We've spent many nights just sitting at bars, drinking while talking about life. He knows me better than my own father, better than any man I've called a friend over the years.

But then it all shifted.

A complete turn of events in which, if he knew the extent of our relationship, he'd never approve.

I'm not stupid. He taught me everything I know, and when the master himself has taught you all his tricks, you know well enough that his proposal for me to move is because he knows the secret we've been keeping.

The forbidden affair between his nineteen-year-old daughter and me.

My throat begins to tighten, the same time my knuckles turn white around the pen still resting in my hand. Pressing hard against the paper, the pen glides across as the blank spot above the line is filled with my signature.

Without a thought, the pen falls against the table as my head slowly lifts to the ruthless stare of the man who pulls all the strings.

The same man who Amelia chooses over me.

Her father.

Lex Edwards.

The new stakeholder in my soon-to-be billion-dollar company.

I rise from my chair without a single word and exit the boardroom. Instead of going to my office, I walk the streets aimlessly, desperate for this pain to subside. Trying to gain some sort of control over this, I head back to my apartment to pack.

Inside my living room, all I see is her. Laying on my bed, all I see is her. Everywhere I look, the memories become as painful as the next. I stomp toward the liquor cabinet, not bothering to pull out a glass and drinking straight from the tequila bottle. Desperate to numb the pain, I busy myself by packing my suitcases, standing them near the door.

Lost in my misery, there's a knock on the door.

Still dressed in the suit I wore today, I open the door to see Amelia on the other side.

Just like me, she appears worn out, even more so than the last time I saw her. I ache to touch her face but restrain myself, willing to shield myself from further pain.

"Can I come in?"

I pull the door completely open as she walks past me, keeping her distance.

"Will," she breathes, lowering her gaze while tugging her sleeve. "I'm sorry."

"What are you sorry for? Choosing your flesh and blood?"

Her lips press tight, still avoiding eye contact with me. "It's too hard, we're too hard together."

My hands clench into fists until my head falls, hanging with a pained expression. The truth is we're too hard together. We are tearing each other apart and fighting for something which neither one of us have the strength to fight anymore.

"I'm going to London."

Her gaze lifts, then falls on the suitcases near the door. "You're leaving?"

"I think it's for the best."

Silence falls between us, but then I allow myself to stare into her eyes one more time.

"Amelia, I never wanted to hurt you nor make you choose. But we're at different stages in life. I can't have you give up everything for me."

"And I can't have you give up everything you've worked hard for just for me."

Our breathing echoes in the room, the weight of our gaze locked into a catatonic state. Neither of us blinks an eye until my hand reaches out to caress her cheek. She rests into my hand, a tear escaping her.

"Don't say goodbye," I tell her. "I need you to walk away."

"But, Will..."

"I'm begging you," I plead, struggling to control my emotions. "Please walk away to a life you deserve."

Some may call it selfless to encourage Amelia to go live her life without me holding her down.

Or maybe I'm the selfish one. The second I step foot on English soil, I'll have leveled up to billionaire status.

Lex Edwards officially won the bet.

Yet all the money in the world means nothing if I can't have the woman I love.

The beautiful woman still standing in front of me.

Amelia Edwards.

THIRTY-TWO

AMELIA

For the longest time, my theory on love has been conceptualized to be a feeling of overwhelming happiness.

It's the holding of hands on a beautiful summer's day, the endearing smiles while eyes lock together as if the rest of the world doesn't exist.

It's the gesture of holding the door open or pulling out a seat in a restaurant.

It's offering to drive, to removing your coat when the other person is cold.

Love, in my eyes, is the hardest of lessons if ever fate is *not* on your side.

I turn to lay on my side, the complete view of Will asleep beside me. His body appears worn, tired after our emotional goodbye which led to truthful admissions, then one last night together—no sex, no lovemaking, just in each other's arms.

We both want the best for one another, yet neither of us is the best for each other.

I drink in the sight of him, knowing this will be the last

time. The small pout of his lips, lips which have kissed every single part of my body. The bridge of his nose, sitting between the bluest of eyes. Above them, his dark lashes curl so naturally. Against the black satin pillowcase, his hair appears lighter than the usual dark shade of brown. His usual controlled style is nothing but a wild mess, making me smile softly.

My gaze falls upon his shoulders, broad and toned, to his perfectly sculpted chest. My fingers ache to run their tips on the edge of his skin but touching him will wake him up. I need to savor this moment for as long as I can.

Something drags my eyes to his chest, watching the rise and fall and what appears so effortlessly. Beneath the movement lays his heart. I so desperately want to be everything it fights for, the only thing making it beat. But the longer I sit here and stare, the deeper my own heart weeps. Every inch of me feels like an open wound, a pain so visible you're unable to escape the severity of its presence.

I can't do this—pretend it doesn't hurt when not one part of me has been affected.

Beside me, Will stirs softly before his eyes open wide, the blue ocean torturing my already weakened heart.

"I have to go," I whisper, lowering my head. "It's time."

He takes a deep breath, twisting his body, so he's flat on his back. Staring at the ceiling, his cheekbones tighten while he bites down on his lip.

"It doesn't have to be this way." His change of mind comes across uncertain, and I know him well enough to know he's scared of the unknown.

"And love isn't supposed to be this hard," I tell him.

His gaze shifts, and perhaps the word *love* was premature to use. Our feelings are strong, our emotions run deep, but love doesn't end by saying goodbye.

"So, this is it..." he states, rather than question. "We go our separate ways. Pretend this never happened."

I shake my head. "I'll never be able to forget, Will."

My hand reaches out for my jacket which so carelessly lays on the foot of the bed. I admire the fabric inside my hands, but, of course, this jacket will be another memory of him amongst everything else.

"I don't know what you expect me to do, Amelia."

I stand up, placing my jacket on, ignoring the pain crippling my simple moves. Adjusting the skirt of my dress, I find my boots on the ground and grab them.

With a forced smile, so much so that my mouth hurts, my eyes struggle to follow in suit. I allow myself to look one more time at the man my heart cries for.

"I expect nothing, Will," I say, until my voice waivers. "London is the right decision."

As I turn back around, a shuffle occurs behind me, and Will has stopped me in my tracks. His hand caresses my face, the pain rippling through as I beg myself not to cry. Slowly, he lifts my chin, so our eyes meet.

"I wish things were different," he chokes.

How I wish the same—that we don't feel compelled to lie to our loved ones, that this relationship almost destroyed our families, and that we had the freedom to express our love without the restraints of age or what society deems appropriate.

If our love has a chance of lasting forever, all these hurdles would come second, not be the priority.

"If they were different," I whisper, unable to look him in the eye. "There's still no guarantee."

He moves forward, placing his lips on mine. There's no urgent rush, no sexual gratification in our kiss.

This kiss comes from a different place, and despite my

willingness to mask the pain, I'm so close to falling apart in front of him.

"Goodbye, Amelia," he murmurs with an ache. "I just want you to be happy."

And perhaps that's the biggest catch of all. My happiness falls dependent on him.

I remove his hands from my face, choke back my words, wishing I can return the sentiment, but I need to walk away now.

Just one step at a time, I tell myself. The room is behind me, the hallway leading to the door appearing impossibly long. I walk past the dining room, the living room, every room carrying its own memories of us.

But the hardest part is seeing the suitcases beside the door.

Taking a deep breath, I close my eyes tight, my hand resting on the doorknob as I leave the apartment, closing the door behind me.

I have no recollection of walking toward the car, or climbing inside, or even starting the engine. I pull out of the parking lot, and just before I drive on the street, I stop at the top of the driveway and grab my phone to send a text.

Me: *You won, as always.*

And there is the final nail in the coffin, no more lying to my father. He wants the truth. Well, there it is.

The streets are dead on Sunday morning, and the radio plays lazy tunes without the idle morning chit-chat. I switch to my playlist, but every lyric runs deep, and eventually, I turn everything off to complete silence.

The fog is clouding my vision from the heavy rain which lashed the East Coast last night, and when I'm only a few blocks away from campus, the red light prompts me to stop.

The traffic lights are buried amongst the fog, and as I count down to the light turning green, my heart rate begins to accelerate. Unwillingly, I clench the steering wheel, trying to ignore my skin flushing. My shoulders bear tight, but they feel like they are quaking, causing me to choke out a gasp.

Everywhere I turn, everywhere I look, all I see is Will—his smile tormenting me, his laughter, and the way he caresses the back of my neck and draws me in for a deep kiss.

I breathe faster, but each breath begins to turn into a sob until my eyes cloud, and warm streams of tears fall down my face.

It all hurts, every piece of me. I don't want to be here, not without him. I contemplate turning around, driving to the airport to beg him not to leave until my phone beeps beside me, and my focus shifts to the text on the screen.

Dad: *It's for the best.*

Anger ripples through me as I open my window and throw the phone outside the car. It smashes against the road, falling into pieces.

Gulping for air, the light turns green, my foot slamming on the gas until the sound of a loud horn catches my attention on my left.

Fuck, what's that?

I try to control myself, but all I see is the parked car in front of me. I slam my foot on the brake, my white knuckles clutching the steering wheel with panic.

I let out a scream before it all becomes a hazy vision of

lights, and my car drives up an embankment, the impact releasing the airbags. My head knocks front forward against the blown-up bag, a sharp pain ricocheting across my temple.

My breath is caught in my throat, shock paralyzing me while strangers rush to my aide.

The voices are panicked, none of it registering. Someone yells, "Call 9-1-1." A woman opens my door with a phone in her hand. I hear a dial tone, then a voice on the other end saying state your emergency.

It all drowns out—the accident, the noise, the strangers around me.

My emergency isn't my catatonic state, nor is it the gash on my head with a trickle of blood falling down the side of my face.

It's a broken heart.

Unrepairable, damaged, and writhing in pain.

And that's the trouble with love.

It's the greatest feeling in the world, if only for a fleeting moment.

Yet, a broken heart will last a *lifetime*.

To Be Continued

SNEAK PEEK – THE TROUBLE WITH US

Next to the only window inside the room, I sit at the head of the table.

Outside, the cluster of gray clouds form in the sky, rainfall predicted as usual. It's your typical day in London—dreary, wet, and cold. Nothing at all like home.

I welcome the momentary silence.

The last two weeks have been chaotic. Non-stop travel between different countries across Europe. Endless meetings, networking, conferences—nothing remotely pleasurable aside from a day trip to the Greek Islands courtesy of a client. If it wasn't for my personal assistant, I wouldn't know what day it is as I barely set foot on English soil. Right after this meeting, I am scheduled on a flight to Brussels for a convention where I am the guest speaker.

Yet these moments of solitude, its purpose of disconnecting me from the world if only for minutes, is a blessing and a curse.

My eyes close, silence drowns out all distractions while I take the deepest of breaths. I've formed a bad habit, cracking my knuckles to loosen my joints. With my eyes still shut, my head tilts left, then right, releasing the built-up tension in my shoulders.

The door opens, and noise from outside the room filters through. Some of our executive team arrive early, entering with a welcoming nod before taking their places at the table. Jensen, our head of IT Infrastructure, takes a seat beside me without considering my personal space and starts rattling off numbers with which he seems displeased. I listen attentively, nodding my head in agreeance, but my focus is elsewhere.

And the very reason is about to walk in the room at any minute now.

Lex Edwards.

If you listen carefully, you can hear the weighted steps, each one taken with a sense of pride. The voices around me slowly filter out, and then suddenly, the energy in the room changes.

Lex's entrance is not subtle.

His presence demands attention.

The team respectfully rise from their chairs, acknowledging his arrival.

Not me, though.

I don't even bother to look his way.

It's been four years since I last spoke to him—all of our business dealings executed through our management team. The moment he gave me the ultimatum—organized that contract to ship me to London with strings attached—we ended our relationship then and there.

I'd been called a fool to go up against the man who deals all the cards, often warned of the risks and ability to lose everything I have.

But the damage is done.

I've lost everything.

All that matters.

My wealth, if measured, is rather impressive. Yet money is the devil's playground. There's the freedom to do things people only dream about, but none of these things nor possessions will ever replace the heartache of letting go of the woman you love.

A phone inside the room rings, forcing everyone to silence themselves so Lex can answer.

"Hello," he states, almost void of emotion. "I'm sorry, now is not a good time."

My gaze shifts to where Lex now sits, and I observe a man who I once considered family. There's resignation in his expression, despite the lowering of his head to grant himself some privacy during his call. And then, he closes his eyes, momentarily, before they spring open and lift to meet my unrelenting stare. The usually emerald eyes appear dark, however despite the change in shade, his presence inside this room onsets memories.

Memories I have long-buried in an effort to move on with my life.

"Congratulations," is all he says, without the usual jovial response attached to the sentiment. "I love you, too."

The call ends, prompting Jensen to suggest we start our meeting. As usual, he leads while I try my best to immerse myself. There are a few disagreements that encourage others to weigh in with their opinions. After two hours, I begin to lose interest, my mind drifting elsewhere.

Bored with the discussion, I respond to an email on my cell then exit my inbox, the Insta icon in the corner of my phone showing me a notification. I barely check any of these platforms, uninterested in connecting with people who serve me no interest.

I don't bother to scroll. I simply watch the first few

stories, which are mainly of my friends from college. And then, in the fourth story, Ava's picture catches my attention. My fingers move on their own accord, swiping to view the story again.

It's a picture of a hand with a diamond ring and a caption reading, 'She said yes!'

My heart stops to what feels like a complete standstill. I'd recognize those fingers anywhere. They touched me in intimate places. Caressed my face so lovingly. Those same fingers ran through my hair softly until they found their way to the back of my neck, where they would often rest.

The kickstart of adrenalin knocks the air out of me, my breathing ragged as my skin begins to crawl with heat beneath the suit I wear.

I scramble through Ava's profile, where the last few photographs are of her, and nothing out of the ordinary. My lips press together as I contemplate stalking Amelia's profile, something I refused to do for the last four years.

The name alone is a trigger, yet her profile is nothing but scenic pictures or objects, with not one picture of her. There's nothing to suggest the ring is hers, and perhaps my eyes have imagined it all wrong.

Heading back to Ava's profile, I scroll further. There's an image of a *Grey's Anatomy* scene in which she tagged Austin Carter. Clicking on his name takes me to his profile which is open to view.

My eyes widen in disbelief.

With a hard swallow, I try to ignore the pressure inside my chest, but it feels impossible—the pain has become unbearable.

It's the same picture—the hand with the diamond ring. On the top right-hand corner, the image says one of two. So I swipe left, my stomach hardening at the second photo, which sends a stabbing pain straight to the middle of my chest.

Austin is on what appears to be a clifftop, kneeling with the ring box in his hand. And standing there, with a happy expression, is Amelia.

Anger thrums through my veins, unapologetic with its ferocity. My nostrils flare, the temperature inside this room unbearable. The four walls surrounding us begin to close in, trapping me in this fucking nightmare called life.

"Are we done, gentlemen?" I demand, unable to control myself.

No one says a word, yet all eyes are staring at me curiously, confused by my sudden outburst.

I push my chair out, ignoring everyone in the room, and head toward the exit.

"Romano," Lex calls, his artic tone gaining my attention.

My sweat-filled palms rest on the doorknob while trying to control the anger which is tearing me to pieces. I refuse to turn around, but like the sadistic fool I am, I do so and fall victim to the man who ruined my damn life.

"Leave her alone," he demands, with an insulting stare. "It's over."

I give him nothing.

The bastard doesn't deserve anything from me.

Exiting the room, I head straight to the restroom. Inside, I slam my fist against the stall door, the pain connecting through my entire body. But the physical pain is nothing compared to leaving her behind or the moment I chose to give up because she deserved better than me. And this pain can never compare to the last four years of hell without her.

I have a choice—follow Lex's command once again and leave her alone.

Or—go back to the States and fight for what I should have all along.

I refuse to let him win.

It may be the biggest fight of my life, but I will battle until the very end, even if it kills me.

Amelia Edwards is mine, and this time, no one is going to stop me.

Printed in Great Britain
by Amazon

79269634R00181